KV-636-049

Jean Rowden lives in Peterborough with her husband. She has two grown-up daughters and she spends her free time horse riding and gardening.

DEADLIER THAN THE SWORD

Constable 'Thorny' Deepbriar anticipates a peaceful interlude as Minecliff prepares for its summer fête. However, following an incident involving an illegal mantrap, there is a suspicious death on the arterial road, and suddenly he has more than enough work. Adding to his troubles, Deepbriar's childhood friend has returned home with his fiancée to plan their wedding, unaware that the village is harbouring dark secrets . . . With someone causing mayhem on the local byways, and malicious letters, written anonymously, to members of Minecliff's community, the constable faces a serious challenge to his detection skills, and ultimately, a threat to his own life . . .

JEAN ROWDEN

DEADLIER THAN THE SWORD

Complete and Unabridged

ULVERSCROFT
Leicester

First published in Great Britain in 2008 by
Robert Hale Limited
London

First Large Print Edition
published 2009
by arrangement with
Robert Hale Limited
London

British Library CIP Data

Rowden, Jean.
Deadlier than the sword
1. Police- -England- -Fiction. 2. Detective and mystery stories. 3. Large type books.
I. Title
823.9′2–dc22

ISBN 978–1–84782–784–5

Published by
F. A. Thorpe (Publishing)
Anstey, Leicestershire

Set by Words & Graphics Ltd.
Anstey, Leicestershire
Printed and bound in Great Britain by
T. J. International Ltd., Padstow, Cornwall

This book is printed on acid-free paper

1

A pain, sharp enough to bring an involuntary grunt, jabbed at Deepbriar's ribs. He tried to turn away but found himself unable to run; panic surged through him. Words were being hissed into his ear, but his fuddled brain could make no sense of them. Another jolt directly below the sternum forced his eyes open, and he stared up at the familiar expanse of off-white plaster above his head, recognizing the stain shaped like a lizard, where the water pipe had burst in the winter freeze-up three years before.

'There's somebody knocking at the door!' Mary said, for the third time, aiming another accurate thrust of her elbow into his ribs.

Some people can come out of a deep sleep and be instantly awake. It was an ability Constable 'Thorny' Deepbriar much admired in his fictional hero, Dick Bland, but one he himself sadly lacked. He came far enough awake to realize his wife was right; somebody was not just knocking, but positively hammering on their front door.

It was daylight, but since it was midsummer that only told him that it must be later than 4.00 a.m. Mary was sitting up, one hand trying to free his legs from the tangle of sheet wound round them, while pointedly rubbing the bruise on her shin, delivered as he tried to kick his way out of his dream. Finally released, Deepbriar swung his feet over the side of the bed and groped for his slippers. Groggily he headed for the door.

'Not like that,' his wife protested, sinking back against her pillow.

'What?'

'You can't go to the door in those, Thorny.'

'Bit thin, that's all,' he muttered, grabbing his dressing-gown from its hook and putting it on over the threadbare pyjamas. He'd rescued them from the rag bag when the weather turned hot, but they showed altogether too much of his manhood.

As Deepbriar flung open the door, the rector's hand was raised to make yet another assault on the knocker. 'Rector.'

'Sorry — urgent.' The clergyman was red-faced and breathless, 'Can you come?'

'Two minutes,' Deepbriar said, almost dragging the man inside and pushing him into a chair. 'Sit there and get your breath back.'

Not needing to be awake to get dressed, the constable had his uniform on in less than the allotted time and ran back downstairs.

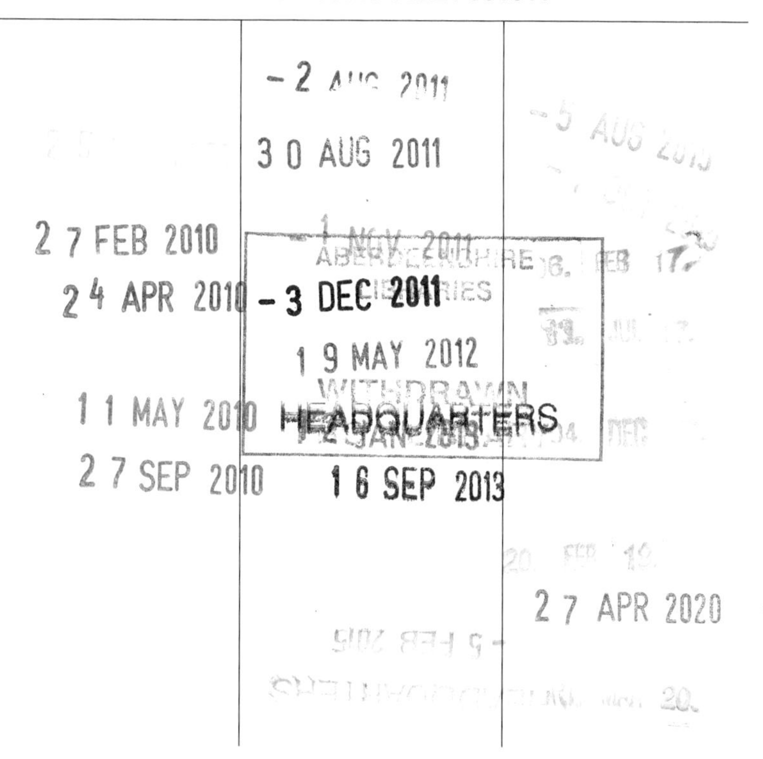

A L I S
1866243

The Reverend Robert Pusey had recovered his breath but remained agitated. 'I wasn't sure what to do,' he began.

Deepbriar ushered him outside. 'If it's that urgent you'd better tell me on the way.'

'Yes, of course. It's by the church wall. In Back Lane.' And with that he took off at a run, arms and legs pumping, his speed putting the younger man to shame. He gasped out his story while he ran, and some disjointed phrases drifted back to the constable as he struggled to keep up, but the early morning haze was still fogging his brain and he made no sense of them. They were turning down the alleyway beside the church, passing between high stone walls, before one word brought Deepbriar abruptly upright and fully awake. 'Did you say you *found a body?*'

'There.' The parson bent double, hands on knees, gasping for breath.

It had been a terrible death. The thin lips were drawn back in an horrific rictus, to show stained teeth. A swarm of flies buzzed around the tongue that protruded from the mouth, puncture wounds showing where it had been bitten through. Though swollen and discoloured, the tongue had only bled a little, so perhaps that self-inflicted injury had happened in the last agonized moments of life.

A petal from a dog rose, fallen from the

overhanging hushes, was stuck incongruously to one eye, which, once sparkling with life, now stared blindly at the sun. There was a great deal of blood on the shoulder, blackening as it dried. A flap of skin lay loosely against the rusty iron that had inflicted the deadly wound.

Deepbriar was a humane man; he hated to see an animal suffer needlessly, even when it was a predator, a killer of chickens as this fox had doubtless been, but to have been woken from sleep for this . . . He opened his mouth to give the rector a piece of his mind, but then he took in the whole of the scene before him and the words that actually escaped him weren't quite what he'd intended.

'Bloody hell!' Deepbriar tore his gaze away to stare wide-eyed at the rector. 'Sorry,' he added automatically.

Mr Pusey had got his breath back. 'My own reaction was similar, though I refrained from expressing it in quite that way. You see why I called you.'

Deepbriar nodded, leaning down to peer more closely at the huge metal jaws locked around the fox's body, the rusty points embedded deep into its flesh. 'It's a ruddy mantrap!'

'Here, of all places.' The rector wrung his hands together. 'The children will be on their way to school in a few hours. Do you think there could be more of these things about?'

'Let's hope not.' Something like a shiver ran up Deepbriar's back, as if this discovery had chilled the warmth of the perfect summer morning.

'You were right to fetch me,' Deepbriar said. It was a hard admission to make; relations between the village constabulary and All Saints Church had been rather strained recently. The rector didn't reply, though his nod seemed to hold more than mere acknowledgement.

'Is this church land?' Deepbriar asked, staring along the narrow pathway. It ran, with many twists and bends, between the churchyard and the back gardens of the houses in Meadow Row, barely four feet across and with walls on either side about six feet high. To the best of his knowledge, the track had no official name, but the locals called it Back Lane.

'Not as far as I know. I believe it must be a public road, despite being so narrow. Of course, the local children make frequent use of it; I've seen as many as two dozen at a time playing here.' He waved a hand towards the Ash Meadow council estate. 'It's conveniently close, yet out of sight of adult eyes.'

'I spent a few happy hours here myself,'

Deepbriar admitted. 'We used to call it Indian Gulch. It was the best place in the village for an ambush. Plenty of cover.' He gave a faint smile, remembering. With sticks for guns and grubby handkerchiefs tied over their faces, he and his friends had got a hiding for holding up old Job Taylor, one time landlord of the Speckled Goose.

Deepbriar pulled his attention firmly back to the matter in hand. 'Public property or church land, it makes no difference,' he said. 'Either way this is a serious business. We need to find this maniac. It doesn't bear thinking about, a child stepping into that thing.'

'I was under the impression that gin traps had been banned,' the rector said. 'Didn't I hear something about it on the wireless recently?'

'The law's not been passed yet,' Deepbriar replied, 'though generally gin traps aren't used so much now, thank God. There're plenty of alternatives that don't cause this much suffering. But I've never seen one this size — mantraps have been illegal for over a century, even the Victorians didn't use them, not officially at least.'

He bent over the big dog fox, noting how the trap's jaws had ripped into its shoulder, breaking the bone. He'd heard of animals biting through their own legs to get free, but this one hadn't had a chance; it had lain here dying in terrible agony, a process which probably took several hours. The size of the trap might account for the animal being caught in such a way, or maybe the fox had leapt off the top of the wall, coming from one of the gardens in Meadow Row.

'Foxes may be vermin, but I don't believe any creature deserves such a death,' the rector said.

'In my experience few of us get what we deserve,' Deepbriar responded drily, the old antagonism resurfacing.

'True.' The clergyman sighed. As if prompted by the constable's words he made what might have been an oblique reference to their past disagreement. 'Few of us intend to do harm, Constable; indeed, we try our best to do the opposite, although we often fail.' He paused as if there was more he wanted to say, then sighed again. 'An act like this shows a grave disregard for the well-being of others.'

Deepbriar pulled out the stake that anchored the trap to the ground by means of a rusty chain. The peg had been firmly hammered in.

'Do be careful,' the rector cautioned, as the constable set about releasing the body.

'Safe enough if you know what you're doing,' Deepbriar replied. 'I never handled one quite this size, but I helped my uncle set a few of these in my time. He used them for rabbits, until my aunt persuaded him against it. She couldn't stand to hear the poor things screaming half the night.'

Mr Pusey shuddered. 'As a city dweller I came here with quite the wrong idea about country life. I thought violence was an urban occupation.'

'Violence to other human beings, perhaps,' Deepbriar said, 'although we have our share of that too.'

'So I have found.' The rector nodded. 'But I don't understand why anybody would wish to cause such suffering, surely there are other ways to deal with pests. Even foxes and rabbits are God's creatures.'

'Mmm.' Deepbriar concentrated on his task, relaxing once the trap's bloodstained jaws had snapped safely shut again. 'What brought you out here so early, Rector?'

'The inability to sleep, and a fine morning,' the clergyman replied. 'A little time alone, a chance to reflect, is a rare thing. Maybe you find that too, Constable.' He sighed again, his voice dropping a little as he went on. 'It is thirteen years this week, since my son died. Coming across evidence of a violent death, even though it is only that of a dumb animal, brought back memories I would sooner forget. There are times when I believe those men born without imagination are extraordinarily fortunate.'

Deepbriar nodded mutely. His had been a 'good' war, and he had lost none of his nearest and dearest, but he knew many who had. Mr Pusey's son had died during a ferocious and bloody battle in the Far East, and the rector had never been able to discover the exact circumstances of his death.

It seemed like the right time to repair their friendship. Their disagreement had arisen when the rector allowed Bella Emerson to supplant Deepbriar as church organist. It wouldn't have been so bad if she was a better musician, or even a likeable person. In fact she was simply persistent, and hard to refuse. Setting his anger aside, Deepbriar acknowledged that the rector probably hadn't had much choice in the matter.

The constable cleared his throat, but before he could put his thoughts into words the rector had returned to the matter in hand. 'How can you find the man who did this?' he asked.

Deepbriar gave it some thought. 'Maybe somebody in the Row has been losing their chickens, though if that's the case I'd expect to have heard about it. People usually shout long and loud when they're being robbed, and I'm the first one they complain to, even if the culprit's a fox. Though where the heck they laid their hands on a trap this size, heaven only knows.'

He looked up at the church clock, now showing 5.15. 'If somebody from Meadow Row set this trap then I might give them the benefit of the doubt, but only if they're out here removing it before anyone else is out and about. They'll get the rough edge of my tongue, though, and they won't be trying any stupid pranks like this again.'

'And if nobody owns up?'

'Blowed if I know.' Deepbriar shook his head. 'I can think of a dozen people who'll have a stack of gin traps dumped in the back of a barn or hanging up in a shed. I can even think of one or two men who'd be willing to use them, come to that. But who's going to have a mantrap? And why put it here?'

'Would it be helpful if I inspected the rest of the lane,' Mr Pusey asked, 'just for the sake of safety?'

'It would, thank you, Rector. And maybe you'd ask old Sam to get along here with his scythe, so at least we won't have to worry about anyone hiding a trap where it can't be seen.'

'Of course.' The clergyman inspected the corpse, putting out a finger and gingerly touching the rich red fur, as if in benediction. 'Poor creature. I'll ask Sam to dispose of the body too, if you wish.'

* * *

'Blimey, I've not seen one of them since I was a nipper.' Cyril Bostock stared at the contraption Deepbriar held with something like awe. 'Old Grubb, who was gamekeeper on Lord Cawster's estate, 'e used to keep one 'angin' in the yard. When 'e caught poachers 'e'd take 'em to see it, tell 'em they were lucky they 'adn't put a foot in one just like it. Not that 'e 'ad any more, it was just to put the wind up 'em.'

The old man led the way round the side of his house, slouching along in his grubby nightshirt and carpet slippers. 'I've not lost no birds, not since Christmas.' When he pulled open the door of his shed the whole building shook. 'Them's all the traps I got,' he said, pointing to three small gin traps hanging from a nail on the far wall. They had plates no more than four inches across, and were covered in rust; it looked as if no amount of oil would ever make them usable.

Bostock slammed the door shut and a piece of wood fell from the frame, a puff of dust exploding from it as it hit the ground. 'Wood don't keep like it used to,' he grumbled. 'You never found out who 'ad them two chickens, an' I still reckon that were a two-legged animal,' he added darkly, favouring the constable with a sour look as he led the way back through a tangle of briars. Deepbriar didn't answer. Bostock was probably right. It was a rare fox that broke into a chicken coop and took two plump pullets without leaving a drop of blood behind. Although Deepbriar had had his suspicions at the time, he'd been unable to run the culprit to ground.

Bostock sniffed, giving the ramshackle fence that surrounded his hen house a quick shake as he passed it. 'Be out 'ere every night with me shotgun come December,' he said, 'An' I'll make sure them rogues down the Goose knows it. Mind, it's a wonder the Row ain't overrun with foxes, what with 'er an' the way she carries on.' He jerked his head towards his neighbour's fence. 'Feeds the bloody vermin, she does. Throws out bits o' bread an' stuff. Always at it she is.'

Deepbriar looked over the fence. The garden on the other side couldn't have been more different from Bostock's wilderness. Vegetables grew in orderly rows, the hen house stood on six solid wooden stilts, with a miniature door, closed and bolted, and a ramp leading down to a run at the edge of the neat lawn, the whole thing entirely enclosed in wire mesh. 'Reckon it would take a pretty smart fox to break in there,' Deepbriar remarked.

'Good morning, Mr Bostock. Constable Deepbriar.' The voice came from close above their heads and the two men looked up, startled. A head was poking out of the upstairs window of the next cottage, the grey hair neat, a pair of wire-rimmed glasses perched on the end of a beaky nose. 'Is something wrong? Only it isn't yet six o'clock.' It was a gentle reproof, but a reproof none the less.

'Sorry, Miss Cannon. I don't think this can concern you,' Deepbriar replied. 'There was a fox caught in a trap last night.'

'Hmph.' The woman gave her neighbour a look of contempt. 'Trapping foxes is quite unnecessary. All that is required to keep stock safe is good husbandry. My hen house and run are perfectly secure, as you can see.'

'That don't mean you should go feedin' the little red b — ' — Bostock caught a look from the constable — 'blighters,' he finished, scowling.

'I feed the birds, Mr Bostock,' Miss Cannon replied tartly. 'And the hedgehogs, which can be very beneficial in the garden. I can hardly be held responsible if the occasional scrap is picked up by a passing fox. Now, perhaps we may be permitted a little peace and quiet? If I may say so, this hardly seems a serious enough matter to warrant disturbance at this early hour.'

Deepbriar touched a finger to his helmet by way of a salute as the woman ducked her head inside and noiselessly closed the window.

'She's got a point,' Bostock said, leading the way to his back door.

'Miss Cannon didn't see the trap,' Deepbriar said grimly.

'Well, you seen mine. Ain't bin used in years.' Bostock yawned widely. 'Reckon I might get another 'alf hour in bed, if it's all the same to you.'

Deepbriar watched him go then headed home. His stomach grumbled. Maybe the affair would make some sense once he had a meal inside him. He had his orders for the day, and they wouldn't leave much time for anything else, he thought irritably; there were two summonses to be delivered, and a couple of traffic offences to follow up. After that he had to complete a cycle beat around the neighbouring villages. Failure to report from the police box outside Cawster at the correct time would get him in trouble with Sergeant Hubbard in Falbrough. Any enquiry into the business of the mantrap would have to be fitted in at either end of the day.

With a good helping of egg and bacon inside him, and suppressing a yawn, Deepbriar swung on to his bicycle at 7.30. Immune to the uplifting effect of summer sunshine and birdsong, he set off for Minecliff Manor.

⋆ ⋆ ⋆

Colonel Brightman shook his head vigorously. 'I won't have those contraptions on my land, Thorny, not even for rabbits,' he said. 'Wicked things. When I was Master with the Gadwell pack we lost a couple of hounds to them. Nasty way to die. But by all means have a word with Job Rowbotham if that'll set your mind at rest. Not that he'd object to using a gin trap if I let him; he's a bit set in his ways. He's getting on in years, of course.'

Deepbriar nodded, straight-faced. The colonel was eighty, while Rowbotham was at least twelve years his junior. It wasn't so much the gamekeeper's age that made the difference; he was of the old school, a man who would be happy to see poachers deported. Deepbriar had heard some of his bloodcurdling tales; if Rowbotham was to be believed, his predecessors had thought nothing of swinging a poacher from the nearest tree, like men in the American Wild West, and burying the body deep in their master's woods, where it would be neither sought nor found.

It wasn't Rowbotham he tracked down first though, but young Watts, the assistant keeper. Terry Watts was a bit of an unknown quantity, having only been in the area for a year. He and his wife lived in one of the tied cottages behind the manor gardens. According to Mary Deepbriar, Sylvia Watts was a nice girl, not very clever, but eager to enter into village life, and already a keen member of the Women's Institute. Her husband, on the other hand, kept himself to himself.

Deepbriar couldn't recall ever seeing the man in the Speckled Goose. There was nothing wrong with a chap being a teetotaller, though that usually went with being a churchgoer, and Watts didn't frequent All Saints either, or the Methodist chapel.

'Good morning, Constable.' Watts stood by the kennels, one hand on the latch. 'Were you looking for the colonel?'

'No, I've just seen him. I was hoping to find Job, but you'll probably do. I gather you're not allowed to use gin traps on the estate?'

'No.' Watts volunteered no more.

'Somebody set a trap last night and caught a fox,' Deepbriar said. 'It was on a footpath in the middle of the village, one that the local children use.'

'Daft thing to do,' Watts commented.

'Yes, especially as it was a mantrap.' Deepbriar watched the man's expression, hoping for some reaction, but his face showed nothing more than polite interest. 'I was wondering if there's anything like that kept on the manor, maybe left over from the old days?'

'I wouldn't know.' Watts turned away from the kennel, leaving the gate shut. The two retrievers inside barked their frustration. 'Quiet,' he said, not raising his voice. The dogs were immediately silent. 'You'd need to see Mr Rowbotham, but I can show you where we keep our equipment, if you want.'

'Yes, thanks.' Deepbriar followed him to an old stone building adjoining the tack room. Watts took out a key and unfastened the large padlock from the door.

'Always kept locked, is it?' Deepbriar asked.

'Yes. We've got a bit of bait in here, for the rats. The colonel's very strict about keeping it where the farm cats can't get at it. Guns and cartridges are kept in the house, of course.'

As Deepbriar had expected, there were

traps in the store, but they were all of the more modern type, designed to kill an animal quickly, not leave it suffering. 'Nothing missing?' he asked.

Watts looked around. 'Not that I can see,' he said. 'Mr Rowbotham would know for sure.'

'I'll call another time,' Deepbriar said. 'Thanks.' He waited while Watts closed the door and put the padlock back in place. 'How are you settling down in Minecliff? I don't suppose it's easy coming to the manor, not when the rest of the men here have known each other all their lives.'

Watts nodded briefly. 'Suits me all right,' he said.

Deepbriar watched as the man walked away. The under-keeper strode past both Ernie Pratt, the groom, and Mrs Brant, on her way to the kitchen, without a word or a sign of acknowledgement to either; he'd been right, Watts wasn't the sociable type.

2

Memory was a strange thing, Deepbriar reflected an hour later, as he walked in through the school gate, though that strange twinge of concern as he entered by the front entrance was more reflex than memory, beaten into him at an early age when Mr Visby was headmaster. The man had been over-fond of using the cane; he required boys reporting for Saturday morning punishment to enter at the front door, so passers-by would witness their shame.

There had been great rejoicing when the gentle Mrs Harris had taken Mr Visby's place. With the reign of tyranny ended, little else had changed. The boys' entrance and playground were still segregated from the girls' by iron railings with spikes along the top, while the pervasive smell of cabbage and urine remained ever present. Despite all Mrs Harris's pleading, the outside lavatories hadn't yet been replaced.

Everyone was in the hall for assembly. Trying to tread quietly in his size ten boots, Deepbriar made his way to the door at the back of the hall and looked in through the small glass panel at the top.

The children were just rising to their feet, and prompted by a chord from the ancient piano, they launched into '*All Things Bright and Beautiful*'. One enthusiastic but particularly tuneless voice reminded Deepbriar of his young friend Harry Bartle, and he smiled. Harry was nearly at the end of his training with the police force, and already a legend. He was the only man to have been turned down at an audition for the county constabulary choir before he'd even been issued with a uniform. Harry was tone deaf, but he refused to believe he didn't have a fine singing voice.

Mrs Harris had seen the burly shape outside the door, and with the children starting on the second verse of the hymn, she whispered briefly to one of the other two teachers and stepped down from the platform. Deepbriar held the door open for her and shook her proffered hand.

She gave him a sweet smile. 'We weren't expecting you this morning, Thorny. I hope nothing's wrong?'

Swiftly Deepbriar explained his mission to the headmistress. Having expressed her shock she gave a brief nod. 'Certainly you can talk to the children, though you may find them a little inattentive. We're preparing for the fête, and some of them are already overexcited.'

'I'll do all I can to make them listen. If there are more of those traps set around the village there could be a nasty accident.'

Mrs Harris frowned. 'Perhaps it would be better to advise parents to keep their children home for a few days, especially the infants.'

Deepbriar rubbed a hand round the back of his neck. 'I'd thought of it, but to be honest I'm afraid that's just likely to make the older ones even more determined to go looking for the darned things, rather than trying to avoid them.'

She nodded. 'Yes, you may be right. I'll have a few words with them after you've gone.' She smiled again, her cheeks dimpling. 'I believe it won't hurt to remind them that they don't want to get on the wrong side of Constable Deepbriar!'

'Very true,' he said, doing his best to look formidable. He'd been known to give particularly unrepentant boys a swift clip round the ear, but, recalling his own suffering at the hands of Mr Visby, he didn't make a habit of it.

He kept the talk short and to the point. These were country children, not likely to be upset by tales of sudden death, particularly when the victim was a fox.

'Of course foxes have to be kept down, or

we'd have no eggs for breakfast, and we wouldn't like that, would we?' Deepbriar concluded, giving his comfortably rounded stomach a gentle pat. He waited for the brief ripple of laughter to die down then went on, 'But Back Lane's no place to go setting a trap, particularly such a big and vicious one. It had a very strong spring' — he clapped cupped hands together loudly, making several of the children jump — 'and it was big enough to grab hold of any one of you, even young David at the back there. Size eight boots now, is it, David? Reckon it's time you changed your name to Goliath.' He addressed this remark to a member of the Hopgood clan, an eleven-year-old who could have passed for fourteen. As his school mates laughed the boy grinned cheerfully.

'Yes, well, it isn't really funny,' Deepbriar went on. 'I'm here to warn you that there might be more of these things about, so you need to keep your eyes open. I'm not saying don't go out to play, but I'm asking you to be very careful. And I'm asking you especially to look out for your younger brothers and sisters. I'll be organizing searches, but in the meantime it's up to you to be on your guard, every one of you.'

A small child in the third row raised a hand. 'That's Jane,' Mrs Harris whispered.

'Did you want to say something, Jane?' Deepbriar asked. 'Go on,' he urged, as the little girl nodded.

'My granny's cat got caught in a trap. Now it's only got three legs.'

This brought sniggers from the older boys, swiftly silenced by a look from their teacher.

'Yes, well, that's my point.' Deepbriar nodded gravely. 'Unlike Jane's granny's cat, you've only got two legs each, so you can't afford to lose one. We don't want any of you having to hop around school all day, do we? Think about what I've said, and take care.'

Deepbriar gave them a moment for his message to sink in, waiting for total silence. 'Just one more thing, then I'll let you get back to your assembly. If any of you find a trap,' he said sternly, 'or if you know where this one came from, I need to know. If you don't want to come and see me yourselves, you can tell your mum or dad, or your teacher. Will you do that for me?'

There was a pause, an uncertain murmur, then one voice was raised above all the rest. 'Yes, sir.' At that, it was as if a dam had burst, and every child present added their voice, until at last Mrs Harris had to clap her hands for silence. 'I believe you captured their attention, Thorny,' she said softly, escorting Deepbriar to the door.

'I just hope they don't see it as permission to go looking for trouble,' Deepbriar whispered in response, as the children rose to their feet and began to sing another hymn.

Down the road Deepbriar could see activity in the church field, where Minecliff's summer fête would be held. He glanced at the church clock and decided he had a few minutes to spare, letting his bicycle freewheel down the hill and through the open gate. Colonel Brightman's elderly Humber stood by the refreshment tent, and Deepbriar was surprised to see the colonel himself, supervising the unloading of a large basket from the boot of the car.

'Hello, Thorny, we meet again,' the old man called cheerfully. 'And in rather happier circumstances, I hope. You'll be joining the festivities tomorrow?'

'I'll be here in an official capacity to start with, I'm afraid, making sure nobody blocks the lane. But all being well I'll be along later to try my luck at some of the stalls.'

'Ah, yes, I seem to remember you're an expert when it comes to guessing the weight of the pig! Well, I trust you'll be here for the opening, in or out of uniform. I think you'll be rather surprised by our special guest this year.'

Deepbriar raised his eyebrows. Usually the

fête was opened by the colonel himself, or Lady Cecilia Downham-Bloom, an even older cousin from a distant branch of the Brightman family. 'Don't tell me you've found us a real live celebrity? Who is it, somebody off the wireless?'

'Better than that. Charles is coming home. He'll be on the afternoon train.' The colonel's lips curved in a faint smile as he dropped his bombshell. 'And he's bringing his fiancée!'

* * *

It was past one o'clock when Deepbriar rode his bike back into the village. He went home for a quick sandwich then set about organizing a search of all the footpaths in and around Minecliff. Knowing he couldn't get the job done alone, he called at the Speckled Goose, and found news of the incident in Back Lane had gone before him.

'I'll come and give you a hand,' Don Bartle said, polishing a glass, 'and I reckon Phyllis can spare young Frank too, once we're shut.' Frank was the new barman, employed to fill the gap left by Harry's departure.

'I suppose,' Phyllis agreed, with a martyred smile as she headed for the door to the saloon bar, 'I can cope with clearing up on my own, just this once.'

Ferdy Quinn ambled up to the bar. 'I'll join the hunt,' he said, mellowed perhaps by Don's best bitter. 'It's a quietish time.' This brought similar offers from a couple more regulars, men who were semi-retired, idle during slack seasons, but still fit enough to put in a day's work when there was some to be had. Deepbriar jotted down the names in his notebook. With the hay in, and harvest not yet started, he could probably find some more farm labourers with an hour or two to spare, but he didn't have the time to ride around and ask their bosses for the loan of them.

At that moment the door to the saloon bar opened and Phil Golding squeezed his huge bulk through the doorway. The general chatter was instantly silenced and a couple of men headed for the door.

'Afternoon, Deepbriar,' Golding said, ignoring the rest of the bar's customers as he waddled across the room. The death of his father a few years before had left him in control of an estate bigger than Minecliff Manor. Now Golding's was the largest market garden in the county, employing a great many men. The area of cultivated land Phil Golding had under glass was expected to double in the next two years, and he was tipped to become a millionaire.

'Good afternoon, Mr Golding,' Deepbriar

replied. Although Golding had figuratively spread his wings, physically he was becoming less mobile with each passing year, his size increasing in proportion to his ever-growing fortune. Puffing slightly from the exertion needed to walk a few yards, Golding leant heavily on the bar next to Deepbriar.

'Bartle's wife was just telling me about that trap,' he said. 'Rather an unpleasant business by the sound of it. If you want more help, I can let you have half a dozen of my hands for the afternoon.'

'That's good of you, sir,' Deepbriar said. He would have preferred not to accept any favours from Golding; the man would chalk this up and expect something in return. However, on this occasion the constable decided he had no choice, the sight of a child in place of that dead fox was likely to feature in his nightmares. 'Thank you, that should make the search a lot easier.'

Golding waved an expansive hand. 'I'm a father myself.' He gave a throaty chuckle. 'Not that you'd find any child of mine playing in the mud down a back alley.'

There was an inaudible muttering from the group at the far end of the bar. Golding didn't seem to notice, though Deepbriar caught a jaundiced glance between two of the pub regulars, one of them making a face behind the oversized nurseryman's back, the other winking at Deepbriar.

'That makes eleven of us,' Deepbriar said, snapping his notebook shut, 'reckon that should about do it. We'll meet at two-thirty outside the Goose.'

'I'll send the boys down in the lorry.' Phil Golding departed, the room seeming both larger and more airy once he'd gone. His sleek cream Wolseley stood outside, and as Deepbriar left the pub the man was still squeezing his bulk in through the door; if Golding got any larger he would have a job finding a car big enough to carry him.

When the men from Golding's arrived it turned out five of them were Italians who spoke very little English. Luckily the sixth member of the party was George Hopgood, the foreman, who'd learnt how to get through to his Latin workers with a mix of hand signals, mangled English and a smattering of their own language. 'Don't worry, Thorny,' he said, 'tell me what you want done and I'll see to it.'

Before Deepbriar could reply, several members of the Women's Institute, led by the formidable Miss Cannon, erupted from the village hall, all suitably attired in sensible shoes and equipped with sticks to beat down the nettles.

'Mr Quinn told me what happened,' Miss Cannon said, striding up to Deepbriar. 'If you have other things to do, Constable, you can leave this to me.' She unfolded a large map of the village and its surroundings. 'I had plenty of experience of handling volunteers during the war; I'll soon get this lot sorted out.'

'Well, thank you, Miss Cannon. I'm supposed to look after my regular beat, no matter what else crops up. Perhaps you'd be kind enough to report to me at the police station once you're finished.'

Ignoring George Hopgood's anguished expression, Thorny handed his volunteers over to Miss Cannon and set off to cycle his beat. A mile from the village he passed Golding's nursery, where a brand new fence had been erected along the side of the road, solid metal and six feet high. Deepbriar sighed, a frown appearing between his brows. Golding was always complaining about people trespassing on his property, but surely it hadn't been necessary to grub out a perfectly good hedge and put up a monstrosity like that.

By the time Deepbriar returned the search was complete; for the moment Minecliff was declared free of mantraps. The Italians were being entertained with tea and home-made cakes in the village hall, provided by several

WI members, among them a simpering Bella Emerson, who naturally hadn't been part of the working party. George Hopgood had reportedly gone home with a blinding headache. As Mrs Emerson and one of the Italians launched into a chorus from *Aida*, Deepbriar couldn't blame him, making his own excuses as soon as he could.

Shortly after five o'clock, his routine work out of the way for the moment, Deepbriar started a tour of the farms and smallholdings around the village, visiting anyone who might once have owned the lethal trap. By the time he'd finished he'd seen a huge number of deadly devices, including one gin trap almost as large as the one that had killed the fox, but it was cobwebbed and rusted solid. He was no nearer to finding the source of the contraption he'd got locked in a cupboard in his office.

The heat had gone from the day when the constable eventually cycled wearily back home.

'You're late.' Mary stood on tiptoe to kiss him, taking the helmet from his hands and pushing him towards the kitchen door. 'Get changed and have a quick wash, I'll have your supper on the table in ten minutes.'

'Thanks, love. I'll need to try and get a few hours' sleep, before I'm off out again.'

'Out? What's happened now?'

'Nothing, I hope, but I'll not chance this beggar setting another trap during the night. Assuming it's some kind of nutcase, getting somebody hurt on the day of the fête might appeal to him. I've a couple of lads offered to help; the last two I visited today. Billy Tapper and his brother Fred are meeting me.'

'That pair of rogues!'

He smiled wearily. 'As reformed poachers they decided it was an insult, me asking them about mantraps. They reckon it'll be a gamekeeper.'

'Well, they would say that,' Mary said thoughtfully. 'But I can't imagine either of the Tapper boys risking a child getting hurt. After all, Billy's got a little girl of his own now.'

'Yes, I saw her. Bright little thing. Anyway, I'll take help wherever I can get it. I think the Tappers were tickled at the idea of being on the right side of the law for a change.' He yawned, heading for the stairs. 'Sorry, love, shan't be long.'

Half an hour later Mary was clearing away the plates. 'I hope you'll be awake enough to come to the fête tomorrow, Thorny,' she said, as he drank the last of his tea.

'I'm on duty until three,' he replied. 'I'll have to come home and phone in, then get changed. It won't leave me much time.'

'I've already thought of that. I've arranged it all with the rector's wife. You can use the phone at the rectory; you only need to tell Miss Strathway at the exchange where to find you if you're needed. You can get changed out of your uniform in the rectory too; I'll take your clothes down when I go.' She put up a hand to stop him as he made to interrupt. 'I know you and the rector don't see eye to eye over this business with Bella, but I've already asked Mrs Pusey, and she says you'll be very welcome. It's all a bit silly; you and the rector used to be good friends.'

'I know, love. As a matter of fact I'd already decided it was time to bury the hatchet.' He pushed back his chair. 'I'll come to the fête, though you'd better pack a couple of matchsticks with my clothes, so I can keep my eyes open. I'm going up now, I'll try not to wake you when I go out later.'

* * *

The day of the fête dawned fine. Deepbriar was more than pleased to see the sun; the overnight patrol had failed to turn up any shifty characters, and at first light, around 4.20, he crept wearily back to his bed, waking with a start two hours later when the alarm clock rang.

Mary bustled around the kitchen even more energetically than usual, setting his breakfast down before him, along with a fresh pot of tea, before putting on her coat and hat.

'It's barely seven o'clock,' Deepbriar protested.

'I'm taking the cakes down first,' she replied. 'We're leaving them in Mrs Pusey's parlour until it's time to set up the stall. Then Mrs Harvey is coming to help with the pink elephants, and we'll have to do another trip with the sweets. I'll be home before twelve, so you won't need to get your own meal.'

Two baskets stood on the dresser, full of home-made fudge, toffee and other sweet things. 'They look good,' he said.

'Prizes for the children's pick-a-straw, and I know exactly how many there are,' Mary retorted, 'so keep your hands off.' She bent to kiss him. 'I did save a bit of coconut ice for you; it's in the larder. Don't eat it all at once, or it'll make your teeth ache.'

Deepbriar had barely finished his breakfast before he was called to the village hall in Possington. A cash box had gone missing overnight. He pedalled to the neighbouring village, where it took him most of the morning to establish that the suspected robbery was actually no such thing.

'I'm so sorry, Mr Deepbriar.' Mrs Appleby,

the treasurer of the Possington Music Club, was apologetic. 'After that robbery at Harwayes Bank last month — well, it makes you think, doesn't it? An armed gang in Belston, it makes thieves breaking into our village hall seem so much more likely.'

She glared at the club secretary who had finally arrived and solved the mystery. He was still holding the cash box she had reported stolen. 'Really, Mr Morgan, you might have come sooner. I woke up this morning and suddenly remembered I'd left the money out on the table after last night's meeting. Then when I got here I found the door wide open, and no sign of the box. You can't blame me for calling the constable.'

'No, the money certainly could have been stolen,' the secretary retorted, 'if I hadn't noticed it left lying about and taken it home for safe keeping. As for the door, I had my hands full; it must have just slipped my mind.'

'No harm done,' Deepbriar assured them. 'I'll be on my way.' The sound of raised voices, one tenor and the other soprano, followed him halfway back to Minecliff. Returning to the police house, the constable found things barely less fraught at home. His wife was looking positively harassed. 'You'll have to make yourself a sandwich,' she said. 'I've no time to cook. There's a bit of a crisis.'

3

'What's up, love? Anything I can do?' Deepbriar asked, picking up the kettle. 'Tea?'

His wife shook her head. 'I'm off out. And no, you can't help, not unless you're free to help run the cake stall this afternoon! Mrs Twyford's let us down.'

'Let you down?'

'Yes. She sent a message. I hope she's not poorly, I haven't time to go and see, not until this evening. The stall's going to be a problem; it's such short notice! I'll pop round and see if Bella will help. She can't stand for long because of that trouble with her feet. Still, even a couple of hours would be useful. She was going to be giving a short recital while the band are taking their break, but she has a sore throat and isn't able to perform.'

'Let's be thankful for small mercies,' Deepbriar said, but not loudly enough for his wife to hear. Bella Emerson was convinced she had a beautiful voice, but only her most sycophantic adherents in the operatic society shared her conviction. As for the cake stall, he couldn't see Bella Emerson putting herself out for anyone. Mary however, had a sublime faith in human nature.

Once he was alone, the constable ate a hasty meal, keeping half an eye on the clock. More and more people were coming to the fête by car each year, so there might be as many as twenty vehicles for which to find spaces; he didn't want them blocking the road. As he picked up his helmet somebody knocked at the front door, which served as an entrance to both his office and the house. Muttering a silent prayer that it was nothing serious, Deepbriar went through to answer the summons.

'Well, if it isn't Charlie!' Deepbriar smiled. 'Your father told me you were coming.' Major Charles Brightman stood on the doorstep, clad in his dress uniform and looking hot. Deepbriar felt briefly smug; the day was already very warm, but luckily county headquarters in Belston had finally sent permission for short-sleeve order. Beside the major was a pretty woman, maybe a year or two younger than her escort, wearing a cool-looking cream linen suit and matching hat. Her hand was linked firmly through the major's arm.

'Hello, Thorny,' Brightman said, offering his hand. 'How's police work going these days? Solved any more murders? I've brought the love of my life to meet you. Elaine, meet

Constable Deepbriar. Thorny, this is Miss Elaine Barr. Improbable as it may seem, Elaine, when I was a child this chap used to be my best friend; he was the only village boy who'd have anything to do with me. The rest of them didn't want to know a little squirt who went to a public school. Luckily Thorny was so big, the rest of them didn't argue with him.'

Elaine Barr shook Thorny's hand, a slight smile on her face. 'I'm never quite sure when Charles is teasing,' she said, 'but I'm very happy to meet you, Constable.'

'My pleasure, Miss Barr. Actually your fiancé was very popular, because his friends were allowed to fish in the colonel's pond. I was just that bit quicker to realize the advantages than the rest of them. I'm afraid my wife isn't here; she's down at the church field, setting out the cake stall.'

'It looks as if you were going out, too,' Miss Barr remarked.

'Just to the fête. I have to make sure nobody blocks the entrance by parking his car in the wrong place. Presumably you'll be heading that way, since you're doing the honours this year.'

Charles Brightman groaned. 'I couldn't persuade the old man against it. He expects everybody to enjoy this Lord of the Manor thing as much as he does. You don't think they'll throw eggs, do you?'

Deepbriar laughed. 'Not likely. The prodigal son returns. They'll probably see it as a fairy story, particularly when you turn up with a lovely lady at your side.'

'Mmm,' Elaine Barr laughed. 'I seem to recall the prodigal son had been up to all sorts of mischief. I believe there are things you need to tell me about your old friend Charlie, Constable Deepbriar.'

'Not now, or we'll never be finished,' Major Brightman said hurriedly. 'Look Thorny, joking apart, Elaine's a bit nervous about all this fuss. I wondered if you'd go ahead and make sure my father doesn't lay it on too thick.'

Deepbriar glanced at his friend's companion. The knuckles of the hand clutching his arm were white. 'Not to worry,' he said, 'as soon as I've sorted out the cars I'll station myself at the gate and make sure nobody's carrying rotten tomatoes or old cabbages. Seriously, Miss Barr, both your fiancé and his father are very well thought of in Minecliff. You'll be made thoroughly welcome, I promise. Just cheer the tug-of-war teams and buy an oddment from a stall or two and they'll be eating out of your hand.'

She gave him a slightly tremulous smile. 'Thank you, I'll bear that in mind.'

'We'll walk with you as far as the church, Thorny, then Elaine and I will go and inspect the family memorials until we're needed,' the major said.

'Not a bad idea,' Deepbriar said, 'it'll be cool in there.'

'Yes, probably better than lurking in the bushes beside the churchyard,' his friend grinned. 'Talking of the churchyard, what's all this about somebody setting a trap down Indian Gulch? It sounds as if everyone's making a lot of fuss. I mean, nobody wants a cat or dog getting hurt, but it's not that serious, is it?'

'It was the size of the thing that had me worried,' Deepbriar replied, putting on his helmet and pulling the door closed behind him. 'It was a mantrap.'

Elaine Barr exclaimed in horror. 'I never knew there were such things!'

'It was a favourite way of dealing with poachers a couple of centuries ago, Miss Barr. There's a new law banning all gin traps, but it won't be in force for a while yet. Mantraps are already illegal of course.' He sighed, shaking his head. 'Only a madman would set that trap where children might be running about. Maybe I should have been checking the local asylum yesterday, rather than the farms.'

The woman went pale, and the hand that held on to the major's arm trembled a little. 'I — it sounds — I mean, what will you do?'

'Don't worry, darling,' Major Brightman cut in, patting her hand soothingly. 'It's probably some local rogue with a grudge against the rector. Thorny will catch the blighter. Come on, we'll slip into the church via the vestry door, so nobody sees us. Let the old man know where we are, Thorny, there's a good chap.'

* * *

The fête was in full swing. A group of proud parents and grandparents were watching the children dance round the maypole, while the tug-of-war teams were assembling under the shade of the elm trees. Nineteen cars, the greatest number that had ever turned up for the occasion, had been guided safely into their allotted spaces, and Constable Deepbriar's working day, thanks to a special dispensation issued by Inspector Martindale, was about to come to an end. The constable stood looking out of the rectory window, hearing the church clock striking three. He telephoned Falbrough station, listening patiently to several minutes of clicks and crackles before he was connected.

'All right for some,' Sergeant Hubbard's deep bass voice grumbled down the line, having admitted that no new orders had been issued. Minecliff's constable wasn't required to remain on duty. 'Some of us have to work a full day.'

'If I win the pig this year I'll save you a couple of chops,' Deepbriar promised rashly. A slightly mollified grunt was the only reply, and the constable grinned as he put down the receiver. He picked up Mary's ancient shopping basket, peering inside to check that she'd put in his comfortable shoes. It would be good to get out of uniform.

As he put one foot on the stairs, a distant rumble of sound from outside made him turn back to the window. The noise grew louder, almost drowning out the laughter and shouts of merriment from the crowd in the field. Craning his neck, Deepbriar could see a motor cycle coming down the lane from the arterial road, swerving a little when it hit the bend. The engine was straining as the bike topped the slight rise and began to drop the last 200 yards into the village. As the machine passed between Mill House and the alms-houses the din was muffled briefly between the solid stone walls, then there was a final deafening roar and a frantic screech of brakes as the bike shuddered to a halt at the entrance to the field.

Recognizing both motor cycle and rider, Deepbriar abandoned the basket and ran. Jim Hopgood, George's middle son, wouldn't be speeding like that without good reason.

'Mr Deepbriar!' In his agitation Jim had dropped the bike on the ground, not bothering to push it on to its stand. 'There's been an accident. On the arterial road. There's a woman in the ditch. A lorry hit her.' The young man was breathless and, as he untangled the scarf from around his neck and took off his goggles, Deepbriar could see that his face was pasty white.

'Take it easy, lad,' Deepbriar said. 'You weren't involved yourself?'

Young Hopgood swallowed hard, his colour taking on a tinge of green. 'No.'

Deepbriar glanced around. He was relieved to see Major Brightman and Dr Smythe heading towards him.

'Something wrong?' the doctor asked.

'An accident. It sounds as if we'll be needing an ambulance. Tell me exactly where it happened, Jim.'

'Right by the crossroads. Near the bus shelter.'

The doctor nodded briskly. 'I'll go and phone.' He vanished into the rectory

'She wasn't moving. I think — ' Jim

Hopgood swallowed again, his eyes flickering from Deepbriar to the major and back again. 'I'm afraid she might be dead.'

Deepbriar turned to Major Brightman. 'No need to spoil everyone's day.' He looked at the field with its scattering of gaily coloured stalls. The festivities had faltered into a watchful quietness, and several men were beginning to stride purposefully in their direction, Colonel Brightman at their head. 'Perhaps you'd ask your father to tell people there's no need to stop the fun,' he added. 'Let them know I've been called to an incident on the arterial, will you please, Charles? Oh, and send somebody to find the rector, there may be people needing him as well.'

'Of course.' The major half turned away then paused. 'Look, I can drive you up there. The old man's car will be quicker than your bike.'

'Thanks, that would be a help.' As soon as the major had gone Deepbriar returned his attention to the young motor cyclist. 'Tell me what happened, Jim.'

'I was coming from Belston, and there was a lorry in front of me. I didn't see the woman, but I knew something was wrong when the lorry braked suddenly. It pulled up so quick I'd have run into it if I hadn't been slowing down for the turning. Soon as he'd stopped the driver jumped out of his cab and ran to the verge.' He gulped and put a hand to his mouth. 'Sorry. I'm feeling a bit odd, like.'

'It's the shock,' Deepbriar said. 'Go on, you're doing fine.'

Hopgood wiped his hand over his damp forehead. 'Right, well, I'd just got off my bike when a car came from the other direction. This old gent sort of took charge. He had a quick word with the lorry driver, and — and had a look . . . ' he faltered, then rallied. 'Well, he came over to me and said he knew a bit of first aid, and did I know where to find a phone box because we'd need the police and an ambulance. When I told him I was sure you'd be here, he said it was best I came to fetch you.'

'So nobody else was hurt?' Deepbriar asked, 'just the woman?'

'That's right. There wasn't a lot of traffic. There was a car coming past me, just as I was pulling up. It had a couple in it. I reckon they might have seen more than I did.' For the first time since he'd arrived he looked around and seemed to notice where he was. He took in a great gulp of air, his colour beginning to return to normal. 'I'd forgotten about the fête. That's why I was coming home a bit early . . . Sorry,' he said again, 'seems daft thinking about that after what's happened.'

'Nothing to apologize for, lad. That's all for now, nothing else you can do. Get yourself home, have a cup of tea and a sit down. I might be along to talk to you later.'

In the house, Dr Smythe was just replacing the telephone receiver as Deepbriar appeared. 'Ambulance on the way,' he said. 'My bag's in the back porch, won't take me a second to fetch it, but I didn't come by car.'

'We're going in the colonel's Humber,' Deepbriar told him, glancing out of the window and relieved to see the old soldier, with Miss Barr's hand tucked protectively under his arm, shepherding the last few curious onlookers back towards the stalls. The major drove up to the door then, with the rector already in the front passenger seat.

The colonel rarely drove his elderly Humber at more than a brisk walking pace, but the major showed none of his father's caution, gunning the ancient engine unmercifully. In minutes they reached the crossroads, and the brakes squealed a mild protest as the car rolled to a stop on the grass with its bumper just inches from the bus shelter.

Deepbriar unclenched his teeth. 'Thought we'd end up in the ditch too,' he muttered to Dr Smythe as they got out of the car. 'A bike's fast enough for me.'

'You're likely to get left behind that way,' the doctor replied. 'It's a high speed world we're living in.'

'But we wouldn't have this sort of thing happening if everybody wasn't so keen on dashing about,' Deepbriar shot back.

There was a lorry drawn up slightly askew at the side of the arterial road, skid marks showing where it had started braking, the black parallel lines beginning by the cross-roads. About halfway along, the tracks left by scorched rubber were smeared over with something that shone wetly in the bright sunshine.

Several cars had pulled up nearby, two of them in the middle of the carriageway, effectively blocking the road. Deepbriar glanced over his shoulder as the sound of an engine announced another vehicle on its way. 'Charles,' he said quietly, as the major came to join him, 'can you find out who owns those cars and get them moved out of the way? We don't want any more accidents. Don't let anyone leave though, not for the moment.'

Nearly a dozen people stood in a group at the side of the road. Beyond them lay an old army blanket, looking as if it had been flung down haphazardly on the long grass. Some of the onlookers were staring, as if transfixed, at the shapeless khaki-covered mound, while others kept their heads averted. One young woman stood in the bus shelter, her face unnaturally pale and her gaze fixed unseeingly on the trees across the road.

The small crowd moved aside to let the two newcomers through. 'If you'd all just step back, please,' Deepbriar said, 'and give us some room here.'

'Constable.' An elderly man stood his ground.

'Not just now, sir, I'll be with you in a moment.' Deepbriar shooed him back with the others, until there was a clear space around the blanket. Only then did he notice the large man in shirt sleeves and cloth cap, who sat on the kerb a little way off, his head in his hands. Deepbriar made half a move in the man's direction, then changed his mind. If that was the lorry driver he was obviously going nowhere; he could wait.

Doctor Smythe took hold of a corner of the blanket, and Deepbriar went to look down briefly at what lay beneath. As a country bobby, months could pass without him encountering death in any form. Twice in two days seemed too much. Although the previous day's body had been that of a dumb animal, the terrible nature of the death had left him shocked. Now here was a woman who should have had many more years of life ahead of her, lying face-down, discarded among the sun-scorched weeds. Her hair was a mousy brown with no sign of grey, one side still neatly curled, the other a mess of blood, the skull seriously misshapen.

The rector whispered a few words and made the sign of the cross. 'Nothing I can do here, Thorny,' he said quietly. 'I think that young woman in the shelter might need help.'

Deepbriar nodded, saying nothing. On this same stretch of road he'd dealt with an incident two years before which had left three people dead, but it got no easier; he never became hardened. He steeled himself to be professional, to do the job he was paid for. The woman's limbs were flung wide in apparent abandon. She wore a pink dress decorated with small yellow flowers. The constable felt a vague churning in his stomach as he realized it was familiar. He had seen somebody wearing that dress, or an identical one, only days earlier.

Deepbriar moved round and bent down, trying to see her face, but only her cheek was visible, the rest buried in a tangle of grass and oxeye daisies. Since she had evidently been on foot perhaps he should have suspected that she was local.

'Hmm, sad business,' Smythe said. 'I'd say

death was instantaneous,' he added quietly, crouching down beside the constable and gently easing the body over a little so they could see the face. He drew in a sudden shocked breath. 'Oh, Lord. It's Mrs Twyford.'

4

Deepbriar watched the ambulance drive away. He'd spoken to most of the witnesses, but he hadn't yet interviewed the young girl who had been a passenger in the car following the lorry. He found her still hiding in the bus shelter.

'She took a few steps across the grass, and she looked at the lorry,' she told him, her voice a little shaky. 'She stared straight at it. Then she ran.'

'You're sure she wasn't looking at somebody on the other side of the road?'

'There wasn't anybody there.'

It hadn't been likely, Deepbriar reflected. The lane twisted and turned without going anywhere, then rejoined the arterial road a mile further on.

'Could there have been anybody else in the bus shelter?' he persisted.

'No, I'm sure it was empty. I looked. I mean, what she did was so strange.'

Perhaps Mrs Twyford had been distracted, staring into space rather than at the approaching lorry. Perhaps she was unaware of the danger. But why was she there at all?

'It's a bit odd,' Dr Smythe said, when Deepbriar rejoined him a few minutes later. 'She can't have been waiting for a bus; there's nothing due at this time on a Saturday.'

'She could have been expecting a friend to pick her up.' Villagers from Minecliff would wait in the bus shelter if they had arranged a lift, since it was on a direct road from Belston, but no distraught friend had arrived, although it was now nearly an hour since the accident had occurred.

Deepbriar stared at the smeared blood-stains on the grass near his feet. It had been out of character for Mrs Twyford to let Mary down over the village fête; she was usually meticulous to a fault. What brought her here? Even if she had something important to do later in the day, she could have helped her friends to prepare the cake stall first.

It felt strange to return to the village and find the last of the revellers still drifting away from the festivities. Deepbriar let out a long slow breath. Normal life had carried on whilst he presided over the scene of violent death; it was like coming to the end of a long and arduous journey, and this time his discomfort had nothing to do with the major's driving.

All the other vehicles had gone from the lane by the field gate, and Major Brightman stopped the Humber right at the entrance.

'You won't want me again, will you Thorny?' he asked, slamming the car door. 'I'm afraid Elaine must be feeling neglected.'

'You can tell her I'm sorry for keeping you, Charlie,' Deepbriar said. He grimaced. 'I'm sure we'd all have preferred to spend the afternoon bowling for coconuts.'

Deepbriar found Mary in the tea tent, helping to pack the empty plates and tins that had once held food; they would be carried back to the village hall for eventual return to their owners. He skirted round a large figure in a floral print dress, seated in a camp chair and taking up a great deal of space, to give his wife a quick peck on the cheek. She stared at him in surprise at this public display of affection, then responded with a smile before she went on with what she was doing.

Mary's two helpers were also busy, and there was still a pile of washing up waiting to be done. The woman who sat watching, and getting in the way, was Mrs Bella Emerson. Her large feet, crammed into a pair of fashionable shoes that looked several sizes too small, were stretched out before her.

'I'm so sorry not to be more help,' Mrs Emerson said plaintively. 'You'll understand, Thorny, dear, I gather you police officers suffer with your feet too. It's very hard to sit here watching everyone working, when I'd far rather be making myself useful.'

Something seemed to snap in Deepbriar's head. The use of his nickname was a privilege reserved for his friends. He didn't care for Mrs Emerson, unlike the mousy little woman whose broken body had been carted away in the ambulance that afternoon. Widowed during the war, Mrs Twyford had never complained about her solitary state. She was the kind of person few people noticed, but she'd always been a worker, quietly helping out whenever and wherever she was needed. In fact she'd been the total opposite to the impossible Bella.

'Tell you what, Mrs Emerson,' Deepbriar said brusquely, picking up a tea towel and speaking with a firmness that brooked no refusal. 'Let me move that chair for you. I'll wash and you can dry. I don't like to see you sitting there suffering.'

'You're still in uniform, dear,' Mary Deepbriar demurred, as Mrs Emerson reluctantly rose so he could place her chair beside an empty trestle table.

'Nobody to see,' he replied, picking up an apron that lay nearby and tying it round his waist; right now a little bit of normality was just what he needed.

But the heap of dirty crockery wasn't enough to occupy his mind, and once

Deepbriar had collected a bucket of hot water from the vicarage, emptied it into a bowl and plunged his hands into the suds, his thoughts wandered. Something was troubling him. The most obvious answer to the mystery was one he didn't want to consider: Mrs Twyford might have run in front of the lorry deliberately.

With a sigh Deepbriar knew he mustn't put off a visit to the woman's house. She might have left a note. He hoped he was wrong; suicide was regarded by the church as sinful, and by the law as a crime. Deepbriar didn't want the little woman's memory to be stained with that kind of stigma, but it was his duty to discover the truth. It was an unpleasant part of his job, delving through the personal effects of the deceased. For some reason his thoughts flickered back to the previous day and the fox, dead in the cruel trap. He sighed again. There were times when he almost wished he'd gone to work for the railway, like his dad.

With the washing up done, Deepbriar threw out the dirty water and removed the apron.

'All done, love?' Mary asked cheerfully, looking around at the tent, which was almost empty. 'It's such a shame you were called away. You'll be wanting something to eat.'

Deepbriar nodded absently. He could put off his visit to Mrs Twyford's house until he'd had his tea, but it must be done. Suicide note or no, like most people in the village the woman usually left her door unlocked, and he had to make sure the place was secure.

There was another job he wasn't looking forward to. He would have to tell his wife the identity of the woman who had died up at the junction. Mary had a soft heart, and although they hadn't been best friends, she'd known Mrs Twyford a long time.

Thorny Deepbriar walked alongside his wife, pushing his bicycle homewards with two baskets and a bulging shopping bag hanging from the handlebars. Strictly speaking that was against regulations; he'd be in trouble if a senior officer saw him abusing police property, but it had been a long hard day and he was past caring.

Deepbriar stared glumly at the baked path as it passed beneath the bicycle's wheels; he wished he could expunge the last few hours from his memory. The lovely summer afternoon was slipping quietly into an evening of soft blue skies, the perfume of honeysuckle and sweet peas wafting to them on a gentle breeze, as if to point a contrast to his state of mind.

'Funny thing,' Deepbriar said, 'it poured

with rain for the fête last year, but I had a smashing afternoon. Do you remember?'

Mary smiled. 'I remember you enjoyed that bottle of whisky you won in the raffle.'

'I did. The pork was good too. And I knocked down a couple of coconuts. Bit different this year. Goes with the job, I know, but it doesn't get any easier.' He fell silent, knowing he would have to tell his wife soon, but not wanting her spoil her day.

'How did you find out that Mrs Twyford wasn't coming to run the cake stall?' he asked suddenly.

'Whatever made you think about that?' When her husband didn't answer she glanced at him. Deepbriar grimaced. 'Looking for a change of subject,' he lied gruffly.

'Oh, right.' The look she sent his way this time was sympathetic. 'Well, Gladys wrote a note. It was a bit strange; she didn't address it to anyone in particular, it was just a scrap of paper saying she wasn't able to come. The boy who lives at the end of her row brought it. The one with the reddish hair. I can never remember his name.'

'Geoff Berdale?' Deepbriar hazarded.

'That's it. He came tearing into the field on his dad's bicycle. If Mrs Harris hadn't been there helping set up the area for the maypole dancing I think he would have ridden right into the tea tent! Anyway, he practically threw this note at Sylvia Watts, and he was gone before she'd even had a chance to look at it. Of course once she'd read it she showed it to Miss Cannon, who brought it to me.'

'I don't suppose you've still got it?'

'What?' She stopped then, staring up into his face. 'Thorny, what on earth would you want that for? Are you sure you're feeling all right?'

'Let's just get inside,' he said wretchedly, gesturing at the garden gate which was only a few yards away. 'There's something we have to talk about.'

Thorny sat his wife down at the kitchen table and told her about her friend's untimely death. As Mary's eyes filled with tears he patted her clumsily on the shoulder then turned away to light the gas under the kettle. A few minutes later he put a cup of tea down in front of her. 'I'm sorry, love, I meant to wait and tell you in the morning; you've had such a busy day.'

'And you haven't?' she retorted, drying her eyes and reaching across the table to grab his hand. 'There are times, Thorny Deepbriar, when I don't think you understand me at all.'

He grinned briefly. 'I'd say that's most of the time. I've never been able to figure out how women's minds work.'

She gave a theatrical sigh. 'You and every other man in the world! But why were you interested in that note Gladys sent?'

'Because I want to know what the heck she was doing up on the arterial road this afternoon!'

'I don't think the note will help much.' She pulled one of the baskets across the table and began to rummage inside. 'There's just a chance it's in here, I threw in all the rubbish at the end of the day. It's strange isn't it, Gladys can't have been running for the bus, not at that time of the afternoon. And why didn't she come to help us set up the stall this morning? But maybe she didn't want the local bus. Isn't there a coach on a Saturday afternoon?'

'Yes, at five to two. And the next one's not till five to four. That can't have been why she was there, unless she didn't know the times and just went on the off chance.'

'No, she knew all the timetables by heart. It was always a bit of a joke at the WI; everybody knew they could ask Gladys if they couldn't remember what time the next bus was. I really don't understand it,' she mused, 'why didn't she catch the bus at the post office, if she was going to Belston?'

'What makes you think she was planning to go to Belston?' Thorny took a mouthful of hot sweet tea, and leant back in his chair. His troubles had grown no less, but it was good to be sitting in his own kitchen talking to Mary. A little of the ache was easing out of his neck and shoulders.

'She'd been going there a lot.' Mary Deepbriar glanced up from her search and gave her husband a sad smile. 'It's such a shame. She'd been so happy lately. People have been joking about her having a new man in her life and I couldn't help wondering if it might be true.' A moment later she triumphantly pulled a scrap of paper from among the litter of dirty tea towels, pieces of greaseproof wrapping and crumpled paper bags. 'Here we are.'

The constable smoothed out the note. It was only about three inches across, with ragged edges as if it had been torn from something larger. On closer inspection he realized it was part of an envelope. *Sorry, can't do the cake stall today, Gladys Twyford*. The words had been hastily scribbled in pencil. On the other side, one edge of the paper bore a few letters written in blue ink; *rd*, at the top, below that *ane*, and at the bottom *hire*. No mystery there, just fragments of Mrs Twyford's address.

Mary finished her tea and rose to her feet. 'You must be hungry. Will eggs be all right?'

'Not just yet, love, I've got to go out again,' Deepbriar replied, tucking the note into his pocket and reaching a hand to his helmet. 'I'll be back as soon as I can.'

* * *

Mrs Twyford's cottage was small and neat and not particularly remarkable, a bit like Mrs Twyford herself, Deepbriar thought, as he tried to avoid stepping on the plants growing across the narrow path; he felt clumsy blundering around wearing his size tens in such a tiny space. Knowing there could be no reply, he nevertheless tried knocking at the front door, his fingers leaving marks on the polished brass knocker. He tried the handle. The door was locked.

'Thorny.' The voice from the side of the house made him jump. The rector was standing at the garden gate, looking as furtive as it was possible for an upright man of the cloth to look. 'I was a moment before you. I believe we'll find the back door open, Mrs Twyford rarely locked it.'

With a brief nod Deepbriar followed the clergyman round the house, where the top half of the stable door was hooked back. Deepbriar unlatched the lower half and stepped inside, and was a little surprised when the rector followed him. The kitchen was clean, everything tidy and in its place, as if its owner had just popped out for a few minutes. A large tabby cat stirred and stretched on the rug by the stove, looking up at the two intruders through unworried yellow eyes.

'You said you were here before me. Did you come inside?' Deepbriar asked, turning back to face the rector.

A less dignified man than Mr Pusey might have been said to squirm. 'No. But I admit I thought about it. Mrs Twyford didn't have any close family. I thought maybe I could be of use. Somebody will have to make the arrangements — '

'I'll try and find her next of kin if nobody comes forward, but I don't see there's any great rush,' Deepbriar said. 'She was an organized sort of person; I wouldn't be surprised if she left a will. I'll check the solicitors in Falbrough on Monday.' Sudden enlightenment hit him. 'You don't think it was an accident, do you? You're wondering if Mrs Twyford left a note.'

The rector twisted his hands together. 'If she ran out in front of that lorry deliberately, the coroner will have no option regarding the verdict. And from what I heard at the scene of the accident — It's hard to imagine what might have driven the poor woman to take her own life.' He sank on to the hard wooden chair beside the door. 'Seeing her like that this afternoon, Thorny, it was a terrible shock. Mrs Twyford was a true Christian, and I don't just mean she attended services and came to church twice on Sunday. Yet when she was in trouble she didn't come to me. I let her down.'

'You can't be sure — ' Deepbriar began, but the rector ploughed on, his face bleak.

'No, listen. There's something else, something that was important to her. Unless this affair is handled carefully, I may not be able to bring Mrs Twyford to the resting place she wanted. You'll know better than I do, the Twyford family connections with Minecliff go back for centuries. There are more memorials in the church to Twyfords than there are to the Brightman family.' He looked up and met the constable's eyes. 'You were there when we buried Digby Twyford. It was a rare honour we bestowed upon him, but he was a war hero. It seemed the right thing to do.'

'He's down under the crypt,' Deepbriar said, suddenly seeing the light.

'Yes, along with several of his forebears. The trouble is, our bishop is so old-fashioned.' The rector pulled a long face. 'I suspect if he had his way we'd still be burying suicides miles outside our villages, and probably at crossroads.'

Deepbriar gave a sympathetic nod. 'You may have a problem. But the evidence can't be altered. And there's the living to think about. It sounds as if the lorry driver had no chance to avoid her; he'll be having a few sleepless nights.'

'I know. It wouldn't be fair if any blame were to attach to him. I just thought, if there's no proof of her intentions, the case might be less cut and dried. A sudden aberration, perhaps a touch of the sun after all this hot weather. You never know, she may even have a history of dizziness or fits,' the rector finished, clutching at straws.

'I'm not sure that's much of an improvement on suicide,' Deepbriar said drily, 'suggesting she was mentally unstable, though that might satisfy your bishop. Anyway, so far I don't see any sign of a note,' he went on briskly. 'I'll check the rest of the house. You'd better wait here.' He went through into the little parlour, which was just as tidy as the kitchen. There was a writing case on the sideboard, but it held only unused paper and envelopes. A thought occurring to him, Deepbriar extracted one of the envelopes then studied the note that Mary had given him. They weren't even similar, but there was no reason why they should be, since the remnants of writing suggested the used one had come to Mrs Twyford in the post.

In some households it would be commonplace, to tear up an old envelope and use it to write a note, but in this little home, neat as a new pin and almost obsessively tidy, the use of the scrappy piece of paper jarred. It was out of character for Mrs Twyford to do such a thing when she had a supply of paper to hand.

Deepbriar closed the writing case and went on with his search, but he found nothing, and when he returned to the kitchen he shook his head in response to the rector's enquiring look. 'She didn't leave a note,' he said. 'But there is one funny thing: her handbag doesn't seem to be here.' The brown leather bag had accompanied Mrs Twyford everywhere. It was a large receptacle, almost more distinctive than the mousy little widow herself Nobody had mentioned seeing a handbag at the crossroads, neither before nor after the accident. Deepbriar castigated himself for not conducting a proper search along the grass verge.

There was a shuffling step outside. Mr Pusey leapt to his feet, turning to look at the bent figure who was staring suspiciously in at the open doorway. 'What's going on here?' Mrs Grimes was over ninety, but her brain was as sharp as her piercing blue eyes.

'Good evening, Mrs Grimes,' the rector said. 'You gave me a bit of a start.'

'Were you looking for Mrs Twyford?' Deepbriar asked.

'No, I knew she wasn't here. I came to feed Tibbles.' She looked with fondness at the cat, which rose languidly to its feet and wound itself sinuously around her bare purple-veined ankles. The old lady delved in the pocket of her apron. 'She put this through my door.'

Deepbriar took the note. The paper was from the same source as the one Mary had given him. Again the message was written in pencil, and it was even briefer than the other: *Please look after Tibbles*. He turned the note over. On the other side there was a stamp with a postmark across it, a little blurred, but he could make out the time and place of posting easily enough. As for the words Mrs Twyford had written, they could apply to a few hours, or be seen as a request that her neighbour should care for the cat for the rest of its life.

'She must have left it after I'd gone to the fête,' Mrs Grimes said. 'I went to have tea with Miss Cannon on the way home, that's why I didn't get here earlier. Mrs Twyford must have been called away.'

'I'm afraid there's some bad news, Mrs Grimes,' Deepbriar said. 'Come in and sit down for a minute.'

5

'I'm sure the rumours weren't true,' Mary Deepbriar said, straightening her hat in front of the mirror. She held a lethal looking hat-pin poised as if intending to stab herself in the ear. 'Lots of people go to church without being devout, but Gladys Twyford wasn't like that. She wouldn't have done anything she thought was sinful.'

'You said yourself she was happy recently. And she'd been going to Belston to visit somebody.' Deepbriar shifted his shoulders uncomfortably in his Sunday suit. When he'd made his self-imposed inspection of the local lanes and byways just after dawn it had already been warm.

'I know I said she might have a man friend, but that doesn't mean she was having an affair,' Mary protested.

'I wish I knew what came in that envelope,' Deepbriar mused.

'The one she used to send us the note?'

'Yes. She got the letter yesterday. It was posted in Belston on Thursday evening. It might tell us why she cried off the cake stall. If I could only find her handbag, maybe that — ' He broke off. 'The cat!' he yelped.

Mary jumped, narrowly escaping injury from the hat-pin she was thrusting into place. 'Thorny! Don't do that! What could a cat possibly have to do with Mrs Twyford's letter?'

'Nothing. I just realized I locked her cat in when I shut up the house last night. And I don't know if Mrs Grimes has a key.' He bent to give his wife a quick peck on the cheek. 'Sorry love, I'll have to go and check. I'll see you in church.'

Deepbriar unlocked the door to 4 Stellings Lane, and pushed it open. A stripy grey streak of fur hurtled out past his feet and dashed away down the garden. 'Sorry, Tibbles,' Deepbriar murmured. He hesitated before he stepped inside; the little cottage was full of silence, and he felt a tingle of desolation run through him, as if the house knew what had happened to its owner. Deepbriar shook himself briskly. It was bad for him, this going short of sleep.

The constable placed a hand on the top of the stove. It was cold. He opened the door; the fire had died down to grey ash. It was impossible to say if Mrs Twyford had burnt a letter in there the previous day, but the thought sent him hurrying into the parlour.

The fireplace was hidden by a tapestry

screen, which was why he'd missed the telltale black wisps lying on the bars of the grate. Pulling out the ashcan he drew in a sharp breath. There was a tiny remnant of paper left, one scorched edge still attached to a larger piece which was charred almost to a cinder. A single word was clearly readable, in blue ink and written in the same rounded hand as the fragments on the envelope: '*tell*', it said.

Deepbriar sank back on his heels, disappointed; this could be just another piece of envelope. He reached out a hand to pick it up, then something stopped him. There were letters visible on the carbonized paper below those he had just read, fragments of two more lines below those innocuous four letters. The first of them definitely didn't spell out Minecliff. Deepbriar leant closer, careful not to exhale, since even a breath of air might destroy the fragile scrap of evidence. The first three letters were definitely '*wan*'. After that he wasn't sure. It looked like a rather oddly formed '*b*'. No, he decided, it was '*to*', followed by '*n*'. *Wanton*. The word below wasn't complete, but he couldn't think of many that contained the letters '*urdere* . . . '.

* * *

'I'm real sorry, Mr Deepbriar.' Billy Tapper stood at the front door of the police house, his fingers playing nervously with the flat cap in his hands. 'I wouldn't have bothered you on a Sunday, but you did say to tell you if we found anything.'

Deepbriar suppressed a sigh. The smell of roast beef wafted to him. His years as a married police officer had given him an acute sense of timing where meals were concerned; in exactly thirty-eight minutes his dinner would be cooked to perfection. If he went out, in about fifty minutes Mary would eat her meal without him, and his food would be left to dry out on a hot plate. In around ninety minutes his wife would lose patience and go to visit her sister, leaving him to come home to eat a solitary and unappetizing meal in an empty house. 'That's all right, Billy. What's the trouble?'

'I found another one of them traps,' Billy said.

'Where?'

'The Spinney. Don't go lookin' at me that way, 'cos I wasn't up to nothin'. I'm straight now, no more poachin' for me, not with little Susan to look after. Anyway, my Bessy would have my hide if I got into any more trouble.'

'Then thank heavens for Bessy. So, what has our nutcase caught this time?'

'Nothin'. The trap was right in the middle of Spinney Way, with the grass round it all trampled down, so I saw it plain. It was lucky Gip an' Flo gave it a wide berth though, a young pup might've got nosy.'

'You didn't just leave it?'

'No, I used a bit of branch to spring it, an' I brought it back.' He waved a hand. 'Wasn't no lightweight neither. It's outside your gate.'

Deepbriar followed him on to the road. 'Flipping heck!' He stared down at the rusty contraption in dismay. It looked even bigger than the one that had killed the fox.

'Don't reckon he was tryin' to catch no one,' Billy Tapper said consideringly, 'not with it lyin' out in the open like that. More like it was — I dunno — a warnin' or somethin'.'

'A warning of what, that we've got a madman loose in the village?' Deepbriar reached to pick up the gin trap.

'I carried it by the chain,' Billy said hastily, 'in case there was fingerprints.'

'You can't get prints off a surface like that,' Deepbriar told him, 'nice clean shiny metal maybe, but not on all that rust. Though it was clever of you to think of it, Billy. Look, I ought to see where you found it.' His stomach gurgled, reminding him that it was dinner-time. 'Can you meet me later, say three o'clock?'

'I dunno, I'm supposed to be takin' our little Susan out in 'er pram. Bit of fresh air an' that.' He scratched his head, embarrassed by this admission. Deepbriar hid a smile. Billy had been the village bad-boy until Bessy waltzed him up the aisle. Being firmly wound around her little finger was doing him no harm at all.

'Tomorrow then?'

Billy nodded. 'I ain't workin' till late tomorrow, 'ow about we do it at eight?'

Deepbriar thought quickly. He had a very important appointment at Falbrough Police Station at eleven, and he mustn't risk being late. 'Make it seven-thirty and you're on,' he said. 'I'll meet you by the war memorial. Thanks again, Billy.' He looked down at the sinister object he held. 'You ever see anything like this before?'

He hadn't expected an answer, but young Tapper looked suddenly shifty, more like the man Deepbriar had helped convict of poaching some years before. 'Yeah, once.'

Deepbriar prompted him. 'Well, are you going to tell me where?'

'It was a long time ago. Ten years, nearer twelve maybe. Me an' Fred was in the manor woods, lookin' for birds' eggs. We sneaked up close to all them sheds behind the stables, where they keep logs an' stuff. I saw ol' man

Rowbotham carryin' a couple o' traps just like this across the yard. Didn't see what 'e did with 'em, though, 'cos Fred sneezed an' we 'ad to leg it.'

* * *

Three hours later, hot, splashed with mud and soaked from the knees down, Thorny Deepbriar stomped round to the back door of the police house. Clutched under one arm he held a large brown handbag, which dripped green slime down his shirt. He dropped the bag on the doorstep and eased off a wet boot, screwing up his nose. His sock squelched and steamed as he put his foot down gingerly on the sun-baked path.

The other bootlace had tied itself into an impenetrable knot. The constable stopped struggling with the tangle briefly to slap at his neck; the boggy ground that surrounded the Dally Pond had been swarming with midges, and hundreds of them seemed to have followed him home. Still, he had Mrs Twyford's bag.

Some instinct had led the constable to the pond, no more than a mental itch but every bit as insistent as the ones left by the marauding insects. He put his success down to a lucky guess, prompted perhaps by his addiction to detective stories; the Dally pond was close to a green lane, and that lane took you from the village to the arterial road without being seen.

Having finally divested himself of the other boot, Deepbriar marched triumphantly inside, eager to share his triumph.

'Stop right there.' Mary met him in the hall, an exasperated expression on her face. 'Look at you!'

'I took my boots off,' Deepbriar protested. Reduced in an instant from conquering hero to small boy, he took two steps back, off the hall runner and on to the kitchen lino, the dripping handbag leaving a trail of dirty brown spots behind, alongside the telltale prints of his size ten feet. 'Sorry, love. It's Mrs Twyford's bag.'

'So I see.' She sighed. 'Let me by, before that mat dries.'

'No, don't you bother yourself, go back and sit down. I'll clean up this mess.'

Mary gave him an old-fashioned look. 'Since when are you an expert on cleaning up messes? If you want to be useful then make some tea, and get out the fruit cake; it's in the royal wedding tin.' She laid a thick wad of old newspaper on the kitchen table. 'You can put that filthy thing on there, if you don't mind.'

Some time later, with peace restored and

their tea cups empty, they sat facing each other over the ruined contents of Mrs Twyford's bag. These included a handkerchief, two packets of hairgrips and one of safety pins, a small sewing kit, a powder compact, a comb, two headsquares and two pairs of gloves, but the only paper they found was a single ten shilling note in the purse. 'Nothing,' Deepbriar said bitterly. 'All that effort. I thought at least there'd be an address book.'

'I don't think she needed one,' Mary remarked. 'I told you about the bus timetables. She knew all sorts of things off by heart, and she never needed to write addresses down, she just remembered them.'

'I was hoping to find who this friend of hers was.'

'It must have been a man, I suppose,' Mary sighed. 'But he can't have been married; I'm sure Mrs Twyford wouldn't steal another woman's husband.'

'Why else would she keep things secret?'

'Perhaps he wasn't free. He might have been living with his ageing mother, or maybe it was like that film we saw. You know, *Jane Eyre*, where his wife was mad, but he couldn't divorce her.'

'Highly likely,' Deepbriar nodded. 'I bet there's a whole lot of mad women locked up in big gloomy mansions in the middle of Belston.'

'Well, it doesn't matter now, does it? What will you do with her things?' Mary asked, fingering the disintegrating packet of hair-grips.

'Dry them out and put them in her cottage. They belong to whoever inherits her property.'

His wife straightened her shoulders, suddenly brisk. 'I'm glad you didn't find anything. It must all have been a dreadful accident. I can't bear to think Mrs Twyford killed herself.'

'No,' Deepbriar said. 'Mr Pusey will be glad. He can go ahead and bury her with her husband.' But somebody had sent that letter, he thought, and if his guess was right they had named Mrs Twyford '*wanton*', and maybe mentioned murder. Perhaps the threat to expose some guilty secret to her friends and neighbours had been enough to send her running out in front of that lorry.

* * *

With his boots polished to an even higher sheen than usual, and every item of his uniform spotlessly clean, Deepbriar pedalled out of Minecliff. The feel of Mary's encouraging kiss was still fresh on his lips; she knew how important this day was to him, and her belief in him buoyed up his spirits. He rode slowly, enjoying the fresh summer scents in the air, taking a leisurely look at his beat as it unwound beneath his wheels; today of all days he wouldn't risk getting hot and bothered on his way to Falbrough.

Earlier that morning Billy Tapper had shown him where the second mantrap had been found; Deepbriar agreed that whoever set it hadn't intended to catch anything, either two or four-legged, but that didn't make him feel any easier. God knew how many more of the things might turn up; it could only be a matter of time before somebody got hurt.

Deepbriar pondered on the possible origin of the gin traps for a while, but he came up with no new suspects, and his wandering thoughts moved on to the questions surrounding Mrs Twyford's death. Since he'd drawn a blank with the handbag his only hope was to find her mysterious friend. He would call at the solicitor's office later; if she'd left a will that might give him a lead.

Mulling over his current cases kept Deepbriar calm until he was in the outskirts of Falbrough and only half a mile from the police station, but then his stomach began to perform somersaults. As he parked his bike his heart was beating far faster than it should have been.

'Morning, Thorny.' Detective Sergeant Jakes went by quickly, not pausing to chat. Deepbriar opened his mouth to return the greeting but his tongue seemed to have been disconnected from his brain. Before he could summon up a response Jakes had gone.

Behind the main desk Sergeant Parsons was speaking to an elderly woman with two small children in tow. The sergeant gave Deepbriar a nod of acknowledgement and pointed his pen towards the CID office.

The two children stared up at Deepbriar, mouths open slightly. He wondered briefly if they could hear how loudly his heart was drumming; he'd never been so nervous in his life. The constable glanced at the clock on the wall and, as he hesitated, Parsons gave another quick nod, and again gestured with his pen. Deepbriar took a few reluctant steps. He was nearly half an hour early for his appointment, he'd expected to be given time to hand his incident report sheets to Sergeant Hubbard first. Taking a deep breath, he tapped on the lacquered wood.

Inspector Stubbs looked up briefly from the papers he was reading. 'Come in, Constable. Have a seat, I shan't be a minute.'

Deepbriar obeyed, sitting stiffly upright and resisting the temptation to fidget, though he'd somehow taken up a very uncomfortable position on the hard wooden chair. An unwelcome memory came to him; this was as bad as reporting to Mr Visby, that time he'd cut off Cynthia Down's plait.

He'd wanted a move to CID for years, and just over six months ago Inspector Stubbs had recommended him for transfer. Deepbriar enjoyed being a village bobby; he appreciated his good fortune in being posted to the place that had been his childhood home, but he'd always yearned for something more challenging. Ever since he joined the force he'd wanted to follow in the footsteps of his hero, Dick Bland, the fictional private eye, and become a detective. To make that dream come true he would leave Minecliff without a second thought.

'Right.' The inspector pushed the papers into a file and leant back in his chair. 'Look, Thorny, I shan't beat about the bush. I've got an idea you've always hankered after a plainclothes job, but I'm afraid it's not going to happen.'

It felt as if his face had frozen. Deepbriar gave a quick nod. At that moment he couldn't have uttered a word if his life depended on it.

'I'm sorry.' Stubbs took a paper from the

drawer beside him. 'I did my best, but Inspector Martindale and Chief Inspector Swift overruled me. I'd like you to see their comments, because I'd hate you to think that you've been rejected by the CID. It's just that the uniform branch are refusing to let you go.'

His eyes wouldn't focus properly, but he made an attempt to read, a few words holding his attention. '*Valuable local knowledge — wealth of experience — shortage of mature officers —* '

Were they telling him he was too old? It wasn't his fault the CID had always turned him down in the past.

'Listen.' Stubbs leant forward. 'This isn't absolute. You have a right to put in a request to the superintendent, and if you do then I'll back you. Even if you don't appeal, this decision has to be reviewed in three months' time. I've looked through your record, and you've shown an aptitude for the sort of job you did last winter; it just hasn't been noticed.'

Deepbriar dredged up a reply. 'Good of you to say so, sir. I imagine the problem is it's a bit late in my career.'

'They did raise that point. Most DCs start when they're younger, but I believe you have a lot to contribute. I'd still like to have you working with me, Constable.' He gave a small smile. 'We don't want another murderer at work in Minecliff, but if you were to have a case which proved that the Crimmon affair wasn't a fluke — '

The constable managed to summon a grin in response. 'As it happens I'm investigating a violent death right now, but the victim was a fox.'

Stubbs laughed. 'This I've got to hear. Hang on, I'll get somebody to bring us a cup of tea. And I've got an idea there are some chocolate biscuits left.'

More like Mrs Harris than Mr Visby, Deepbriar reflected wryly, as Stubbs went to the door to call to the young constable in the outer office, but he didn't think tea and biscuits, even chocolate ones, were going to make him feel better. He'd happily have settled for a good hiding, if only they'd given him the job.

6

'That's not fair!' Mary's indignation rang down the telephone line, warming Deepbriar's heart. 'The inspector promised — '

'It's not up to Inspector Stubbs,' Deepbriar put in, 'he did his best. And he said there's still a chance, the decision will be reviewed in three months. Look love, I've got a few things to do while I'm here, which means I'll be late. I'll have something to eat in the canteen. They're auditioning at the society tonight, aren't they, and you won't want to miss that.'

'I don't know. *Tosca*'s a bit ambitious for us. Maybe I shouldn't take part this time.'

'Don't be silly, you're the best singer they've got,' Deepbriar said bracingly. 'I'll come and walk you home from the village hall, after you've finished.'

'Are you sure? I don't have to go.' She hesitated. 'Oh, Thorny, I'm so sorry. I thought we'd be celebrating. I bought a really nice piece of mutton this morning.'

'Put it in the meat safe and save it for tomorrow. You go off to the operatic society, I'll be fine. Anyway, you never know, after the fiasco with *Carmen* maybe Mrs Emerson won't insist on taking the lead this time. Then we'd really have something to celebrate!'

* * *

The chair in the solicitor's office was comfortable, and the place had a warm somnolence about it in the summer afternoon heat. It was an effort to stay awake; Mr Morton's face lost focus for a moment.

'Mrs Twyford named us as her executors,' the solicitor said, peering at Deepbriar over the top of his glasses. 'I trust I can rely on your total discretion?'

'Of course, Mr Morton. It's kind of you to help me.' Deepbriar gave his thigh a painful pinch, forcing his eyes a little further open.

'Hmm. It's an unusual will. We are instructed to read it at the first meeting of Minecliff Parish Council to take place after her funeral.'

This revelation had the effect of waking Deepbriar up. 'The rector and I are trying to trace her next of kin; may I ask if there are any family bequests?'

'We shall be informing several people where and when the reading of the will is due to take place, in accordance with Mrs Twyford's instructions. Naturally we shall also inform them of the funeral arrangements. As far as I know Mrs Twyford had no surviving relatives.'

'None at all? So, there's no major beneficiary?' Deepbriar's hero, Dick Bland, had once dealt with a case where an apparent accidental death had turned out to be murder, the criminals having been prompted to kill their aged uncle to get their hands on a legacy. He bit his lip, feeling a little ashamed of his disappointment; it must be the heat, making his mind wander.

'I can't reveal the details of Mrs Twyford's will before the official reading, Constable, though I can see no harm in allowing you a little hint. She was a generous and public-spirited woman, who felt that her husband's deep roots in Minecliff should be remembered.'

Deepbriar nodded. Mrs Twyford had presumably bequeathed her money to the church, perhaps for a memorial window, or maybe, he thought, suddenly optimistic, a new organ. That aroused thoughts of Mrs Emerson. He frowned and cleared his throat, annoyed to find himself so easily distracted. 'I believe Mrs Twyford had a close friend in Belston.'

'Ah, yes, Mrs Ethel Vennimore.' Mr Morton pushed his spectacles up his nose. 'This is in strictest confidence, Constable Deepbriar. Mrs Twyford lived in dread of becoming the object of gossip.'

'I already assured you of my discretion, Mr Morton,' Deepbriar replied, a little nettled. They had skated delicately around the manner of Mrs Twyford's death for several minutes at the beginning of their discussion. That the friend was female came as a surprise, and Deepbriar said no more, waiting for the solicitor to go on.

Mr Morton's glasses slid back to their normal position. 'You'll know that Mrs Vennimore died? Let's see, that must be eight months ago. Mrs Twyford came to us a short time before her friend's death, to alter her will, since Mrs Vennimore was to have been a beneficiary.'

'*Before* her friend's death? Didn't that strike you as a little strange?'

'Mrs Vennimore suffered a prolonged and debilitating illness. I understand her death came as a merciful release.' The solicitor gave a discreet little cough. 'I believe I may disclose without prejudice that she herself suggested that Mrs Twyford remove her name from the will.'

'Vennimore.' The significance of the name had just occurred to Deepbriar. 'Then her husband would be — '

'Gordon Vennimore, yes.'

One of the wealthiest men in Belston,

Gordon Vennimore owned a company that made wireless sets and gramophones. And with a move into the new television era, his business was expanding fast. Gordon Vennimore was a big noise in the chamber of commerce, and, if the local newspaper was to be believed, he was also a personal friend of half the members of the city council. It seemed Mrs Twyford had moved in exalted circles.

'Mrs Vennimore died eight months ago.' Deepbriar mused. 'Yet I believe Mrs Twyford continued to visit Belston regularly.' Was it possible that the quiet, mousy little woman had been comforting the widower?

'I wouldn't know about that,' Mr Morton replied stiffly.

Deepbriar knew better than to press him, and after thanking the solicitor for his help he left, grateful to get back into the air. Gordon Vennimore was a powerful man, with friends in high places, any further enquiries would have to be handled with care.

Mrs Twyford was the subject of another conversation that day. Deepbriar sat across a table from Sergeant Hubbard in the canteen, viewing his doorstep beef and pickle sandwich with little enthusiasm.

'Don't often see you eating in here, Thorny,' Hubbard said morosely, picking up the last crumbs from his sausage roll. 'You having a wife to go home to.'

'She's at the operatic society,' Deepbriar replied. 'Besides, I have to go and see a witness.'

'That business at the crossroads?' Hubbard buried his nose in his mug of tea. 'I read the incident report and I didn't need to be a genius to read between the lines. You reckon that woman did herself in.'

'Maybe.' Deepbriar certainly wasn't going to admit to considering another possibility. Could that letter have been an invitation to a rendezvous at the crossroads? And if so, had the meeting ended in murder? It was exactly the sort of thing that happened in a Dick Bland mystery.

'Some women go a bit odd when they get to that age,' Hubbard offered sagely.

Deepbriar nodded and chewed silently on his sandwich, trying not to think about that 'nice piece of mutton' Mary had mentioned. Both bread and beef were so dry they had to be helped down with a mouthful of tea. He wondered if the cheese sandwich would have been any better. 'You ever have any experience of poison pen letters, Sarge?' he asked, when he'd finally managed to swallow.

'There was a case before the war,' Hubbard replied. 'A woman started writing insults to all her neighbours. Used red ink, splashed it about so it looked like bloodstains. Mad as a hatter. Why?' he winked broadly. 'Your past catching up with you?'

By way of answer Deepbriar took out the envelope containing the two notes and the fragment of charred paper, explaining about his guess at the letters that had been visible before the wafer crumbled to soot.

'What was she like, this Mrs Twyford?' Hubbard asked.

'Very respectable. Quiet little soul, but got on well with everybody. The rector called her a real Christian, not one of those who goes to church on a Sunday and forgets how to behave the rest of the week. Look, do you think I should have shown these to the CID?'

Hubbard shook his head. 'Not enough here to build up a case,' he said, 'just a theory on your part.' He gave the constable a shrewd look. 'Besides, if she was a decent sort of body you don't want her labelled as a suicide, do you?'

'No. But suppose somebody drove her to it'? Suppose this *was* a poison pen letter? Whoever it was could have a go at somebody else.'

'Until they do, you've got nothing but a wild idea that could just be your imagination working overtime. Take my word for it,

Thorny, you did the right thing keeping it quiet.' The sergeant stood up, pushing back his chair and picking up his mug and plate. 'We've all got enough to do without chasing wild geese.' He leant across the table and lowered his voice. 'You want to stop reading those penny dreadfuls, Constable. Addle the mind, they do.'

Deepbriar returned the pieces of paper to their envelope and replaced it in his pocket. He had known what Hubbard would say, the sergeant always favoured the option that gave him the least amount of work. It took Deepbriar ten minutes to finish the sandwich, and by that time his jaws ached. On his way outside to fetch his bicycle he found himself caught up in an argument between two of his colleagues and a pair of belligerent drunks.

Unable to avoid getting involved, Deepbriar escaped a few minutes later with a bruise on his cheek and a splash of vomit on his best uniform trousers. That required a few minutes in the washroom as he tried to get rid of the smell. Fed up to his back teeth, he wanted nothing more than to go straight home. It hadn't been one of his better days.

There was nothing to stop Deepbriar going back to Minecliff, but he had one more job to do, and if he didn't see to it now he'd only have to come back later in the week.

Reminding himself that Mary wouldn't be home, he made up his mind and checked the address he had to find. Deborah Williams lived on the other side of Falbrough. Naturally.

The girl who had hidden herself in the bus shelter on Saturday afternoon was quite willing to be interviewed. She no longer looked pale and fragile, getting to her feet with a smile as her mother showed Deepbriar into the front room.

'Perhaps we should leave,' the older woman offered, giving her husband a meaningful look as she turned off the wireless.

'That's not necessary, Mrs Williams,' Deepbriar replied. 'This won't take a moment. I only wanted to check up on a couple of things I forgot to ask your daughter after the accident.'

He wasn't greatly surprised to find the girl had nothing new to add to her statement. 'All my friends have been asking about it,' she told him, evidently enjoying the notoriety of having witnessed a fatal accident, 'I've gone over it lots of times. It all happened just the way I said.'

'You're absolutely sure she wasn't carrying anything when she ran across the road?' Deepbriar persisted. 'It could be something quite small, like a piece of paper.'

'No. I think I would have noticed. I'm sure

her hands were empty. I mean, I can still see what happened in my head, as clear as day. That poor woman, she must have been round the bend, mustn't she, dashing out into the road right in front of that lorry.' She gave a melodramatic shudder. 'I hope I never ever see anything like that again.'

'I hope so too,' Deepbriar said, rising from his chair and giving the girl's parents a friendly nod of farewell. 'I won't trouble you any further.'

Although it wasn't yet eight o'clock, the evening had suddenly turned dark. As Deepbriar put on his cycle clips it started to drizzle.

* * *

The village hall offered a haven of light and life, and Deepbriar gratefully shook out his cape, hanging it on a peg beside the door. The meeting of Minecliff Amateur Operatic Society was evidently breaking up. Mary waved a hand at him as she headed for the little kitchen, carrying a tea tray.

'Auditions over?' Deepbriar asked, as Mr and Mrs Harvey passed him on their way to the door.

The man mumbled something in reply and swept out. Mrs Harvey gave her husband a worried glance. 'Nice evening, Constable,' she said quickly, and inaccurately, before she too scurried away. Intrigued, Deepbriar scanned the remaining members of the society. It didn't take long to locate the cause of Mr Harvey's ill-temper.

Bella Emerson stood with a dark, square-shouldered figure, her shoulder tucked possessively against his as their two heads bent over a musical score. Thorny recognized the man. He was the oldest of the Italians who had helped search the village paths after the first trap was found, and obviously he had a better command of English than George Hopgood realized. He was managing to carry on a conversation with Mrs Emerson quite adequately, when she gave him a chance to get a word in.

'Evening, Thorny.' Will Minter strolled over to the constable and gave him a knowing wink. 'Got ourselves a new star,' he added, lowering his voice. 'Our leading lady thinks he's the bee's knees.'

Deepbriar nodded. 'I heard them singing together a few days ago. *He*'s not bad.'

'The way Bella tells it you'd think he was from flipping La Scala.' The farmer chuckled. 'Nothing to do with the way he keeps flashing those dark Latin eyes at her, of course.'

At that point Mrs Emerson noticed the

newcomer and headed towards them.

'Look out, Thorny, you've been spotted,' Minter said, showing an uncharacteristic turn of speed as he made for the door, giving a vague wave of farewell to the room in general. 'Goodnight, all.'

'Thorny, you dear man, have you been working all this time? And you're wet; you've been out in the rain!' As Will Minter vanished, Bella Emerson descended upon Deepbriar, dragging the Italian behind her. 'You must meet Mr Bonelli — Antonio. He's to be our Cavaradossi. He's a very talented tenor. It's such a shame you don't have time to join us these days; I do believe this production will be our best ever.'

Deepbriar had stopped attending operatic society meetings a few weeks after Mrs Emerson joined, claiming pressure of work. Before that he'd enjoyed playing piano for their rehearsals, but listening to Bella Emerson's singing on a regular basis was really too much for a serious music lover to take.

'It's one of the penalties of being a policeman,' Mary said, coming up behind Thorny to take his arm, and relieving him of the necessity of finding some suitable response. 'Excuse us, Bella, we'll be off now; it's been a long day. Goodnight, Mr Bonelli.'

* * *

'Nice bit of rain last night,' Job Rowbotham commented, by way of greeting. 'Were you looking for the major? He and Miss Barr have gone riding.'

'No, it was you I wanted, Job. You'll have heard that I took a look at your traps a few days ago. Somebody told me you used to have some more. I'm looking for gin traps. Big ones.'

'We had some. It's no secret.' Rowbotham's weathered face gave nothing away. 'The colonel ordered me to throw them out, years back.'

'Yes, that's what I heard. The trouble is, Job, I've known you disobey orders when it suited you. Do you want to tell me where those traps are now?'

'I might want to, but I can't.' The gamekeeper took tobacco and cigarette papers from his pocket, offering the packets to Deepbriar once he had the makings of a roll-up.

'No thanks,' the constable said. He waited for the other man to snap a match into life against the stone wall and inhale his first mouthful of smoke. 'So, what happened to those traps?'

There was a long silence. 'They vanished.'

Rowbotham said at last. 'Somebody stole them.'

Deepbriar's scepticism must have shown on his face.

'Honest as I'm standing here,' the old man said. 'Come on, I'll show you.' He led the way out of the stable yard, past the barn and the log store to a small stone-built shed, its slate roof sagging and covered with moss. Wild roses and old-man's beard hung down over the door, which didn't look as if it had been opened in years. 'There.' Rowbotham pointed at the door frame, alongside the ancient lock. Deepbriar stepped closer and whistled. There were pale splinters of wood showing on both the door and jamb, and the lock hung loose.

'The damage isn't exactly recent. When did you discover this?' Deepbriar asked.

'Yesterday. Terry Watts said you'd come calling, and that started me thinking. I put them old traps in here years ago, buried under a heap of other stuff. I swear I'd forgotten all about them.'

'So why did you keep the things?'

'Not sure I know. I never was one for throwing anything away.' As Rowbotham struggled to pull the door open against the tug of brambles and thick stems of clematis, the constable could see what he meant. The little hut was full of every kind of junk, with dusty rotting sacks piled over old farm tools that must have been obsolete when the gamekeeper was a boy. By moving aside an ancient plough and a cartwheel with most of the spokes missing, the two men managed to reach the far corner, where an old bench was piled high with willow baskets and trugs, all of them falling apart.

'They were under here,' Rowbotham said. 'All that's left now is the small ones, the sort we used for rabbits.'

'So it's only the big ones that have gone missing? Two or three, were there?'

'Can't be exactly sure, but I reckon there was maybe seven or eight.'

'That many!' Deepbriar winced. 'So far we've got two back, and we've been darned lucky nobody's been hurt. Who else knew they were here?' he demanded, keeping a check on his anger. Raging at the old man for disobeying the colonel's orders would do no good.

The gamekeeper pondered a while. 'Reckon the major knew,' he said. 'Wouldn't be surprised if most of the men had a good idea too; they knew I wasn't keen on throwing stuff out. This place is a bit of a joke, like.'

'How about the new man, Watts?'

Rowbotham shrugged. 'I've had no call to tell him, but he could have found out. He's got a key to this place, I gave him all my spares when he started the job. I know he had a look in here a time or two.'

'Then maybe he's the next one I should talk to. Where will I find him?'

* * *

The gun-room smelt of oil, leather and polish. Heavy panelled doors stood open, revealing the colonel's collection of shotguns. 'You come to check they're all safe and sound, Constable?' Terry Watts asked. He put the box of cartridges into a drawer and closed it, then locked the gun cupboard.

'No, but I'm interested in the theft of something almost as dangerous,' Deepbriar said. 'I was wondering if you know who broke into that old shed, round the back of the log store?'

Watts shook his head. 'I don't know who it was,' he replied, 'but I know exactly when they broke in. It was the twenty-third of January. We had a shoot on.'

'That long ago? You're sure about the date? The damage isn't very noticeable until you get close.'

'I'm sure. There'd been a fox coming and going down that track by the side, and I was keeping an eye out for it. Mangy-looking thing, but it was a cunning beggar, must've been nearly Easter before I finally nailed him. Best bit of cover was right by the shed, I spent a lot of time leaning against that door. I'd swear to it, Constable, the shed was broken into during the night of the twenty-third. I found the door half open, the morning after the shoot. I took a quick look inside and all I could see was junk. I pushed the door shut and forgot about it.'

Having jotted this down, Deepbriar looked up from his notebook. 'You didn't tell anyone when you saw that the lock had been broken?'

'Like I said, I forgot. There was a problem with one of the horses and I was sent to fetch the vet.' Watts shrugged. 'I didn't think there was anything worth stealing anyway.'

Before Deepbriar could reply, a sound from the doorway made both men turn.

'Oh sorry.' Sylvia Watts giggled. 'I thought you'd be on your own, Terry. I know you said I shouldn't come in the house unless I'm asked, but I thought I'd better tell you I'm off to town. It's such fun, I wish you'd come too sometimes. What's the point of having it if you don't — '

'Sylvia!' Watts looked irritated. 'I'm busy. And didn't we agree you wouldn't go telling everybody our business?'

'Yes, but Mr Deepbriar won't tell anybody.' She looked at him coyly. 'I had a little windfall, Constable. A legacy.'

'And she's trying to spend the whole lot in a month,' Watts said. It sounded as if he wasn't quite sure whether he was joking or serious, so Deepbriar made no comment.

'I couldn't do that,' the woman replied. 'Better go, or I'll miss the bus.' She planted a fleeting kiss on her husband's cheek, leaving them with a jaunty wave of her hand.

'Sorry,' Watts turned back to Deepbriar, a little crease between his eyebrows. 'About the shed. Has something gone missing?'

'Half a dozen big gin traps. Mantraps.'

'I didn't know,' Watts said instantly, looking concerned. 'I was told the boss wouldn't have gin traps on the estate.'

'Hmm.' Deepbriar licked his pencil. 'This shoot. Can you tell me the names of any of the people who were here that day?'

'Nearly all the men on the estate turn out as beaters, and there's a list of the ones who come from outside. Here.' Watts picked up a book from the table. 'The colonel insists I write down the names for each day. Those who turn out regular get a Christmas box.'

Deepbriar scanned the list for 23 January. The writing was distinctive, with the letters sloping steeply backwards, but it was easy enough to read. He recognized most of the names. 'I'm surprised Mr Rowbotham allows Fred Tapper and Bert Bunyard anywhere near the colonel's birds,' he remarked, copying the list into his notebook.

Watts shrugged. 'Reckon he likes to keep them under his eye,' he said. 'They can't do much harm when they're beating.'

'Question is, how would any of these people have known where to find those traps?' Deepbriar pondered. 'I think I'd better have a word with one or two of the other men. By the time I've done that, maybe Major Brightman will be back.' He would have to tell the colonel that the traps turning up around the village were actually his property; the old man wasn't going to like it.

* * *

'He'll have to go!' Colonel Brightman's narrow face was bright pink and his white moustache quivered. 'Rowbotham has been getting away with things for years, and I've turned a blind eye, but this . . . '

Deepbriar fidgeted, wishing himself elsewhere. He was standing in the great hall of Minecliff Manor, surrounded by hunting trophies and ancient portraits of the Brightman family. Elaine Barr, her cheeks attractively flushed from her ride, was looking uncomfortable too, but she kept her arm firmly linked with the major's, as if she had no intention of abandoning him.

The constable had hoped to talk to his friend before he broke the news to the colonel, but Rowbotham had forestalled him, seeking out his employer while Deepbriar was talking to Terry Watts, and admitting that he'd hidden the traps instead of destroying them. If the major hadn't arrived and intervened, the gamekeeper would probably have been dismissed on the spot. As it was, he'd been sent back to work with his ears still ringing from his employer's furious dressing down.

'You can't place all the blame on old Job,' Charles Brightman said reasonably. 'I knew about those traps; maybe some of the men did too. And he wasn't the one who blabbed about them still being on the estate: I'm afraid that was me.'

7

'You knew those traps hadn't been destroyed?' Colonel Brightman stared at his son, and for an instant Thorny imagined he saw the old man as he'd been half a century ago, poised to tear a strip off some young subaltern.

'Yes, I did. I'm sorry. I came across them by accident years ago.' The major caught Deepbriar's eye briefly, his mouth quirking down. 'In the light of what's happened I wish I'd done something about it. And I'm truly sorry I mentioned the traps at the shoot. My mind was on my dinner date; Elaine had hinted that she might give me the answer I'd been waiting for.' He gave his fiancée a sheepish grin. 'It's the only excuse I have for acting like an idiot.'

'Do you remember if anyone specifically asked about traps?' Deepbriar queried.

'I'm sure they didn't. It just came up in conversation. It may have had something to do with the Tapper boys being out as beaters. Phil Golding mentioned that he was having trouble with people trespassing on his land, and somehow we got on to poachers. We were joking about finding ways to deal with them;

you know the sort of silly banter that goes on. The traps were locked away; there was no reason to suspect anyone could get hold of the bloody things.' He turned to the woman at his side, 'Sorry, Elaine. Look, I expect you want to go and change.'

She shook her head, the very smallest of smiles on her lips. 'No, thank you, as your fiancée I think I should offer moral support. I'll keep you company on the carpet until your punishment is dished out.'

Major Brightman laughed, though with half an eye on his father.

The colonel snorted, his anger subsiding. 'Miss Barr, my son doesn't deserve you. As for you, Charles, you're probably past redemption. We'll just have to do all we can to get the rest of these wretched traps back before anyone's hurt. Tell us how we can help you, Thorny.'

Deepbriar left a few minutes later, with a list of all the people the major thought had been present when he mentioned the traps that were stored in the shed, and another of all those invited to shoot that day. The task ahead of him looked impossible; two of the guns weren't local, and could probably be eliminated, but that left nine others, as well as any number of hangers-on, and nearly thirty beaters. If he could think of a conceivable motive it would help, but any person who set traps where they were likely to snare a child was simply beyond his comprehension.

* * *

The inquest into the death of Gladys Twyford was held in a small room in Belston Courthouse, on the hottest day of the year so far. An airless sticky heat hung over the proceedings, and Deepbriar ran a finger inside his collar as he stepped up to give his evidence. He made his report, consulting occasionally ~~with~~ his notebook. The coroner asked one or two questions regarding the scene of the accident, but nobody queried Mrs Twyford's reasons for being by the arterial road that day.

'Thank you, Constable Deepbriar, you may step down.' Deepbriar heard the words with a mixture of relief and unease, wondering if he should have voiced his doubts. As he took a seat Deepbriar glanced at the public gallery. There were half-a-dozen onlookers, but none of them looked like wealthy businessmen; it seemed Gordon Vennimore hadn't come.

Doctor Smythe took the stand after Deepbriar, followed by the driver of the lorry.

'I never dreamt she was going to try to cross the road,' the driver said. 'I was sure she'd seen me.'

'What speed were you doing at the time?'

'Around thirty-eight mph, sir. That's the most my motor can manage unless it's going downhill with the wind behind it.'

'And when you saw Mrs Twyford step into the road, did you attempt to stop?'

'Of course I did, but there wasn't time to do much. And she didn't so much step, more like run.'

A low murmur of sound ran round the room at that point, but the coroner didn't pursue the issue, dismissing the man from the witness box. The driver hesitated.

'I'm really sorry for what happened, honest, but there wasn't a thing I could do. I've been driving for over twenty years, and I've never had an accident.'

'Thank you,' the coroner said. 'Your good record as a motorist had been noted. Kindly step down.' He rushed through the next two witnesses with almost unseemly haste. Deborah Williams was the last to be called. By now the heat was so unbearable that nearly everyone had dropped into a stupor.

Deepbriar wiped away the sweat that was threatening to drip into his eyes, envying the coroner the glass of water his clerk had fetched for him. He missed the first couple of questions, his mind lingering on thoughts of a pint of bitter.

'Miss Williams, you say Mrs Twyford ran into the road. Where did she appear to be going?'

Deepbriar held his breath. The girl bit her lip, then a nervous giggle escaped her lips. She clapped her hand over her mouth, looking contrite. 'I'm sorry,' she said. 'It was . . . that silly joke, you know, about the chicken. She was going to the other side.'

There was a snort from the single member of the local press who was still awake, the sound earning a withering glance from the coroner. The little distraction got them over the awkward moment, the query about the woman's motivation evidently forgotten. A few minutes later the coroner gave his verdict. Mrs Twyford's death had been a tragic accident, with no blame attached to the lorry driver.

'We live in an age of machines,' the coroner said sententiously, 'with cars and lorries becoming ever faster and more powerful. It behoves us all to take extra care, and to remember that the arterial road was built for motor vehicles, not pedestrians.'

'Was that right, do you think?' Dr Smythe asked quietly, catching up with Deepbriar outside the courthouse. 'He didn't pursue the question of her frame of mind. I rather thought you suspected suicide.'

'Suspected, no more.' Deepbriar looked unhappily at the doctor; if only they knew what had taken Mrs Twyford to the crossroads. An appointment to meet somebody? Nobody had come forward. The letter? It might have been irrelevant, and his gut feeling just the result of reading too many detective novels. Deepbriar had reluctantly accepted that murder could be discounted; even if Mrs Twyford was lured to the crossroads by some means, the lorry driver was innocent of any ill intent. The woman had run in front of him and she hadn't been pushed. Not physically, at any rate.

'You didn't mention your doubts,' Dr Smythe said.

'No. What difference would it have made?' The heat of the sun was beating down on the cobbled street and the stone walls, making the centre of the city as hot as a furnace. Deepbriar could feel a river of sweat running down his back, though his mouth was desert dry. 'The rector will be pleased; there's nothing to prevent him burying Mrs Twyford with her husband.'

'That's true. Well, I don't know about you, Thorny, but I need a drink. I've sweated a couple of pints in there.'

'I wish I could join you,' Deepbriar said

forlornly, 'but I'm still on duty, and I'm due back in Falbrough in an hour.'

* * *

The Twenty-third Psalm swelled to the wooden rafters, momentarily blocking out the sound of the rising wind gusting over the church roof. The solemn procession made its way down into the crypt, the voices of the choir fading as they descended. Thorny Deepbriar continued to play more quietly, muting the organ's power, though uncomfortably aware that this meant the elderly tracker action was clearly audible during lulls in the gale.

From time to time he glanced in the mirror above his head, angled so he could see the congregation. Every seat was taken. Mr Morton was there with his wife, and even his elderly partner had turned out; Archibald Childs rarely troubled himself with business these days. The full contingent from the WI had come, with the notable exception of Bella Emerson. Since Mrs Emerson thought the atmosphere at funerals was bad for her artistic nature, she would doubtless be suffering from some short but convenient indisposition. Deepbriar was surprised to see that Miss Strathway had come; she must have arranged for somebody to relieve her at the village telephone exchange. Mrs Rose, who rarely left her invalid son, was there to pay her last respects too, and sat next to old Ada Tapper in the back row. There was no doubt about it, Mrs Twyford may have been a quiet little woman, but she'd had a lot of friends in Minecliff.

When the ceremony was over people began filing out of the church. Once they'd all gone, Thorny sat at the keyboard allowing the last solemn notes to fade away. A little later he stepped down to follow the mourners, but as he passed a column, a hand grabbed him by the elbow, and he turned to find himself facing the diminutive figure of Mrs Grimes, her eyes bright in the comparative darkness of the nave.

'It's about Tibbles,' she said, without preamble.

'Is something wrong?' Deepbriar ushered her into a pew; the old lady was so bent that it was hard for her to look up at him. 'Not got lost, has he?'

'No.' She clutched at his sleeve again with arthritic old fingers. 'I need to be sure. She wanted me to take care of him. But somebody else might want him, and I've got no proof.' Her tone was suddenly reproving. 'You took that note she wrote me.'

'I did, and I've still got it, if there's any query. I don't think you need to worry. I'm sure Mrs Twyford would be glad her cat has a good home.'

'So nobody can take him away?' It was a desperate plea, and there was a hint of moisture in her eyes that hadn't been prompted by the solemnity of the funeral service.

'Not unless he's specifically mentioned in the will as a bequest,' Deepbriar reassured her, 'and I don't think that's very likely. Besides, cats are very independent animals. If Tibbles wants to stay with you then he will, won't he, and possession is nine points of the law, so they say.'

The old lady nodded vigorously. 'My mother lived to be a hundred and two,' she said, with apparent inconsequence.

'You'll see us all out,' Deepbriar said, offering her a helping hand as she rose to her feet. 'It's a bit breezy outside; do you want me to see you home?'

Mrs Grimes gave a most unladylike snort. 'I do not. The day I can't walk to my own front door will be the day they carry *me* up the aisle in a wooden box.'

Deepbriar watched her leave, a little cheered by the encounter. Outside some of the mourners hadn't yet dispersed. Despite the wind it was a warm day. Groups of people stood among the gravestones, holding on to their hats as they talked, the gale making it impossible to converse in the subdued tones normally considered suitable for a funeral.

One man stood back a little from the villagers, a stranger to the constable and yet with something familiar about him. Aged between forty and fifty, he was dressed in a sober grey suit that looked too warm for the occasion. He'd given up fighting to keep his hat on and was carrying it, his dark hair blowing in the wind.

Suddenly the stranger bent his head and lifted a hand as if to push back his hair out of his eyes, but actually to brush a knuckle swiftly across his cheek. The constable looked away, letting his gaze drift beyond the lych gate to the lane. There was a car parked there which he didn't recognize. He knew nothing about makes or models of cars, but he was sure this one was expensive.

'A very impressive turnout, Thorny,' the rector said, coming to Deepbriar's side and almost shouting to make himself heard as the wind howled ever louder overhead. 'I'm glad the inquest worked out well, things could have been a little difficult.'

'Nobody here would have disagreed with Mrs Twyford being laid to rest beside her husband,' the constable replied, 'whatever the coroner decided.'

'No,' Mr Pusey gave a rueful smile, 'but I'm the one who has to deal with the bishop. Thank you for playing the organ at such short notice, I really thought Mrs Emerson would want to be here, since she and Mrs Twyford were fellow members of the WI.'

Deepbriar let this pass, watching as the mourners began to move away, most of them drifting towards the village hall, where a gathering in the dead woman's memory was to be hosted by members of the Women's Institute. Apart from the well-dressed man there was nobody whom Deepbriar didn't know; it seemed Mr Morton was right, Mrs Twyford had no family.

Deepbriar looked around for Mary but found himself facing the solitary stranger, who held out his hand. 'Constable Deepbriar? I'm Gordon Vennimore. I asked Mr Morton to point you out to me,' he added in explanation. 'I'd be very grateful if you could spare me a few moments.'

'Of course. Shall we get out of this wind?' As he led the way out of the churchyard and into the street, Deepbriar realized why the man's face was familiar: Vennimore often featured in the local paper with other leading lights of the Belston Chamber of Commerce.

Having left the gale behind it seemed unnaturally silent as they entered the police house. Deepbriar showed his visitor into his office and offered him a seat. The man sat down, then abruptly dropped his head into his hands. 'Excuse me,' he said, his voice muffled. 'I'm sorry, this has all been rather difficult.'

'I think we should have tea.' Thorny backed hastily from the room, closing the door gently behind him. When he returned bearing a tray a few minutes later the man was sitting erect, his features set into a rigid calm.

'It's less than a year since my wife died,' Vennimore said. 'And then this . . . I do apologize.'

'No need,' Deepbriar assured him. 'How can I help you?'

'I was wondering if you could tell me what really happened to Mrs Twyford.' The man had a haunted look, his dark eyes staring intently at Deepbriar as he spoke. 'I only know what I was able to glean from the report in the newspaper, and the little that Mr Morton learnt from the inquest. You see,' he went on, 'Mrs Twyford was a very good friend to my wife. She was almost like a sister to her, especially during those years when Ethel was so ill. By the end, the three of us had become extremely close.'

Vennimore paused, as if unsure how to continue. Deepbriar handed him a cup of tea, giving him time to marshal his thoughts. 'That's perfectly understandable. Sugar?'

'No, thank you.' Vennimore sighed. 'My wife's death was a release; she suffered for so long. I mourned her, of course, but it was impossible not to be glad that her ordeal was over. After she had gone, Mrs Twyford continued her visits. At first she helped me to dispose of my wife's possessions, but later, once everything was settled, we began to take comfort in each other's company. It was naïve perhaps, but we scarcely realized that our friendship was developing into something more.'

'Mr Vennimore,' Deepbriar said, 'there's no need for you to tell me all this.'

'I believe there is.' The man straightened and met Deepbriar's eyes. 'Gladys Twyford did me the honour of agreeing to marry me, just as soon as a suitable period of mourning was over. We had thought to announce our engagement at Christmas.'

Deepbriar murmured something sympathetic, hiding his surprise. Vennimore made a helpless little gesture with his hands. 'Poor Ethel was ill for a long time, but there are always people who are prepared to think the worst, maybe even suggesting that her death was suspicious if I was seen to consider remarrying too soon. Gladys and I were very discreet. She was a very private person; any hint of gossip would have been anathema to her. There was never any impropriety between us. I wanted to announce our engagement as soon as she'd accepted my proposal, but she insisted on the delay. I agreed, although, as I told her, things are a lot less rigid these days; we've left the Victorian attitude to mourning behind, thank heavens.'

'Not everyone is so broad-minded,' Deepbriar said. The words half seen on a charred scrap of paper, now crumbled to ash, seemed to resonate in his mind, as if waiting to be revealed.

'No. That's why I humoured Gladys and allowed the delay. She thought it might harm my reputation if we appeared to be rushing things. It never occurred to me that she might be the one to suffer from wagging tongues. Yet I'm told there have been rumours.'

Vennimore broke off, now gazing blankly over Deepbriar's head as if what he had to say was too painful to address directly to him. 'I'm told she was suspected of committing suicide. It can't be true, Constable. In the eyes of the church suicide is a sin, and Gladys was a devout Christian.'

Deepbriar drank some tea, trying to think of a suitable answer. 'I wish I had something definite to tell you,' he said at last. 'Mr Morton will have informed you of the coroner's verdict. There was no concrete evidence to suggest that Mrs Twyford's death wasn't an accident. Her actions that day were out of character, but I don't think we'll ever know why. There's one thing I'd like to ask you though, Mr Vennimore. Did you send Mrs Twyford a letter a day or two before she died?'

'No.' The man continued to stare at the wall behind the constable, his eyes focused on something only he could see. 'It seems senseless now, being so careful not to arouse suspicion. We denied ourselves the pleasure of writing letters to each other. I don't believe I have a single line of her handwriting. Even that small comfort would be beyond measure now.'

'Do you know of anyone who corresponded with her? Some old friend, perhaps?'

'I'm not sure she had any friends outside Minecliff, except for myself and my wife. Is this relevant?'

'She received a letter the day she died,' Deepbriar replied. 'It probably wasn't significant, just a minor detail I would have liked to clear up.'

Silence stretched between them, Vennimore's thoughts obviously far away.

'You know the will is due to be read at the parish council meeting on Tuesday week?' Deepbriar said finally.

'Yes, Morton told me. I'll be there.' Vennimore rose to his feet. 'Thank you for your time, Constable.'

'I'm sorry not to have more to tell you.'

'I hardly know what I was hoping for. Some reassurance perhaps, that it really was an accident. She was so happy the last time I saw her. We both were.' His face was grey and drawn, like that of a man suffering from a severe illness. 'We talked of having a spring wedding, here in Minecliff. Gladys said she'd invite every child in the village, and deck them all out as flower-girls and pageboys. Silly, at our age.'

'Not at all.' Deepbriar was uncomfortable with the man's grief, wanting to offer him sympathy but wishing him gone. 'I can only remind you, Mr Vennimore, that the coroner recorded a verdict of accidental death.'

As he closed the door Deepbriar wondered if he should have been honest and told Vennimore the little he knew. The facts were few, but eloquent. After receiving a letter that Saturday morning, Mrs Gladys Twyford had immediately informed her friends that she would not attend the village fête. Sometime later that same day, she arranged for her cat to be taken care of. Taking the footpath that led past the Dally Pond, a route where she was unlikely to meet anyone, she threw away her handbag. Very soon after that she was dead. Deepbriar was as certain as he could be that Mrs Twyford had decided to end her own life.

* * *

'There's something about putting a pair of slippers on your feet.' Thorny Deepbriar said, slumping down in his armchair. 'The end of another day.'

His wife looked up from her knitting, a slightly alarmed look on her face. 'Don't go tempting fate. If — '

She was interrupted by a sharp rap on the front door. 'I told you.'

'Maybe it's nothing,' Thorny said, getting to his feet.

Nev Butcher stood outside, one hand raised in readiness to knock again. 'Constable.' He stepped in without waiting for an invitation, and when Deepbriar saw the object he held in his other hand he didn't protest. Like the others that had been found, the gin trap was large, old and rusty, but the parts that mattered had been oiled so it was still in working order and therefore lethal.

'This was on the bridleway that runs through my yard, only a stone's throw from the farm,' Butcher said, his face red with anger. 'My kids ride their ponies that way nearly every day. Can you imagine what would happen if a pony put its foot in that thing? It would go berserk, and God help the child on its back! You'd better find this bastard, Deepbriar, before somebody gets hurt.'

8

A shrill cry rent the early morning quiet. Deepbriar quickened his pace. The sound was familiar from childhood, as unwelcome now as it had been then. He ran through the straggly copse of trees that skirted Hurdles Farm, where Bert Bunyard lived with his retarded son, Humphrey, following the frantic high-pitched squeals.

The noise guided him to a spot just outside Bunyard's boundary, close to a massive beech tree. Deepbriar bent to pick up a fallen branch. The rabbit's whole body was jerking, its mouth wide as it screamed in pain, and Deepbriar put plenty of power in the blow, striking just behind the head. As the animal went limp, Deepbriar's shoulders sagged. This time the trap was small, aimed at catching one of the rabbits that had colonized the headland; until the new law came into force it was still legal.

Leaning his back against the beech tree, Deepbriar waited for his pounding heartbeat to return to normal, turning away from the trap and its pitiful victim. Around him a lovely summer morning glowed; it was six-thirty, and the patchwork of fields was laid out in green and gold, backed theatrically by the row of dark elm trees bordering the road. But Deepbriar didn't notice the beauty of the birdsong or the slight mist rising around the church tower; he was staring back into the past, his face set. It was a weakness he'd never admit to, but he'd always hated that noise; rabbits were silent, secretive animals, except when driven to extremes of pain or terror.

At last the constable turned away from the pathetic bundle of fur; it was only a rabbit, and God knew there were far too many of them, but there were kinder ways to deal with pests.

Deepbriar trudged down the lane to Bunyard's farm, abandoning his search for the moment. He was tired, suffering a bone-deep weariness that wasn't just caused by the way he was depriving his body of sleep. Three mantraps had turned up so far, and there were at least three more still missing. What lunatic would do such a thing? And why? The questions seemed to scorch the inside of his head.

Hurdles Farm had a neglected air. Even the heaps of rubbish in the yard were slowly disappearing under a tangle of brambles. Deepbriar had called here, the day the first trap turned up, but Bert Bunyard hadn't been home, and his son had shown the constable around the farm. Young Humphrey had been emphatic, his childlike face screwed up as he shook his head. 'Mum didn't like traps,' he said.

'What about your dad, though? He doesn't like foxes.'

'Got a gun,' Humphrey replied, as if that was the end of the matter.

It was Bert who met him this time, coming out of the barn to silence the dog as Deepbriar reached the gate. 'You want something?' Bunyard asked, his paunch thrusting belligerently against the restraints of a filthy stock coat. His tone was surly, his face almost as red as the grubby neckerchief he wore.

'A bit of civility would be a start,' the constable replied. 'I need a word, Bert.'

'I got nothin' to say to you, Deepbriar. After what you done, gettin' a decent man sent to prison, I don't know 'ow you got the nerve to come round 'ere.'

'What I did, Bunyard, was get you off with a six-week sentence when you should have had a year.' Deepbriar pushed open the gate. 'Not to mention I kept an eye on that boy of yours and made sure he didn't starve while you were inside. Now, let's start again, shall we? You'll have heard about these mantraps.'

'I've 'eard. An' if you think you're goin' to pin that on me, you got another think comin'.'

'Believe it or not, Bert, I'm sure you had nothing to do with it. There's a small gin trap up by the big beech tree though. Got a rabbit in it. I reckon that might be yours.'

'What of it?' Bunyard looked even shiftier than usual.

'Your Humphrey seems to think you don't use gin traps.'

'What the boy don't see won't 'urt 'im.'

Deepbriar looked at Bunyard with distaste. 'I'm just letting you know, Bert, all gin traps will be illegal soon, and that's a law I'll be enforcing, with no exceptions. Anyway, that's not what I came to talk about. You're a great one for hearing things.' Deepbriar paused. It was no good trying to appeal to Bunyard's better nature, since the man didn't have one. He did, however, have an inflated view of his own cleverness.

'I hear a sight more than any bloody copper,' Bunyard agreed.

'Maybe you do at that.' Deepbriar nodded. 'Maybe you can confirm something for me. I reckon those traps might have started out on Quinn's farm.'

'You what?' Bunyard spat expressively. 'Not

that I wouldn't like to see Ferdy Quinn get what's comin' to him, but you got it all wrong as usual. They was on the manor, locked up tight. I know a man who was laughin' fit to bust about it, a few days after we'd been out there beatin'. Seems 'e 'eard the toffs talkin'. Reckoned the colonel didn't know they was there, an' 'e was sayin' he could get ol' Rowbotham chucked off the manor if 'e wanted.'

'When was this?'

'Beginnin' o' February. Not likely to forget,' the farmer said sourly, 'seein' I'd only just finished servin' that nice short sentence you got me.'

Deepbriar ignored the gibe. 'You heard this in the Speckled Goose?'

'No, it was a market-day, I was in Falbrough. An' don't you go askin' who told me 'cos I ain't goin' to tell you.'

'Fine. Though that's a shame, because if I knew who he was I could eliminate him from my inquiries.'

Bunyard looked puzzled, then suspicious. 'How come?'

'Well, he wouldn't go bragging to you if he was planning to use the traps, would he?' Deepbriar said. 'Then again, maybe you're just making this up and it was you all the time.'

There was a moment's silence as Bunyard thought about this. 'It was Ernie,' he said.

'Ernie Pratt, Colonel Brightman's groom?'

'You know any other Ernie what works at the manor?' Bunyard made to turn away. 'You finished now? I got work to do.'

'Work? You? Humphrey poorly is he?' Deepbriar jested, returning through the gate.

'Gone to the village with Ada Tapper.' Bunyard scowled. 'It was better when 'e stayed 'ome. An' that's all your fault.'

'How do you work that out?' Deepbriar said, turning back to face the farmer. 'When you weren't here Humphrey had to buy food. Walking into Minecliff was his idea; I just went along to keep him company.'

Humphrey Bunyard was over six foot tall and as broad as his father, but he had the mind of a seven-year-old. In the past Deepbriar had always brought him some chocolate on his visits to Hurdles Farm; there was a peppermint cream bar getting warm in his pocket at that very moment. If Humphrey was happy to shop for himself from now on it wasn't needed.

Bunyard did his best to slam the gate shut behind the constable, but the top bar was rotten and snapped in his hand. As it gave way he almost turned a somersault over the second rail. Thorny Deepbriar chuckled to himself as he walked away, his good humour restored. He groped in his pocket as Bert's colourful language drifted after him.

Licking chocolate from his lips, Deepbriar swiped the back of his hand over his mouth to remove any remaining traces as he turned into the drive that led to the manor. Eating sweets in public while he was in uniform was against regulations; he'd destroyed the evidence, though there was still a suspiciously strong smell of peppermint on his breath.

He found Ernie Pratt in the tack-room, polishing a bridle that was hanging from a hook above his head. 'Morning, Thorny.' The groom gave him a gap-toothed smile. 'You're a mite early for the major; he and Miss Barr will be along in an hour for their morning ride.'

'I was looking for you, Ernie.'

The groom returned the bridle to its place among a dozen others. 'You found me. What can I do for you?' he asked.

'You can tell me what you were doing drinking in the Queen's Head in Falbrough on a market-day, and shooting your mouth off to Bert Bunyard. First week in February wasn't it?'

Pratt was instantly defensive. 'Could've been. What's it to you?'

'Funny time for you to be in town.'

'I was picking up a saddle from Greenways, after it went in for restuffing. I didn't think the old man would mind me having a quick half while I was waiting for the bus.'

'But you had more than a quick half,' Deepbriar replied. 'Made you a bit talkative, didn't it, Ernie, drinking at that time of day? How many people were there when you opened your mouth and put your foot in it? Thanks to you and Bert Bunyard I reckon half of Minecliff could have known about those traps Rowbotham had hidden in the shed.' If Terry Watts was right, the traps had been long gone by the time Ernie told Bunyard about them, but there was no need for either of them to know that.

'Now hold on.' The old man looked alarmed. 'You don't think them traps have got anything to do with me! What would I want with setting traps?'

'What would anyone?' Deepbriar shot back. 'Did you know Job hid them, all those years ago, instead of getting rid of them like the colonel told him?'

The groom removed his cap and scratched his head. 'No, don't reckon I did.'

'So, you found out on the day of the shoot.'

'That's right. See, I was in the stables and the major was chatting to some of the guns, before we set out, like. They was talking about catching poachers, and Mr Golding, he said they knew how to do things in the old days.' He shrugged. 'The major made a joke about it, said they'd got just what he needed locked up in the shed behind the wood store.'

'Were any of the other beaters about?' Deepbriar asked. 'Could anybody else have heard what Major Brightman said?'

'No, only the gentry. The rest of the beaters were already going down the drive. I would've gone too, but I was just taking a quick look at a mare that was a bit off colour.'

The constable took out his notebook. 'Right. Now, Ernie, this is important. Which of the guns were there? Who was the major talking to?'

* * *

Back in his office, Deepbriar scanned the two lists. There were a few discrepancies, some names the major had suggested didn't tie up with those Ernie Pratt and Job Rowbotham had given him. But then Ernie couldn't be expected to know all the guns by name, unlike Rowbotham. He would only be familiar with the local men. Ernie was sure he hadn't mentioned the existence of the traps to anyone before he told Bunyard. Of course there was still the possibility that somebody else had known about the traps all along, but their theft the very day after the shoot suggested otherwise.

Deepbriar was facing a big problem. If he discounted the beaters, as the latest evidence suggested he should, then the thief must be one of Colonel Brightman's guests. Questioning men who were well respected, not to mention influential, wasn't a job for a lowly village bobby. Come to that he doubted if anybody from the local CID would be too keen on doing it either. But it was the only lead he had, and he couldn't think how else he was ever going to find out which one of these men was giving him nightmares.

Two of the guns had come from outside the area. According to the colonel two more were away for the summer. As for the others, he could hardly see Lord Cawster or Sir Arthur Drimsbury sneaking around the manor after dark and breaking into a shed to steal a load of mantraps.

He rubbed those two names out, then with a sigh he wrote them back in. Eight names. He tried dividing the list into two columns. One was headed *Possible*, the other, simply from what he knew of their characters, *Highly improbable*.

'You ought to have one labelled *Likely*,'

Mary commented, looking over her husband's shoulder when she brought him a cup of tea.

'I suppose I should,' Thorny said, 'but I still can't imagine anybody doing it. That's half the trouble.' He stabbed at the names with his pencil. 'I mean, look at them!'

'Surely you could put more names in the improbable list,' Mary said, 'Old Archibald Childs, the solicitor. He's far too old to be wandering around the village in the dead of night. And he lives in Possington.'

'One of the traps wasn't that far from his house,' her husband pointed out. 'Anyway, if you look at it that way, Phil Golding's never been known to walk further than a hundred yards in his life; I can't see him doing it either.' He threw down his pencil in frustration. 'I come back to the same question every time: what possible motive could anyone have? There are twisted people about who enjoy causing pain, but what's the point if they're miles away? Men of that sort are more likely to go badger baiting, or stay home and knock their wives and children about.' Deepbriar rubbed wearily at his forehead, which was starting to ache.

His wife looked concerned. 'Must you keep going out early every morning?'

'I don't know what else to do. I'll be in

trouble for not patrolling my beat if I try to fit the paths in during the day, and there's not enough time. I daren't risk some child running into one of those bloody things. Sorry, love,' he said automatically. 'It's the worst possible time of year, with the schools breaking up in a few days.'

'Maybe you ought to tell people to stay off the paths,' Mary suggested. 'You're wearing yourself out. You can't get by on four hours' sleep.'

Deepbriar hardly heard her. 'You know what children are; there's no way we can keep them shut up all summer, they have to get out and play. And they've always used Back Lane and the The Spinney.' Deepbriar pushed back his chair and stood up. 'There's nothing else for it, I'm going to have to talk to the people on this list.'

'Before you start, there's something I forgot to tell you. I met Mrs Rose in the village earlier, and she was wondering if you'd go and have a word with Oliver.'

Deepbriar ran a hand over his hair. 'Did she say why?'

'No. She was in a hurry.'

'Maybe the lad's poorly again. She didn't bring him to the fête this year. I haven't had time to think about going up there, with all that's been going on.' He looked at the bit of paper in his hand. 'I'll do it first.' It would be good to put off the evil hour; he was about to do something that would get him in deep trouble with his superiors. If he told them he wanted to question the likes of Lord Cawster about the theft of half-a-dozen gin traps, they'd think he'd lost his mind.

* * *

'I'm so glad you could come.' Mrs Rose threw the door open wide. 'It's hot today, let me get you something to drink. Come into the kitchen for a moment. Would you like a cup of tea? Or I've some lemonade, I just made it this morning.'

'That sounds nice,' Deepbriar said, 'thanks. But I mustn't stay long.'

'No, of course.' She vanished for a moment into the larder and came back bearing a tall china jug. 'We heard about this dreadful business with the traps, and we've been quite worried about Barney.'

'Barney?'

'Oh, you won't have heard. We took him in a week ago. A stray. Sweet little thing, Oliver loves him.' Worry lines appeared between Mrs Rose's eyebrows as she handed the constable a glass. 'We thought it might encourage him, having a dog to take for walks.'

'Walks?' Deepbriar asked vaguely, pulling himself together. He'd been miles away. 'He's got his calipers then.'

'Yes, he's had them for a while. The trouble is he hates them. We knew it would be hard of course, they cause him quite a bit of discomfort, but that's not the problem. It's being different. He's afraid of being laughed at.'

'He's always been such a brave little lad,' Deepbriar said, staring into his glass. 'I thought he was keen to get back on his feet.'

'It's not helping that we can't use the footpath.' She gestured at the track that followed their drive and went on across Ferdy Quinn's meadows, leading eventually to the road beyond Will Minter's farm. 'He could practise there without being seen. He doesn't like using the road.'

'Can't say I blame him,' Deepbriar said. 'You and Mr Rose could check the path first.'

The woman shook her head. 'Oliver's taken against the whole idea of walking; it's a job just getting him out of the garden. I'm sorry, I know you're busy, but I thought you might have some ideas.' Mrs Rose sounded as weary and beleaguered as he felt, and Deepbriar straightened his shoulders; this at least he might be able to fix.

'Maybe I have at that.' He finished his

drink. 'Is it all right if I go up?'

'He's not in his room, he's outside. At least that's one thing Barney's done for him, he's spending a lot more time in the garden. Come on, I'm sure he'll be pleased to see you.'

Oliver Rose sat on a blanket under the shade of an apple tree, a bright rug over his wasted legs. The polio that had struck him down had left him pale and thin, underdeveloped for his nine years. It was small comfort that he'd been lucky compared to some victims of the disease, the most seriously affected being forced to live out their lives in an iron lung.

The brown-and-white mongrel that lay sprawled against the boy wagged its tail madly as Deepbriar approached, but Oliver seemed not to notice his visitor. He was staring at his fingers in his lap, busy with the rug's fringe, tying knots and undoing them again.

'Hello, Oliver.'

'Hello.' The youngster still didn't lift his gaze.

Deepbriar crouched down to make a fuss of the dog. Barney wriggled ecstatically, offering his stomach to be rubbed. 'Nice dog,' he said. 'I came to warn you to keep him on a lead when you take him out.'

'I'm not taking him out.' The boy looked up at last, his expression wary. 'I don't want to.'

Deepbriar met Mrs Rose's eye and glanced away quickly. 'Well, at least we'll know Barney's all right, if he spends all his time in the garden.' He stood upright. 'If you're not walking then there's no more to say. I was hoping you might help, seeing you cracked that case for me last year, but it doesn't matter.'

'What do you mean?' For the first time some animation appeared on Oliver's face. 'I don't watch the road much now. Barney doesn't like staying upstairs all the time. It's better for him in the garden. He fetches sticks, and he barks at the rabbits through the fence. He doesn't need to go out for walks,' he added defensively, stroking the dog's head.

'It's not keeping an eye on cars this time. I was thinking you might be able to help with the patrols.' Deepbriar lowered himself to the boy's level again. 'You'll have heard about this villain who's been setting traps, leaving them where a dog or a cat might get caught. I'm asking people I can trust to keep an eye on their nearest paths. Of course, it's a risky business, maybe you're too young.'

'What would I have to do?'

'We need somebody to walk the footpath

past your house every morning and check it's clear. Barney would have to be kept on his lead while you did it, but I reckon he'd be a bit of help. Got good noses, dogs have, he'd probably sniff out the scent if anyone had been around. Then you'd have to report in, let us know you'd done your patrol for the day. See, it's useful your mum and dad having a telephone.' He looked up, as if seeing Mrs Rose for the first time. 'We'd have to ask your mum if she'd let you do it.'

Oliver looked from one face to the other. 'I'd really be helping?'

'You certainly would,' Deepbriar lied cheerfully, childishly crossing his fingers behind his back.

'Mum?' He looked up at his mother.

'It's a big responsibility. And it's a long walk, all the way to Mr Minter's gate. I'm not sure you could do it.'

'I bet I could.' The boy's cheeks were flushed, his expression eager. 'Let me do it, Mum, please.'

She pretended to consider the idea. 'Well, all right, if Constable Deepbriar really needs you.'

Deepbriar felt almost cheerful as he cycled away. Mr and Mrs Rose would be sure to check where their son was due to walk before they let him out each day, but he'd take no chances with young Oliver. Fred and Billy Tapper were still eager to help, determined to prove they were on the side of law and order as far as the mantraps were concerned. He'd ask one of them to search that path every morning from now on, just to be absolutely sure.

9

Sleep refused to come. Deepbriar was so tired his eyes hurt, but he couldn't settle. At last he rolled quietly out of bed, careful not to disturb his wife, and crept downstairs. He made tea and took a mug into his office. Slumping at his desk he sat staring at the list again, studying the names of the men he needed to question about the missing gin traps. The sensible thing to do was hand the whole case over to his superiors, but if he did there was a good chance they'd drop it like a hot potato. He had rehearsed the conversation with Sergeant Hubbard a dozen times in his head.

'*Are you insane, Deepbriar? You want somebody to go and ask the high sheriff of the county if he went creeping around Minecliff Manor after dark, so he could break into a shed and steal some mantraps? Then we'll have a little chat with Mr Childs along the same lines. It doesn't matter a hoot that he's a respected solicitor, not to mention being the chief constable's oldest and dearest friend! As for Sir Arthur Drimsbury, maybe it's slipped your mind that he won the*

Victoria Cross during the war. How's it going to look if we go accusing him of being a sneak thief and a madman to boot?'

Deepbriar sat with his aching head resting on his hands; interrogating the VIPs who had gathered for the colonel's shoot was a very bad idea. Only a few days ago he had been expecting a transfer to CID, but the dream was slipping ever further away; if he pursued this line of enquiry without official approval he might even face dismissal.

He finished his tea and let himself out of the house, long before the sun was up. What he needed was a miracle. The trouble was, he'd stopped believing in miracles at the age of six, when a boy at school told him Father Christmas didn't exist.

The village was so familiar to him that he didn't turn his torch on; the faint glimmer of starlight was enough to let him find his way down Violet Lane and on to the footpath. He hadn't seen either of the Tapper boys the day before, and he would walk a circuit that brought him back past the Roses' house. He'd gone some twenty yards through the long grass before he remembered why he was there: walking into the jaws of a mantrap wasn't the most sensible way to find one.

Deepbriar took out his torch, shivering a little in the pre-dawn chill and facing the impossibility of his half-formed hope. He almost laughed at his *naïveté*; he'd imagined that if he set out early enough he might catch the villain red-handed, but whoever this man was, he had the huge advantage of being able to work in the dark without running the risk of stepping into his own traps.

Two hours later, thoroughly disheartened, the constable walked through the village, heading towards Back Lane and the track beyond it which led along by the stream, another favourite haunt of the local children. It was still early, but he was tired to the point of exhaustion. Mary was right, he had to get more rest. The days and weeks seemed to stretch out before him, a long and weary procession of fruitless searching, while every passing day increased the chances of a terrible accident.

'Constable Deepbriar.' He jumped, startled out of his gloomy reverie. Miss Cannon was at her gate. The stalwart of the Women's Institute looked quite forbidding, her hair dragged severely off her forehead, thin lips drawn in a tight line. It was only 5.30, but she was dressed in her usual hand-knitted cardigan and severe tweed skirt.

'Miss Cannon. I wasn't expecting — '

She cut him short with a look. 'Please, come inside for a moment.'

Obediently he followed her into the house. She closed the front door quietly and turned to face him.

'Is there something wrong?' Deepbriar asked. 'What's the matter?'

The woman didn't answer immediately, but stood staring at him in a way Deepbriar found vaguely disquieting. Then, as if coming to a decision, the woman picked up a large envelope from the table beside her.

'I saw you coming. This seemed like a good opportunity to speak to you without being observed.' She thrust the envelope into his hands. 'I received this in the post,' she said quietly. 'I would prefer that you study it in private. If you wish to speak to me once you've read the contents, I shall be at home all day.' Without another word she opened the door again, and Deepbriar found himself back outside. He took a quick glance at what he'd been given. The envelope was brown foolscap, with Miss Cannon's name and address on it in a neat italic hand, and a postmark from several weeks ago.

Tucking the envelope under his arm Deepbriar set off to finish the self-imposed addition to his village beat. Another hour and he'd be back at the police house. He could enjoy a leisurely breakfast, and maybe even have forty winks before he had to be on duty.

Reaching home at last, Deepbriar intended to go directly to his office, but, as he let himself in through the back door, he heard strange noises from upstairs.

'Mary?' He ran, taking two steps at a time, and peeped in at the bathroom door. His wife was draped over the toilet pan, her body heaving.

'Are you all right, love? Mary?' Alarmed, he rushed to her, only to find himself being pushed away.

'Don't fuss, it's just something I ate. Maybe that piece of fish was off.'

'Can't have been,' Deepbriar protested, 'I'm fine.'

'You didn't have the same piece,' Mary said shortly. 'Go and put the kettle on. I'll be down in a few minutes.'

She was true to her word, coming into the kitchen looking rather pale but otherwise her normal self. 'What sort of time were you off out this morning?' she asked, impatiently brushing him aside so she could start cooking his breakfast.

'I don't know. I couldn't sleep.' Deepbriar poured boiling water on to the tea leaves in the big earthenware pot. It was still well before their usual mealtime.

'You can't keep working all hours like this,' Mary scolded. 'You need your rest. And sit down, please, I can't get on with you standing in the way.'

Deepbriar obeyed, the only possible course of action when his wife was in this mood. She began to set the table then frowned down at him. 'If you're not careful you'll make yourself ill.'

'You were the one being sick,' he pointed out. 'I can't get these gin traps out of my mind. I'm having nightmares, only instead of a fox or a rabbit, I keep seeing a child caught in one of the damned things. No matter how early I start I can't walk all the paths every day.'

'Fretting about it won't do any good.'

He ran a hand over his hair. 'If only I knew who it was. That many large traps would be heavy, they must have used a vehicle. You've seen the list. I can talk to the beaters, but all the evidence suggests it was one of the guns. Sergeant Hubbard will have me for breakfast if I go bothering the gentry over what he'd call a petty theft.'

'It won't help anyone if you wear yourself out. If Sergeant Hubbard won't listen then why don't you talk to Inspector Stubbs next time you go to Falbrough?'

'It's hardly a CID matter.' He looked up as she put a cup of tea in front of him. 'Aren't you having any?'

'Maybe later, my tummy still feels a bit queasy. I expect you're hungry; do you want two eggs?'

At Deepbriar's insistence Mary sat down with him once his breakfast was cooked, and he persuaded her to eat a piece of toast. Then he sat on in his chair for a long time, his head nodding, while she cleared the table and washed up. At last Deepbriar roused himself, recalling the envelope Miss Cannon had given him; he'd dropped it on the dresser when he rushed upstairs. As he picked it up the telephone rang. With a sigh the constable went into his office, throwing the envelope down on his desk.

'Constable? I need you to come out here.'

A small frown appeared between Deepbriar's brows as he recognized the voice. 'Mr Golding? What's the trouble?'

'There's no point talking about it on the telephone. Get over here. Don't waste time going to the house, I'll be in my office in the new packing shed. Come through the main gate and to your left, you can't miss it.'

Deepbriar glanced at the clock on the wall. It was eight o'clock. His working day would officially begin in thirty minutes. He took a breath, tempted to tell Phil Golding he'd have to wait, but before the words got past his teeth he'd changed his mind; he'd always known he'd have to pay for the loan of those men when the first trap turned up. Golding's mind worked that way.

The nurseryman probably wanted to complain about trespassers again. Most landowners had a fairly relaxed view about people taking shortcuts across their property, as long as no harm was done, but Golding took every minor transgression as a personal affront.

'Deepbriar? Are you there?' Golding barked peremptorily.

'I'll be on my way as soon as I can, Mr Golding,' Deepbriar replied evenly. At the other end of the line the telephone was put down, none too gently, and Deepbriar stared at his own receiver for a second, brooding. His eye was caught by the list of names on his desk. Phil Golding was there, near the top. According to the colonel he wasn't a bad shot, though he had to be ferried everywhere in the Land Rover, as he wasn't fit to walk more than a few yards.

Deepbriar's mood lightened for a second as he let his imagination run riot. He could see the enormous corpulent figure puffing his way along a muddy track with a mantrap in his hands. Finding out that Golding was the culprit was even less likely than discovering that Lord Cawster, the sheriff of the county, was the guilty party. Come to think of it, though, Lord Cawster's father had been decidedly eccentric. He'd had a Turkish bath built in his study when he was ninety. Maybe his son was going the same way, and had declared a private war on the local wildlife without realizing he was endangering humans as well.

Deepbriar sighed, his depression returning; the idea made as much sense as anything he'd come up with; absolutely one.

* * *

'It was bad enough when they pushed through the hedges and helped themselves to a few pounds of tomatoes or a couple of empty boxes.' The oversized nurseryman was very angry. His face was flushed deep red, and a pulse beat visibly in his fleshy temple. 'This is beyond a joke, Deepbriar. I thought it was part of your duty to keep an eye on business premises and prevent this kind of thing.'

'I ride a beat past your business five times a week, but I'm only one man, Mr Golding,' Deepbriar said, keeping his own temper with difficulty. 'Fact is, I can't see a lot of what goes on behind that new fence you've had put up. Not to mention I'm responsible for looking after several hundred properties, not just yours. Perhaps you'd like to show me exactly what damage has been done.'

'Hopgood can take you,' Golding said shortly, beckoning to his foreman.

'I'd appreciate it if you'd show me yourself,' Deepbriar said. 'It's your property we're talking about here. I'll need to ask a few questions, and it's likely you're the best person to answer them. I imagine you'll be making a claim on your insurance too. The company will expect you to co-operate with the police, so we can find out who was responsible for the damage,' he went on, as Golding hesitated. With a rather surly nod the man turned to lead the way.

The constable took a perverse satisfaction in the big man's discomfort. The day was warming up and they were walking between rows of greenhouses, the glass reflecting the sun's heat back at them. Golding was dripping sweat before they'd gone five yards.

A miserable-looking George Hopgood followed close on Deepbriar's heels. 'Careful, Thorny,' the foreman muttered, as they threaded their way past a heap of wooden crates. 'He's not a man to push.'

'Too flipping heavy,' Deepbriar murmured in response.

At last, with the nurseryman breathing so

hard he could barely speak, they reached the last of the greenhouses. 'Here,' Golding wheezed. It looked almost as if a bomb had hit that end of the row. The sun's glare bounced off the glass, but there were dark spaces for several yards where many of the panes were broken, and the spars that had held them were crooked and splintered.

'It's all tomatoes this end,' George explained. 'Even if the plants survive I think we'll have to clear them all out, there'll be little chips of glass everywhere and we couldn't risk bits getting into the stuff we send to market.'

Through the holes, Deepbriar could see the plants inside, some of them damaged and already wilting, with the ripening fruits still attached. Further on, the door at the end of the greenhouse stood open, and Deepbriar went to it, his feet crunching on broken glass.

'It's a terrible waste,' Golding said disgustedly, once he'd recovered his breath. 'I want this hooligan caught, Deepbriar, and soon.'

'When did you find this?' Deepbriar asked. 'Presumably it must have happened during the night?'

'One of the men came and told me as soon as I got to work this morning,' Hopgood replied. 'I went into the village and telephoned Mr Golding straight away.'

'I'd better talk to this man,' Deepbriar said. 'Presumably you don't have a night watchman.'

'Not exactly,' the foreman removed his hat and scratched his head. 'Bonelli sleeps in one of the sheds at the other end of the nursery, and he's responsible for keeping an eye on the boiler for the heated houses. He stokes up last thing at night, but that's all.'

'Bonelli. I think I've met him. Speaks a bit of English, doesn't he?'

'Yes, more than the rest of them.'

'But he wouldn't come down here during the night.' Deepbriar went inside the damaged greenhouse, keeping a wary eye on the roof, where broken shards of glass were held precariously in place above his head, like Damoclean swords suspended from scraps of brittle putty.

Half bricks and stones lay among the ruins of the tomato plants, but there was something else too, a rusty chunk of metal half hidden by the bright yellow-green foliage of the tomato plants. 'Must have made a heck of a noise. You'd think somebody would have heard something,' Deepbriar said, moving closer.

'The Italians go down to the pub some nights,' Hopgood offered. 'Bonelli might not have been here when it happened. Or maybe he'd had a couple of pints, and he was sleeping a bit sounder than usual.'

Deepbriar nodded, going forward very carefully, his feet crunching over shattered glass. 'I think you'd better take a look at this,' he said, staring down at the metal object in disbelief.

'You sure it's safe in there?' Golding asked, hovering close to the doorway.

'Nothing's fallen on me yet.'

With Hopgood leading, the other two men came inside. 'What is it, Thorny?' the foreman asked, craning his neck. 'Hell's bells! How did that get there?'

Lying on the rich brown soil, its jaws gaping open, the teeth red with rust, was a large gin trap.

'But — ' Golding's face, already dark with exertion, went an unhealthy purple, and his breathing became painfully laboured. He staggered back towards the doorway.

'Are you all right, Mr Golding?' With Hopgood's help Deepbriar got the big man back into the fresh air and eased him down on an old upturned barrow. 'Come as a bit of a shock, did it?' Deepbriar asked, as Golding's colour gradually returned to normal. 'We've been finding traps like that scattered all over the parish. I'm surprised this is the first time one of them has turned up on your land.'

'No, it's not that. Just the heat,' Golding replied, though his eyes darted nervously back to the glasshouse. 'But what's that thing doing in there? You think it's some kind of a threat?'

'Can you think of any particular reason for anyone to threaten you?' Deepbriar asked.

'Of course not!' Golding snapped.

'Are you sure? It could be somebody you've dismissed recently.'

'That's nonsense. This is the work of some layabout with nothing better to do than cause senseless damage to other people's property.'

'Maybe.' Deepbriar said dubiously. 'But this took a fair bit of time, and energy, Mr Golding. Are you sure you can't think of anyone who has a grudge against you?'

'I've told you, no. I don't have time to answer stupid questions, Constable, I have to be at a meeting in Belston shortly. If there's anything else you need to know you'll have to ask Hopgood.' Golding rose clumsily to his feet and waddled away.

Deepbriar made a move to go after him, remembering that he hadn't yet asked the nurseryman about the day of the shoot, but somehow it didn't seem like the time. He turned back to George Hopgood with a sigh.

His investigation into the theft at the manor would have to wait. 'We'd better deal with that trap,' he said.

'Right.' The foreman went into the next greenhouse and returned bearing a spade, which he handed to the constable.

Deepbriar stabbed down at the plate to spring the trap, but nothing happened. He crouched to inspect it.

'Careful,' Hopgood warned.

'It's all right, this one's not going to hurt anyone,' Deepbriar said. 'Look, it's rusted solid, there's no way those jaws will ever close. Funny that; the others were all in working order.' He bent and lifted the contraption, which hadn't been pegged down. It was heavy, but a strong man could have hefted the thing through the roof.

'Hang on, I recognize that,' George Hopgood said, as Deepbriar carried the trap outside. 'It was on the heap.' He pointed to a spot where nettles and brambles grew over a pile of old farm machinery and other rubbish. 'Must've been there ten years and more. I bet that's where he found all those half bricks too.'

'Could be.' Deepbriar was thoughtful. 'Just a coincidence, then. That gets us no nearer to working out who was responsible for the damage. How about it, George, has your boss been upsetting anyone lately?'

Hopgood shrugged. 'No more than usual.'

'Nobody's been given the order of the boot?'

'Not unless you count Fred Tapper. Mr Golding told him he didn't want him bringing his ferrets here any more. Reckons it's easier to use poison to get rid of the rabbits.'

'I can't see that worrying Fred,' Deepbriar said, 'there's plenty of other places where he's still welcome. Well, I'd best have a word with Bonelli, seeing as your boss has run out on us.'

* * *

'It'll be on the table in five minutes,' Mary called, when Deepbriar finally got back home. With a sigh he took off his helmet and went through to the office. Just time to fill in the report sheet on the incident at Golding's. He'd learnt nothing from Bonelli. The Italian had apologized for his bad English, and said only that he 'find the glass broked'.

When Deepbriar pressed him on the amount of noise that must have resulted from so much damage being done, Bonelli gave him a disarming smile. 'I work hard, I sleep good. You are friends with the *bella* Bella *si*?

Even her voice, it would not wake me.'

As he picked up the report forms Deepbriar noticed the envelope Miss Cannon had given him that morning. He moved it to one side, then he recalled the way she had looked at him when she handed it over. With a sigh he tipped out the contents. Another envelope, much smaller, fell on to the desk. Deepbriar felt as if he'd been punched in the midriff. He sank into his chair, staring at the handwriting in miserable disbelief.

10

'Thorny? I've been calling you for ages.' Mary Deepbriar put her head around the door of the office. 'It'll spoil if you don't come and eat.'

'Sorry, love.' Deepbriar pushed the envelope and its contents into a drawer out of sight and followed his wife to the table. He sat silent through the meal, his thoughts far away. At last, with no idea what he'd eaten, he pushed away his empty plate and watched as his wife spooned sugar into his cup of tea before placing it in front of him. 'Thanks, love, very nice,' he said vaguely.

Absently, Deepbriar stirred two spoonfuls of sugar into the tea Mary had already sweetened, put the spoon down and stared unseeingly out of the window. A moment later he picked up the sugar spoon again.

'That's going to taste like syrup,' Mary said, moving the bowl out of his reach.

'Is it?' He swallowed a mouthful and grimaced. 'Sorry, I wasn't thinking.'

'Yes you were, but not about your tea. You look about as cheerful as a wet Monday.'

'Mmm.' Deepbriar drank the over-sweet

tea without further comment. Mary gave an exaggerated sigh and cleared the table as he stood up and returned to his office.

He didn't know what to do. Retrieving the smaller envelope from the drawer, he looked again at the rounded handwriting, now horribly familiar. It was neat and yet somehow unformed, as if it was written by a child, but no child could have composed the vitriolic attack somebody had sent to Miss Cannon. Although only scraps remained from the missive Mrs Twyford had received, the writing was definitely the same. Deepbriar had no more doubts; putting his own knowledge of the woman alongside what he'd learned at his meeting with Gordon Vennimore, he knew Mrs Twyford had been driven to take her own life.

The coroner's verdict was wrong. And yet, nothing had really changed, he didn't have any concrete evidence. And even if he had, should he stir things up? Having seen the vicious threats and wicked condemnation aimed at Miss Cannon it wasn't hard to understand why Mrs Twyford had found the attack on her too hard to bear. Although she was beyond harm now, revealing the truth might cause the bishop to reverse his decision about burying her alongside her husband. Surely it was better to leave her in peace.

Deepbriar wandered into the kitchen, his gaze settling rather absently upon his wife.

'Was there something you wanted?' Mary asked, still looking a little annoyed.

'No, I was just wondering . . . ' Then he realized he couldn't possibly ask her what he needed to know. He had no idea what confidences women shared. It would be improper to ask Mary whether she'd heard rumours about Miss Cannon. Among the women in Minecliff, how many might know that the pillar of the Women's Institute had a terrible secret hidden in her past? There was only one person of whom he could legitimately ask that question.

'Wondering what?' Mary hung up the tea towel. He'd been standing staring at her for almost a minute. 'Are you feeling all right?'

'Mmm. It's nothing. I have to go out.'

* * *

'You know why I gave you this?' Miss Cannon stared at Deepbriar over the top of her reading glasses, gesturing with the envelope she held in her hand. 'The day Mrs Twyford died, she sent a note saying she wouldn't be attending the fête.'

'Yes. A note that was written on a scrap torn from an envelope.' Deepbriar had made up his mind to be open with Miss Cannon; her trust in his discretion had earned her that much. He took his notebook from his pocket and removed three pieces of paper. 'She also wrote a note to Mrs Grimes, asking her to take care of her cat.' He placed the two notes face down on the table between them, putting them together so part of Mrs Twyford's address could be read, keeping the third and smallest fragment in his hand.

Miss Cannon nodded her approval. 'There are those who are fooled by your country bumpkin act, Constable. I always thought there was more to you than that.' She slipped the two sheets of paper from inside the envelope before placing it on the table so the similarity could be seen. 'I naturally recognized the handwriting when this came through my door. You read the letter.'

'I assumed that was what you wanted me to do, otherwise you would have given me just the envelope.' Deepbriar kept his voice level, his face expressionless. There were lines around Miss Cannon's eyes and mouth that he never recalled noticing before.

'Quite. Presumably the letter Mrs Twyford received was written in the same vein. There had been some talk about her over the last few months, though I doubt if there was any substance to it; she was a timid little soul.'

Deepbriar dropped his gaze. Miss Cannon tossed the two pieces of paper down to lie beside the envelope as if further contact with the letter might do her physical harm.

'That's what puzzles me,' Miss Cannon went on. 'I find it hard to believe Mrs Twyford ever committed any act which would have warranted the attention of this . . . person.' She sighed. 'As for my own past, the facts set out here are essentially correct.'

The constable's head jerked up and he found himself staring into a pair of fierce grey eyes.

'The facts,' Miss Cannon reiterated quietly. 'I was engaged to be married when I was nineteen, Constable, but like so many young couples at that time, my fiancé and I had to postpone our marriage because of the war. After nearly two years on the Western Front, David returned for a week's leave. The banns had been read. Early on the day when we should have been married, Mr Barker, who was rector in Minecliff at the time, suffered a heart attack and died. The vicar of Gadwell agreed to fit in a visit to Minecliff as soon as he could, but he was unable to come until two days later, which meant that our wedding would take place just twenty-four hours before David was to return to France.'

Deepbriar fidgeted uncomfortably, wishing

himself elsewhere. He didn't want to hear Miss Cannon's confession. What kind of sick mind had produced this venom, twisting a woman's personal tragedy and threatening to blacken her name?

Miss Cannon noticed his discomfort and gave a small shrug. 'In a time when whole families were being torn apart, our misfortune was almost a commonplace. The vicar never arrived. We didn't know why at the time. Later I discovered that he had set out on his bicycle, only to be recalled by a neighbour. The vicar's youngest son had been involved in a serious accident. The child died in his father's arms some hours later.

'There was no possibility of extending David's leave. He returned to his unit and died shortly afterwards.' Her mouth twisted a little. 'Like so many young men, he was defeated by an illness contracted in the trenches, not enemy action. Such a waste. For me, life went on. The following summer I bore his child, a little girl. I didn't leave home to have the baby in secret, as was usual for women in my position, since my mother was frail and I was caring for her. Of course tongues wagged, as they always do. For a while I was ostracized, but in time the matter was forgotten, or at least, allowed to fade into the back of everyone's mind.'

'The child,' Deepbriar prompted, looking at the letter with disgust.

Miss Cannon gave him a grim smile. 'Still lives, I hope and pray, and no matter what this evil-minded creature says, she is neither a woman of ill repute nor a criminal. The baby spent one week with me, then she was adopted. It was the vicar of Gadwell who found a place for her, with some friends of his. Occasionally I had news of her, until he died four years ago. The last I heard, she was happily married, and her husband had the good fortune to survive the Second War, despite serving in the navy. They have three healthy children. For her at least the story has a happy ending.'

'It sounds as though a great many people in Minecliff knew that you'd had an illegitimate child.'

'Yes.'

'So the threat to ruin your reputation by disclosing your so-called secret is an empty one. In view of your frankness and, if I may say so, your courage in allowing me to see this letter,' Deepbriar said, 'I'll tell you what little I know, and trust to your discretion. The case of Mrs Twyford was slightly different.'

He laid down the last piece of paper. 'This was in Mrs Twyford's fireplace. A charred wafer alongside it bore traces of a few letters, which I copied.' He opened his notebook at the relevant page and put that down on the table with the rest of his evidence. 'It seems,' he went on, as Miss Cannon leant forward to study his offerings, 'that Mrs Twyford was engaged to be married to a widower. His wife had only been dead a short time, so they weren't making the relationship known until a decent period of mourning had passed.'

'Gordon Vennimore! Of course. Mrs Twyford introduced me to his wife, many years ago. They were close friends, and Mrs Vennimore was ill for a very long time.' She shook her head. 'But she, Mrs Twyford, would never have acted with any impropriety. To name such a woman wanton, or to suggest that she had been involved in the murder of her closest friend — ' Words failed her.

'About as accurate as the accusations this letter makes about your conduct,' Deepbriar pointed out. 'But in both cases, the person responsible knew something which was not general knowledge.'

'Many people in the village knew about my past.' Miss Cannon reminded him. 'It was never exactly a secret.'

'Yes, but it was a long time ago.'

'Women chatter, Thorny,' Miss Cannon replied, with a faint and rueful smile.

'So I've heard.' He was silent a moment,

thinking. 'Did everybody know that the baby was a girl?'

'I think not. Of course the vicar knew, and the midwife, but they are both dead now. My closest friend at the time was Edna Hopgood; she is the only one to whom I ever confided anything about my daughter's life since she was adopted.'

'George's wife? She doesn't strike me as the type to gossip.'

'No, I have every faith in Edna,' Miss Cannon said. 'There may have been other people who knew; my mother wasn't a particularly discreet woman, especially during her last illness. Still, it is a very old story. In some ways it is easier to see how this person latched on to Mrs Twyford. A chance sighting of her in Belston with Mr Vennimore perhaps, added to the undoubted lifting of her spirits over the last few months; it would be easy to jump to conclusions.'

Silence lay between them for a few minutes.

'I suppose it wouldn't be seen as murder,' Miss Cannon said at last.

Deepbriar looked back at her bleakly, understanding where her thoughts had led her. 'No. I don't even have enough evidence to prove that Mrs Twyford received a poison-pen letter. Taking any action to pursue the matter would be difficult, if not impossible, and the attempt would almost certainly smear her name.'

'Then we must concentrate on the evidence we have here,' Miss Cannon said, drawing herself up to her full height. Her expression was fierce as she picked up the two sheets of paper and glared down at them.

Deepbriar nodded. 'That letter is libellous. On the other hand, the writer makes no direct suggestion of blackmail; they don't mention money, although the threat to spread these lies among your neighbours suggests they might have something like that in mind. I have to warn you, pursuing the matter may bring you a lot of unpleasantness. Even if we find out who is responsible we might not be able to bring a case against them.'

'Are you saying there is nothing you can do?' Miss Cannon turned on him, her eyes challenging.

'Far from it,' Deepbriar replied, meeting her gaze.

'Then, Constable, you may have this, with my blessing,' she said, putting the letter into his hands. 'And do whatever is necessary. I survived the worst kind of prejudice when I was a young girl; if necessary I can doubtless cope now. One's skin thickens with age, I believe.'

* * *

The Speckled Goose was crowded. Deepbriar fought his way to the bar and caught Phyllis Bartle's eye. 'Heard from Harry lately?' he asked, counting out some coppers for his pint.

'We had a letter yesterday. He asked after you. Said he was busy learning definitions, whatever they may be.'

Deepbriar grinned. 'Definitions set out exactly what criminals can be charged with,' he explained, tapping the side of his head. 'It's all still in here, about the only thing that's guaranteed to stick, the amount of time you have to spend on them. Only a couple more weeks and he'll be on the beat in Belston.'

A loud shout and a gale of laughter drowned out Phyllis's reply. There was a big group at the other end of the bar, with Job Rowbotham at its centre.

'Celebrating,' Phyllis explained. 'The colonel's told him it's time he retired, but he's guaranteed him the cottage for the rest of his life. It's more than the old reprobate deserves, but that's the Brightmans for you, they always were a bit soft.' She chuckled. 'Job says Lord Cawster's offered him a job for two days a week, even arranged that he'll be picked up by car when there's a shoot on. He'll be like a pig in clover. Knowing him he'll spend the rest of his time annoying his lordship's gamekeeper. None of your downtrodden serfs in Minecliff, eh Thorny?'

Deepbriar shook his head thoughtfully as Phyllis hurried away to serve some more customers. There was one man in the group around the old gamekeeper whom he'd never seen in the pub before. Terry Watts stood with his back to the wall, nursing a pint which looked as if he'd barely touched it. Presumably the underkeeper had cause for celebration too, unless the colonel was going to bring in another man over his head.

Lifting on to tiptoes, Deepbriar searched for the man he'd come to talk to; unsurprisingly, he wasn't among those gathered around Job. But he wasn't in his usual spot either, in the alcove by the window. Ada Tapper sat there, massive and unmoving, her elephantine legs stretched out in front of the bench, with her grandson Billy at her side, but there was no sign of his brother Fred. Deepbriar drank another mouthful then squeezed through the crowd towards the old charlady.

'Fred not in tonight?' he asked, having to shout to make himself heard.

The old woman shook her head then

buried her nose in her glass. Deepbriar looked at Billy.

'Gone to see his mate in Belston,' Billy replied. 'Saved me the price of a beer anyway.'

'Why's that?'

'Job's not the only one celebrating,' Ada said proudly. 'Our Billy's got himself a proper job. Will Minter's taken 'im on.'

'Is that a fact?' Deepbriar clapped the youngster on the shoulder. 'Well done, Billy.' He raised his glass and emptied it at a draught. 'Next one's on me, reckon you deserve it.' At this, Ada proffered her glass as well, and he nodded good-humouredly. 'Milk stout was it, Ada?'

'What did you want with our Fred?' Ada asked bluntly, when the constable returned with the drinks.

'Nothing to worry about,' Deepbriar said, 'just a bit of a favour. Though maybe you can help instead, Billy, if you're willing.' And he explained about Oliver Rose, and how he'd given the boy the task of patrolling his own path to encourage him to learn to walk with his new callipers.

'Nasty thing that polio-my-titus,' Ada nodded sagely. 'Poor little mite.'

'Reckon I could go that way to work,' Billy said. 'It'll only take me a couple of minutes more.'

'I'd appreciate that, lad. Mr and Mrs Rose will be walking the path too, before the boy's up and about. I'll see to it myself on a Sunday, so the little chap should be safe enough.' Deepbriar beamed, cheered by his second pint. 'Even if we can't catch this beggar, if I can find a few more like you and Fred at least we'll stop anybody getting hurt.'

Billy nodded. 'Funny thing, I've never known Fred so bothered by anything. He's been out every morning, right over beyond Quinn's and across to the Gadwell lane. He won't let his dogs off, not till he's sure there's no traps about.' He looked past the constable, his eyes widening. 'I think you're wanted, Mr Deepbriar.'

The constable turned and stared through the haze of smoke. Charles Brightman stood just inside the door with his fiancée at his side; they were smartly dressed, Miss Barr looking very much out of place in the public bar. As the drinkers turned to stare she blushed, tipping her head so her jaunty yellow hat hid her face. The major guided her through the crowds, beckoning to Thorny as they approached the door of the saloon bar.

'Join us for a drink, Thorny?' the major asked, pushing the door open as Deepbriar reached them.

'A quick one, thanks,' Deepbriar replied, 'I

told Mrs Deepbriar I wouldn't be long.'

'We've been to the Belston Riverside Hotel for dinner, Constable,' Miss Barr explained, smoothing her skirt as she sat down, 'which is why we're a bit overdressed.'

'You look very nice, Miss Barr,' Deepbriar assured her. 'Please, I already told you to call me Thorny.'

'I will, as long as you call me Elaine. Your wife does,' she added quickly, seeing that he looked doubtful. 'I spent most of the afternoon with her, helping plan the Women's Institute autumn produce show. It's easier now I'm based in the village.'

'Glad to hear you're settling in. I thought Charles told me you were staying at the Riverside?'

'I was, but it was such a nuisance him having to come and fetch me every day. I'm living here now.' She pointed above her head. 'I have a pleasant little room with a window beside the sign. When I look out in the morning there's this big goose staring right back at me. Luckily it's a friendly goose.'

'Excuse my lady friend,' the major said, putting a glass in front of the constable with a grin, 'we pushed the boat out and shared a bottle of wine with our meal.'

'Wine has nothing to do with the way I'm feeling,' the woman replied, smiling serenely.

'Can we tell him our news?'

'I don't see why not. We can't keep it a secret once the banns are read. We've fixed the date, Thorny. Miss Elaine Barr will become Mrs Charles Brightman in the parish church on the 4th of October. It's a little late in the year perhaps, but we'll be off to Scotland for a week's honeymoon afterwards.'

'Near Dumfries.' Elaine smiled, her eyes sparkling. 'It's a favourite place of mine; it reminds me of a very special time in my childhood. Charles insists we go there.'

'Of course. From now on you're going to have whatever makes you happy,' Brightman said, taking his fiancée's hand before he turned back to Thorny. 'Talking of which, we were hoping you might agree to be my best man.'

Deepbriar flushed. 'Surely that's a job for one of your fellow officers? I mean, not that I wouldn't be proud to do it, but — '

'We both agreed it should be you,' the major said. 'Another month and I'll be out of the army. We're having a quiet affair, just close friends and relations and as many people from the village as want to come.'

The woman nodded. 'Minecliff's going to be our home for the rest of our lives, Thorny. Everyone I've met here has made me feel welcome; it's such a friendly place. We want you all to celebrate with us.'

Even as Deepbriar smiled at her enthusiasm he felt a chill engulf him; Minecliff was harbouring a couple of nasty secrets. Not only was somebody writing poison-pen letters, but there was also the matter of the mantraps to deal with. He toasted the happy couple and soon they were eagerly recounting their wedding plans. The constable's thoughts wandered. He had three months to root out the troublemakers, or there was a risk they'd discover Minecliff wasn't quite such a perfect place after all.

11

'Well, it's not exactly a murder case, but it's worth looking into,' Inspector Stubbs said, studying the letter he was holding. 'This is pretty malicious stuff. Any idea if this nutcase has sent any more of these?'

'No, though it's possible this isn't the first,' Deepbriar said. He was grateful for the CID man's interest, and his help should be useful, but he found he wasn't ready to admit to his suspicions about Mrs Twyford's death. Detection was all about proof, not speculation.

'You'll need to keep your ear to the ground,' Stubbs went on. 'Victims of poison-pen letters aren't often willing to come forward. Once rumours get started things can turn quite nasty; people are inclined to think there's no smoke without fire.'

'They picked on the wrong lady this time.' He gave the inspector a quick résumé of the story Miss Cannon had told him. 'She's never really tried to hide the truth, and she had the courage to bring me the letter. There's another thing. She's a leading light in the WI, and she knows nearly everybody in Minecliff. I'm hoping she'll notice if anyone else shows signs of being a target for one of these.' Deepbriar hesitated. 'I thought I might ask my wife to keep her eyes open too, unless you think that would be unprofessional.'

'In a case like this I don't think so; I'm sure Mrs Deepbriar is discreet. It's a good idea. In the meantime I'll have this letter looked at. One thing that's a bit strange about it, people who send abusive letters to their neighbours don't usually write them by hand, unless they use block capitals. Either they use a typewriter or cut words out of newspapers, so this could give us a lead. There's a lecturer at the university who helped me out once before. He makes a hobby of studying handwriting and he knows a bit about paper too.' Stubbs rubbed the envelope between his fingers then held it up to the light. 'The paper looks ordinary, but the envelope is different. That's quite a fancy watermark; I don't think this is something you could buy in Woolworth's. You never know, it might give us a lead. Sergeant Jakes can handle that end of the investigation and he'll let you know if we come up with anything.'

'Thank you, sir.' Deepbriar hesitated. There was another case that was worrying him more than the poison-pen letters. He'd filed reports each time a gin trap turned up, but nobody at Falbrough was taking the matter seriously. 'It's a stupid prank,' Sergeant Hubbard had said, when he'd brought the latest incident to his superior's attention, 'and gin traps aren't illegal, not yet.'

'But these aren't just four-inch traps for catching rabbits,' Deepbriar protested, 'man-traps were banned over a hundred years ago.'

The sergeant waved this aside. 'But they're being put in plain view, so nobody's going to be fool enough to step on them. Folks who keep pets are just as likely to lose 'em to a fox, or a shotgun, if they make a nuisance of themselves. You've better things to do with your time than investigate dead foxes. It'll all fizzle out in a week or two. You're worrying over nothing.'

Deepbriar wished he had the sergeant's faith. Now as he faced the inspector across the desk, the list of names of the men who'd been at Colonel Brightman's shoot on 23 January felt like a dead weight in his pocket. Stubbs sat back in his chair, ignorant of Deepbriar's inner struggle. 'Was there anything else?'

Deepbriar shook his head. 'No, thank you, sir,' and the moment when he might have bared his soul was gone. A second later he was outside the office, cursing himself for a coward. He stomped down to the canteen, and pulled the well-thumbed piece of paper from his pocket as he lingered over a cup of tea and a stale bath bun.

An hour later the constable stood at the door of a house in the most exclusive street in Falbrough.

'Were you looking for my father?' the young man who answered the door asked cheerfully. 'Surgery should have finished by now, he'll be free in a minute.'

'You'd be Mr Richard Williams?' Deepbriar asked, consulting his list, noting that the young man was a student at Oxford University. 'I believe you and your father were guests at Minecliff Manor on the twenty-third of January this year. I'd be obliged if I could have a word with both of you; there are a few questions I need to ask.'

Williams grinned. 'Sounds intriguing. Somebody didn't go shooting another guest instead of the pheasants, did they? Look, come on in, and I'll tell the old man you're here.'

The two men listened with apparent concern when Deepbriar explained the reason for his visit. 'Anything we can do,' Dr Williams said helpfully. 'That's a damn silly thing to do, playing around with gin traps. I remember Charles making a joke about them, and I seem to recall somebody asking where they were kept, though I can't remember who it was.'

'Nor me,' his son chipped in. 'I was chatting to that American chap. He was only in England for a few days, so at least you can eliminate him from your inquiries, Constable. The colonel's old gamekeeper is a bloodthirsty cove. Are you sure he's not the one you're looking for?'

'If the traps were aimed at catching poachers on Minecliff Manor land I might suspect Rowbotham,' Deepbriar confessed. 'The trouble is, the evidence suggests that the culprit was probably one of the guns.'

The doctor was taken aback, but neither he nor his son seemed to take the accusation personally, and when they ushered Deepbriar out of the house a few moments later they both wished him luck with his inquiries.

Deepbriar stood in the street for almost half a minute, breathing deeply and making some pretence of writing a few words in his notebook; two down and eleven to go, if he included the guests who had gone along to watch, without being actively involved in the shoot. He couldn't expect everyone on the list to be as sympathetic as Dr Williams and his son.

Archibald Childs was at his office, which was a rare bit of luck, and the old man was polite, if a little distant, answering Deepbriar's questions with a lawyer's circumspection. 'I do recall,' the solicitor said, 'there was a man in the stables while we were having this conversation about poachers. I imagine he was a member of Colonel Brightman's staff. He did not appear to be engaged on any particular duty, which suggests that might be a suitable starting point for your investigation. Personally I took no part in the conversation about poachers and gin traps, so I regret I am unable to help you on that score.' He peered at Deepbriar shortsightedly. 'I feel it my duty to warn you, as a man of the law, that some of my fellow guests may take exception to being questioned about such a matter, especially by a uniformed constable. They may choose to regard it as an insult.'

Thanking him glumly, Deepbriar went on his way. He paused briefly at the station to telephone Lord Cawster's house, and was a little disconcerted to be told the high sheriff of the county would be happy to see him at 12.15 that day; he had almost hoped to be rebuffed, or told that he would have to wait a week for an appointment. With his heart in his mouth the constable cycled the four miles to Lord Cawster's estate.

'Mantraps, eh?' Lord Cawster stared at Deepbriar and the constable had to steel himself to meet the man's gaze without fidgeting. 'I remember them being mentioned. And now they're turning up all over Minecliff? Sounds as if you've got a crackpot on the loose.' Lord Cawster narrowed his eyes. 'You've heard a few stories about my family, I daresay.'

'I'm visiting everybody who took part in the shoot, your lordship,' Deepbriar said, keeping his tone even. He hadn't forgotten about the baron's forebears, several of whom had been notoriously eccentric, but as far as he knew the current Lord Cawster was not only sane, but extremely shrewd. 'No one person stands out as a likely suspect. What I'm after is information.'

'Hmph. I'll take your word for it. You've got some nerve, I'll grant you that. There's one or two who were there that day who might not give you a very friendly welcome, naming no names. I'm not sure that I can help you. The only person who seemed interested in the subject of poachers was that chap Golding. Never met him before, bit of an oddity, had a bee in his bonnet about people tramping about on his property.' He raised expressive eyebrows. 'New money, isn't he?'

'He owns the nurseries to the south of Minecliff,' Deepbriar replied. 'His father was a farmer. Fell off his horse when he was out with the local hunt and broke his neck.'

'Oh yes, I remember him, mad on riding to hounds. Skinny chap, not like the son. He's not got the figure for scurrying around after dark setting traps though, has he? The man's only half my age but he was puffing like a grampus before we reached the end of the drive.' He thought for a moment. 'There's young Monty Hargraves of course; he's crazy enough for anything. He once set fire to his school dorm. Cost his father a packet to keep the matter out of court.'

'Young' Monty was now a successful businessman, and one of those who had been out of the area all summer, so his name wasn't on the list. Deepbriar thanked Lord Cawster for his time and left, happy to have escaped unscathed. He hadn't learnt much, except that his lordship didn't much care for Phil Golding, a prejudice the constable could quite understand.

Reluctantly Deepbriar decided to attempt one more visit, though it wasn't one he looked forward to. Sir Arthur Drimsbury lived in a cottage tucked away beyond the furthest reaches of Lord Cawster's estate, and it took Deepbriar almost an hour to find it. After several missed turns he pedalled wearily up a steep hill, his mind on the sandwiches

Mary had packed for him before he set off that morning. He wished he hadn't left them at the station; he functioned better on a full stomach.

As he approached the house Deepbriar reflected that at least Sir Arthur had the right sort of pedigree; the man had been awarded a knighthood for his exploits behind enemy lines, so he would know how to skulk around the countryside at night without being seen. Deepbriar grinned to himself; a crazy idea occurring to him. Maybe the man missed the old excitement of the war years, and was looking for ways to liven up his retirement.

Unfortunately for Deepbriar, Sir Arthur was at home, and he was in a bad mood. It might have been his normal frame of mind, but Deepbriar never had the time to find out. Sir Arthur was instantly outraged that the police should want to question him, and didn't even invite the constable over the threshold.

'I've already visited Mr Childs, and Lord Cawster,' Deepbriar said desperately. 'I'm simply trying to find out if anyone showed a particular interest in Major Brightman's comment about mantraps.'

Sir Arthur wasn't listening. He ranted for several minutes about integrity and honour, and made a point of writing down Deepbriar's name and number. 'I shall report your conduct to your superior officers,' he roared. The heavy oak door rattled back into its frame, leaving the constable on the step, flush-faced.

Hungry and dispirited, Deepbriar found his way back to the Falbrough Road. He wasn't even halfway through his list. He'd spoken to just six people. Of those, Phil Golding had walked away before the shoot was even mentioned, while Sir Arthur was probably on the telephone to Sergeant Hubbard right now, lining him up for an official reprimand.

Deepbriar had half hoped to sneak in through the back of the police station, retrieve his sandwiches from the staff room and make a dash for home, but he was called into Inspector Martindale's office as soon as he put his head around the door.

The inspector scowled down at the message he'd been given just minutes before. It had come, by a rather circuitous route, from the chief constable.

'I can't help being disappointed, Deepbriar,' Martindale said, glaring up at the constable who stood at attention in front of him. 'A few weeks ago I was telling the CID what a valued officer you were. Do I need to reconsider that assessment?'

Deepbriar did his best to explain why he'd

tried to interview Sir Arthur Drimsbury, but Martindale interrupted him. 'There's not a man in this station, with the possible exception of yourself, Constable Deepbriar, who doesn't know that our local hero has a very high opinion of himself. If you had something that needed saying to him, you should have consulted me.'

'The matter didn't seem to justify involving you, sir,' Deepbriar said woodenly. 'I was merely — '

'With people like Sir Arthur there is no such thing as *merely* doing anything!' Martindale said acerbically, crumpling the note in his hand. 'Can you assure me that you won't upset any more of the local gentry?'

'I'm not sure that I can, sir.' Deepbriar pulled the list from his pocket and handed it to the inspector, reflecting that he might as well be hanged for a sheep as a lamb. Ten minutes later, chastened but with a spark of righteous anger smouldering somewhere beneath his stoical exterior, the constable collected his lunch and a cup of strong tea, and retreated to a corner of the canteen.

Just like Sergeant Hubbard, Inspector Martindale had refused to accept that the matter was important. 'A very minor risk,' he assessed, when Deepbriar pointed out that these particular gin traps were large enough to injure an adult seriously, let alone a child. 'It's simply a matter of warning everyone to be careful. We'll have no repeat of the altercation with Sir Arthur, if you don't mind, Deepbriar. If anyone is hurt by one of these traps, that might justify action. Until then, I advise you to keep your nose clean.'

* * *

'If they think I'm going to sit back and wait till some child gets injured,' Deepbriar said indignantly, as he watched Mary prepare his meal a few hours later, 'they can think again.'

'But if anybody else complains you'll be in trouble,' his wife cautioned. 'Look, why don't you forget it all for a while? Come to the rehearsal with me this evening. We could do with somebody to play the piano. Mrs Harvey has been a bit awkward since her husband wasn't given a leading role. He was offered Spoletta, but he was talking about turning it down.'

'I wondered why he wasn't looking happy when I came to meet you the other day. Mrs Emerson needs to be careful, upsetting her supporters like that.'

'She's a bit taken with Mr Bonelli,' Mary Deepbriar said, with a little sigh. 'But I suppose you can't blame her, being on her own. He makes such a fuss of her, and he *is* charming.'

'Italians,' Deepbriar snorted, that one word expressing his opinion quite clearly.

Antonio Bonelli was at the village hall before them, making himself useful, tidying chairs and fetching music stands while Mrs Emerson chattered happily to him from the stage. Elaine Barr was next to arrive, coming through the door rather hesitantly and looking glad to see Mary Deepbriar there.

'I don't sing,' she said hastily, when the constable asked if she had a part in the forthcoming production, 'but I paint a bit, so I thought maybe I could help with the scenery.'

'Don't be so modest,' Mary said. 'She knows a lot about dress designing too,' she told her husband, 'and we'll need a lot of new costumes. Most of us can sew, but it will be a great help to have a real expert.'

'I'm interested in foreign costume,' Elaine admitted. 'And I've one or two books that might be useful.' She lowered her voice, a hint of mischief in her tone. 'I'm not just trying to ingratiate myself with Mrs Emerson, honestly. It should be fun. What about you, Thorny, are you in the chorus?'

'He doesn't sing in public,' his wife said, before Deepbriar could answer, 'though he has a nice voice.'

'It's the job,' Deepbriar said. 'I'd never be sure I could make it to the rehearsals, let alone the performance. I only came tonight because Mary says they're short of somebody to play the piano.'

'Oh yes, Mrs Harvey's bad back.' Elaine nodded, though there was a twinkle in her eye. 'Funny, she looked fine when I saw her in the post office earlier!'

Mary laughed. 'I gather you're learning a bit about village life.'

Will Minter came over to them, and swept Elaine away to look at some scenery he'd been working on. Several more members of the society arrived, among them the wife of the under-keeper at Minecliff Manor, who bustled across to them. Unlike her taciturn spouse, Sylvia Watts seemed happy to be in company. 'Hello, Mrs Deepbriar,' she said breathlessly, 'have you been able to learn your part? I hope I'll be all right. I'm getting a bit muddled with the second act.'

'There's plenty of time,' Mary said, 'you can't expect to have the whole thing by heart yet. You've met my husband, haven't you?'

'Oh yes, sorry, Mr Deepbriar, I didn't mean to forget my manners, but I'm a bit nervous. I've never been in a proper production before. You weren't here last week; are you joining us?’

Deepbriar patiently explained again that the demands of police work didn’t mix with performing on stage.

‘Of course, silly me.’ Sylvia Watts shook her head solemnly.

‘Terry told me why you were at the manor. It’s horrid, isn’t it, those traps I mean? I don’t know why anybody would do a thing like that. I don’t like it when Terry has to kill things. Well, of course they’re pests and all that, but it’s not nice, is it?’

‘Let’s not talk about it,’ Mary Deepbriar said firmly. ‘That’s a nice dress, is it new?’

‘Oh yes, I only bought it last week. Do you like it?’ She glanced archly at the constable. ‘Terry gets a bit cross, but it’s my money I’m spending, and there’s plenty more. It’s such fun being able to buy whatever I want.’ She delved into her handbag. ‘Look, I bought this little notebook too, I’ve been writing out the words I have to learn.’ She showed them a page of spidery writing. ‘I expect you’re really good at remembering things Mr Deepbriar, being a policeman.’

‘He sometimes forgets our anniversary,’ Mary said, giving her husband a smile. ‘But then he’s a man; you can’t expect too much. Look, Sylvia,’ she went on, taking her arm, ‘Miss Strathway’s here, I expect she’d like some help with the tea things, ready for later.'

Mrs Emerson noticed Deepbriar then, and he allowed himself to be hurried to the piano, where the woman fussed over the music for several minutes, before her leading man came to fetch her away, a warm smile on his face, a flattering word on his lips.

'She's besotted,' a voice whispered, and Thorny looked round to see George Hopgood's sister behind him. Known universally as Miss Jane, she was probably the most active of the village gossips, a position aided considerably by her job in the village shop.

'She ought to know better,' Miss Jane went on, her tone conspiratorial, 'a woman in *her* position.'

'You think people might talk?' Deepbriar replied, giving her an eloquent look. Miss Jane pressed her lips together, taking his meaning, and offence along with it.

'I speak as I find,' she said, marching away.

Deepbriar sighed and began playing the overture very quietly, just for his own amusement; the people in the hall were making so much noise that they drowned out the music. He was beginning to wonder why he'd agreed to come.

At last the rehearsal began, and despite his misgivings Deepbriar found he was enjoying himself. Mrs Emerson was apparently resting her voice, so he was able to enjoy hearing his wife and Sylvia Watts singing with the chorus. When Tosca's part was needed it was performed by the understudy, who had perfect pitch, though she lacked Mrs Emerson's volume. Bonelli was actually quite an accomplished tenor. His performance might have been better if he hadn't insisted on addressing every note personally to Mrs Emerson although she wasn't on stage at the time. She was at the back of the hall speaking in loud whispers to Elaine, and even over Bonelli's singing and his own offering at the piano, Deepbriar could hear her quite clearly.

'It's so very kind of you to join our little band,' Mrs Emerson gushed. 'Living in our small rural community we've never had the benefit of such a talented designer in our ranks.'

Elaine Barr began to make a deprecating reply, but Mrs Emerson didn't wait for her to finish. 'We were all so happy to hear that dear Major Brightman was coming home. So romantic, for a man of his age to finally find his perfect sweetheart. I do so hope you'll be able to accept my invitation for Friday, these humble luncheon parties of mine are quite a treat for me. A poor widow has to make the most of what little company is available to her.'

Deepbriar couldn't hear the younger woman's answer, and he was sorely tempted to abandon the piano and intervene. Bella Emerson was neither poor, nor a widow, and when it came to imposing on other people's kindness she was positively shameless. He almost lost his place on the page, and there was a fraught moment while Cavaradossi held a note rather longer than he should before the piano caught him up again.

Mrs Emerson, Deepbriar thought sourly, was a menace. The ghastly woman had once been eager to attach herself to him. Bonelli could doubtless look after himself, but there was something fragile about Elaine Barr; he didn't want Mrs Emerson to get her talons into the poor girl. Unfortunately Mary was too good-hearted to see the woman's true colours, and was still one of her admirers. As if in response to his thought, his wife came to his side as Bonelli finished his solo. 'He's good, isn't he?' she whispered happily. 'I think it could be our best show ever. Bella wants to try a duet with him before we finish.'

Deepbriar suppressed a groan. He should have brought earplugs. Before he could sort out the right page in the score, a small figure came racing into the hall, panting noisily, his sandalled feet skidding on the polished floor.

'Mr Deepbriar! Mr Deepbriar!' It was Geoff Berdale, his grubby face pink with excitement. 'There's another one of them traps! We found it. An' it's caught a cat!'

12

Deepbriar sent the boys on their way, silencing their ghoulish comments with a look. He hurried on alone to the place where they'd found the trap. The light was fading fast in the western sky, and once the lads were out of sight he trotted along the track that ran behind the houses in West Road.

For most of its length the path was well used, giving entry to back gates through fences in various states of disrepair, but the last few yards were choked with weeds. Once the thoroughfare must have provided access to Stellings Lane, but that had been before Deepbriar's time. Somebody had put up a fence and now it was a patch of wasteground, a jungle of brambles cut through with a narrow path the local youngsters used to reach an open space at the end. Here generations of boys had built secret dens beneath a couple of ancient yew trees. An even lower and narrower path, made perhaps by a badger, crossed the children's track, and it was here that the trap had been set, far enough from the youngsters' route not to be noticed. The cat's silver-grey stripes must have caught the boys' attention; they shone pale in the twilight, just visible in the gloom.

The tabby cat was mercifully dead. Its end had probably been swift, the metal jaws almost tearing the poor beast in half. Deepbriar stared down at the little corpse, and something inside him gave a tiny leap of apprehension; the cottage where Mrs Grimes lived wasn't far away. Was this Tibbles? It was too dark to be sure, though the cat's fur was certainly the right colour. Furiously, Deepbriar wrenched the peg from the ground, lifting the trap with its pathetic burden, holding it away from him so he didn't get blood on his clothes. He fought his way back out of the brambles. It would be too cruel to take the mangled body back to the old lady. After a moment's hesitation he placed it beside a heap of grass clippings somebody had left outside their back gate.

There was a light on in Mrs Grimes's window, and Deepbriar's knock brought the old lady out from the kitchen to the door. He could see the shape of her through the stained-glass panel as she approached, her footsteps slow and shuffling.

'Sorry to call so late,' Deepbriar began. The old woman looked small and frail. 'I — ' Before he could say more, a sinuous striped body came from behind the old woman's legs. Tibbles stared up at Deepbriar, his amber gaze intense. The constable was irresistibly reminded of Mrs Grimes on the day of the funeral, when she'd waylaid him at the church, ready to defend her right to her new pet. Tibbles was definitely a cat who knew which side his bread was buttered. 'Just wanted to check that your cat was safe indoors,' the constable went on lamely.

Mrs Grimes looked up at him shrewdly. 'Found another one of them traps, have you?'

'Yes, as a matter of fact I have. Just down the alley.'

She nodded. 'I heard those young lads go by a while back. Funny thing, Tibbles woke me up last night. Staring out of the window he was. First time he's ever done that. Maybe he heard something.'

Deepbriar resisted the temptation to ask for more details. He might be getting desperate, but he'd be the laughing stock of the force if he started acting on evidence gathered from the behaviour of a cat. He bent to stroke the tabby's silky head. 'Shame you can't talk, Tibbles.' Deepbriar straightened. 'Sorry to have bothered you.'

'You haven't bothered me,' the old woman replied. 'I was going to come and see you. There's been a lot of talk about this special meeting. I've never taken any interest in the parish council before, lot of nonsense, most of it. But they say somebody's coming to read Mrs Twyford's will. That's right, is it?'

The constable nodded. 'Yes, that's what she wanted.'

'Can I go to this meeting then?'

'Anybody can go,' Deepbriar told her. 'Though if the whole village turns out it'll be a tight squeeze.'

'Tomorrow night, is it?'

'That's right. Seven o'clock.'

'You don't think there'll be anything said about Tibbles?' The worry was back in her eyes.

'I shouldn't think so. Don't fret, Mrs Grimes, I'll do all I can to make sure Tibbles stays where he's best off, and I reckon that's right here with you.'

Going back to collect the trap, Deepbriar saw a shadow lurking at the end of the alley. 'Who's there?' he called.

'Will Minter.' The farmer came to meet him, a small torch throwing a dim circle of light at their feet. 'All right, Thorny?'

'Somebody's missing a pet,' Deepbriar said.

Minter shone the light on the dead animal. 'No,' he said. 'He's wild. That old tom lived in my barn a few years back, before our Bob chased him out. Got careless in his old age,' he added disparagingly.

Deepbriar buried the body at the bottom of the garden, piling a few stones on top to keep the foxes from digging it up. He added the trap to the growing collection in his office. The way things were going he'd end up with them all. Maybe he could wait for the affair to blow over, like his superiors told him. If only his luck held. It would be a miracle if this menace caught nothing worse than a stray tom cat.

⋆ ⋆ ⋆

'Afternoon, Thorny.' Detective Sergeant Jakes put his head round the office door, grinning widely. 'Mrs Deepbriar let me in. She said to tell you the kettle's on.'

'Don't know what you've got to be so happy about,' Deepbriar replied grumpily.

'The inspector sent me on a nice little trip out into the country,' Jakes said. 'He told me to call on Minecliff's favourite sleuth. I've been doing a bit of work on your behalf and I've got a couple of things to tell you.'

'I don't suppose it's good news,' Deepbriar said, not yet ready to relinquish his gloomy mood.

'Can't be sure one way or the other,' the younger man replied cheerfully. 'Still, it might help in the long run.' He opened the folder he was carrying and took out the envelope that had contained Miss Cannon's letter. 'I had a long chat with this handwriting expert. Funny thing, he says he can usually tell if handwriting belongs to a man or a woman, but in this case he can't. To be honest he's a bit baffled. The writing is unformed, so he says, the sort of thing a child might do. No character to it.'

'It's very neat,' Deepbriar said. 'But it'll be a sorry sort of world if a child ever learns to use words like that.'

'True enough. He says the grammar proves it's an adult, as well as the vocabulary, which is a bit on the coarse side.'

'To say the least.' Deepbriar scowled. 'So, this clever expert of yours hasn't been much help.'

'I don't know about that,' Jakes said. 'He reckons this person has found some way of disguising their writing, and he says that's a difficult thing to do. Not for the odd word maybe, but it's almost impossible to keep it up for a couple of pages. Interesting, eh?'

Deepbriar pulled a sheet of paper towards him and began writing, trying to make clear rounded letters like the ones on the envelope. The result was laughable. 'Maybe it just takes practice. I take your point, but it doesn't help us find our culprit, does it?'

'All right, Sherlock, try this for size.' Jakes took out the letter and held it up to the light. 'The watermark tells us that this stuff is in common use, you can buy it at two places in Falbrough, probably ten times that in Belston. *But*,' he added portentously, before Deepbriar could interrupt, '*This* on the other hand, is a rarity.' He flourished the envelope. 'Our expert confessed himself temporarily at a loss. He says he knows a man who could probably pin it down, but he lives south of London and is a bit on the eccentric side, doesn't answer letters and won't have a telephone in the house.' Jakes sighed. 'It's a shame we're not working on a case of grand larceny or murder. The inspector refused to let me catch the first train to London, though I told him I was quite willing to go.'

'So, we're no further on.'

'No, but our man will keep working on it. He's feeling a bit put out. You never know, he might decide to take the thing to Surrey himself. Never say die, Constable! You look as if you've got the weight of the world on your shoulders. You know,' Jakes went on, suddenly serious, 'I was really sorry you didn't get that move to CID. It was Martindale's fault, he had a word with the superintendent.'

'They think I'm too old.' Deepbriar was

plunged back into gloom again.

'Prove them wrong then.' Jakes tapped him lightly on the shoulder. 'Stubbs wants you, reckons you've got a real talent for seeing round corners, and there's a rumour that he'll be made up to chief inspector soon, so maybe he'll be able to pull rank for you. Personally I'm keeping my fingers crossed. I'd rather work with you than young Tidyman; he's about as bright as a fifteen watt bulb when the sun's shining.'

* * *

Every chair in the village hall was taken, and there were people standing at the back. Even though he was out of uniform, Deepbriar was hot, and heartily wished himself elsewhere as he watched the last few stragglers coming in through the door. Bert Bunyard pushed in front of him, arguing loudly with Cyril Bostock.

'Lot o' bliddy nonsense,' Bunyard declared, 'Turns a bit warmish an' folks is worryin' about storms. Be another week before we 'as thunder.'

'You're the one talkin' nonsense,' Bostock shot back. 'I allus know when it's turnin' stormy. My 'ens come in like there was a fox on their tails tonight. Got sense them birds

’ave. Whole darn lot of you’ll get a soakin’.’ He tapped the floor with the ancient umbrella he was holding and gave a gap-toothed grin. ‘I’ll be laughin’ all the way to the Goose.’

On the stage, the parish council was gathering, the dapper little figure of Mr Morton sitting silent and watchful amongst them. When everybody was assembled Ferdy Quinn stepped to the front of the stage and called for silence. ‘Before we get on to our normal business,’ he said, taking out a handkerchief and wiping sweat from his face, ‘As Chairman of Minecliff Parish Council, I’d like to welcome Mr Morton. As you probably know, he is here for the reading of Mrs Twyford’s will.’

‘The cunnin’ beggar wants to get shot of us,’ Bostock chortled, ‘Must be even ’otter up there than it is down ’ere.’

The solicitor rose to his feet and waited for the odd rustlings and murmurs to die away, his gaze fixed upon the sheet of thick paper in his hand.

When there was silence Mr Morton peered over his glasses at the assembled villagers and cleared his throat. ‘I am charged with reading the last will and testament of Mrs Gladys Twyford, late of Number 4, Stellings Lane, Minecliff.’

As the dry toneless voice droned out the

preliminary statement, Deepbriar's attention wandered. He allowed his gaze to roam across the rows of people in front of him, thinking about Mrs Twyford. Was the person who had sent her a malicious poison-pen letter in the hall? Sylvia Watts sat in the front row, wearing a very smart hat decorated with feathers; she must have been spending more of her legacy. She was listening with her mouth open, her face vacant. He gave a tiny shake of his head; that woman wasn't bright enough to have written those letters. And he'd seen her writing, hadn't he, it was spidery and badly formed, totally unlike the round hand of his miscreant?

Moving on, Deepbriar noticed Miss Jane, her head cocked on one side as if she was concentrating hard on what the solicitor was saying, though Mr Morton had hardly got past 'sound of mind' yet. One of the generation of women who'd been robbed of the chance of marriage by the First War, Miss Jane was an inveterate gossip, and she could be spiteful.

Women loved to talk about their neighbours; it was in their nature. But not many of them felt the venom expressed in the letter that had been sent to Miss Cannon. Deepbriar's gaze moved on to Miss Strathway, another single woman of a similar age to Miss Jane. In her position at the telephone exchange she undoubtedly had access to many secrets. Could she harbour a deep-seated hatred for women who'd avoided her solitary fate?

Deepbriar was brought back to the present by a sound like a great wind gusting through the room, as every soul in the hall drew in a breath. Morton had finally got to the point.

'The rest of the estate is to be left to the people of Minecliff, in trust. This legacy is intended to create a permanent memorial to all those members of the Twyford family who gave their lives for their country.' Morton peered over his glasses again. 'You will not need to be reminded that Mrs Twyford's late husband was one such man. A small plaque has already been erected in the church, but it was Mrs Twyford's wish that something more should be done to ensure that his sacrifice is not forgotten.' He returned to reading, evidently close to the bottom of the page. 'The trust is to be administered by Morton and Childs, Solicitors, in co-operation with Minecliff Parish Council.'

A rustle of movement shimmered round the hall. The sky had grown dark although the sun wasn't due to set for two hours, and the atmosphere was so oppressive the air felt thick and stifling.

‘We already got a war memorial,’ Cyril Bostock grumbled, not quite under his breath.

‘Bet they’ll spend it all on the bliddy church,’ Bert Bunyard replied, loudly enough for everyone to hear.

‘Mrs Twyford made her wishes quite clear in a further instruction which was left with me only two months ago,’ Mr Morton replied reprovingly, ‘and which will be presented to the council when we meet to determine how this legacy should be disbursed. She instructed that a sum of money should be released immediately for the purpose of providing Minecliff’s children with a playground, naming the small area of land to the south of the village green as a suitable site. The funds will be made available very soon, and equipment installed. There are other recommendations, which are to be proposed to the council in due course, but I imagine the council may be open to alternative suggestions. Miss Twyford felt that Minecliff might benefit from having its own lending library, and also from improvements made to this hall. If — ’

‘An’ ’ow much is a library goin’ to cost? What folks want — ’ Bunyard’s further interruption was broken short, as Deepbriar’s hand descended upon his shoulder.

'Let the man speak, Bert,' the constable said peaceably. 'You can have your say in the Goose later. And I'm quite sure you will.'

This brought a laugh, then a hush. Mr Morton inclined his head in Deepbriar's direction. 'Thank you, Constable. As yet I can make no more than an estimate of the amount involved, and I am reluctant to speculate concerning the total. However, I can confirm that the trust will be responsible for administering a sum of no less than sixty thousand pounds.'

Ferdy Quinn slumped back in his seat as if he'd been shot, and all over the hall people stared up at the solicitor, open mouthed. Then as if at a signal, just as pandemonium was about to break out, a flash of lightning lit the darkened hall, followed half a second later by a deafening clap of thunder. All conversation was instantly halted as heavy rain drummed on the roof.

* * *

'A bit of a turn-up, eh, Thorny?' Don Bartle pulled a pint and slid the glass across the bar. Having left the empty pub in the charge of their barman for half an hour to attend the meeting, Phyllis and Don Bartle had led the rush from the village hall through the pelting rain, and the man's dark hair was slicked over his head as if he'd overdone the Brylcreem. Phyllis having dashed upstairs to change out of her wet clothes, the publican was holding a shouted conversation with Deepbriar while serving drinks to a steadily increasing queue of customers. 'Come on, Frank,' he called, as the barman dithered over counting out change, 'Get a move on before somebody dies of thirst. There's times we really miss Harry,' he confided, lowering his voice a little, 'but I suppose Frank might get quicker in time. So, Mrs Twyford was a wealthy woman.'

'The family was always pretty well off,' Deepbriar said. 'She didn't have anyone else to leave it to. Sad in a way.'

'Yes, but all that money! You really think they'll build a library?'

'I suppose they might. I can think of something else I'd like them to do though, and it wouldn't cost as much,' Deepbriar said. 'The church organ's worn out. A few thousand spent there would do a lot of good.'

Bartle grinned. 'Bert and his cronies wouldn't like it, but I must say I like a bit of organ music. Anyway, there'd be enough for that a dozen times over,' Don replied, deftly handing over three pints of bitter and a half of shandy without even looking at George Hopgood, who had finally made it to the front of the queue. 'If we're allowed to make suggestions, I'd like to see a new bridge by the mill. The brewery reckon they'll have to send their deliveries round by the arterial if it's not mended soon.'

'The cricket pavilion's falling down,' George commented, as he turned away from the bar, to be replaced by a damp and disgruntled Bert Bunyard.

'Give us a pint, Don, I'm parched,' the farmer said, his purple-veined face glistening from the rain. 'I bet us ordinary folks won't get no say in what's done.'

'Why, what else could you possibly need, Bert?' Deepbriar replied. 'A man can only be in one pub at a time.'

When the laughter had died down Bunyard glowered at the constable. 'We could 'ave some better roads, 'stead of all these ruddy potholes.'

'What, you think the council should repair your cart-track, Bunyard?' Ferdy Quinn came in, the crowd parting to let him through.

'That must have been a very short council meeting,' Don Bartle commented, reaching for another glass.

'We adjourned till next Monday,' Quinn replied, handing over a shilling and waiting for his change. 'Couldn't hear ourselves talk for the rain. Anyway, half the village stayed, trying to tell us how to spend all this money.' He glared at Bunyard. 'Like him. Maybe you should try taking better care of your own property, Bert.'

'Don't you go tellin' me my business,' Bunyard roared, slamming his nearly empty tankard on the bar. 'I know 'ow you got that money to build a new barn.'

'Don't you go spreading your lies about me,' Quinn retorted, his cheeks flaming as red as his hair. 'Maybe you need a bit more of a lesson. Seems like a few weeks in gaol wasn't enough for you!'

'Now now, that'll do,' Deepbriar said. 'Calm down, or I'll help Don throw the pair of you out in the rain to cool off.'

Bunyard retreated, grumbling. Quinn buried his nose in his tankard, while a dozen more men came pressing round, all intent on telling the chairman of the council exactly what they thought should be done with Mrs Twyford's legacy. 'Will you all just leave me alone!' he shouted at last. 'There's going to be a public meeting as soon as the estate has been wound up. You can all have your say then.' And with that he withdrew, diving back into the rain, which was still coming down in a relentless torrent.

'One good thing about this weather, Mr Deepbriar.' Billy Tapper squeezed through the crowd to reach the constable, his glass held high to keep it from being knocked. 'Don't reckon anyone will be out setting traps tonight.'

'Let's hope not. Isn't Fred here? Must be nearly a week since I've seen him.'

'No.' Billy said no more, suddenly very intent on his drink.

'Not in any bother, is he?' Deepbriar asked. He was ready to believe that Billy was a reformed character, but he doubted if Fred had turned over a new leaf.

Billy sighed. 'Not that I know of, but I reckon he's keeping out of sight. Don't ask me, Mr Deepbriar, he doesn't tell me what he's up to any more.'

Deepbriar might have pursued the subject further, but a huge figure came lumbering out of the saloon bar, forcing the regulars to give him room as he made a beeline to where the constable was standing.

'Don't expect to see you in here drinking, Deepbriar,' Phil Golding said loudly. 'Not when there are still villains on the loose. But maybe I shouldn't expect too much from our dimwitted police force; look at that fiasco in Belston when Harwayes Bank was robbed.' He gave a harsh bark of laughter, looking around the bar as if waiting for applause. 'They had a description of the men, but all they did was run around like a lot of headless chickens — couldn't catch a cold. I thought better of you though, Minecliff's very own detective. Why aren't you out there looking for the man who smashed up my greenhouse?'

'Because,' Deepbriar said, pausing just long enough to get a hold on his temper, 'I'm off duty. I've been putting in a nineteen-hour day these last couple of weeks, Mr Golding, and just this once I've rewarded myself with a pint of Don's best. I'll be out before dawn again tomorrow; maybe you'd like to join me and make sure I'm doing my job properly.'

'If you were doing your job properly some damn layabout couldn't come sneaking on to my land trying to ruin my business!' Golding's face flushed. 'You'd better get some results soon, or I'll be talking to your superiors.'

13

The crowded pub had been full of noise. Now there was a silence, a communal holding of breath as Golding glared angrily at Deepbriar, his heavy breathing the only sound, except for a rumble of thunder rolling admonishingly in the distance.

It was too much. Deepbriar was dog tired. When he did get to bed his short nights were punctuated by troubled dreams. He was no nearer catching the bastard who had been setting the traps, and he'd have no peace until he did. The constable clenched his fists. Suddenly words weren't enough to express exactly what was going on in his head, and Golding's fat face loomed at him, as inviting as if it had a target painted across the fleshy features.

'I'm afraid I'm going to have to ask you to leave, Mr Golding.' Unseen, Don Bartle had come round from behind the bar, and he pushed Deepbriar aside to confront the nurseryman. 'I'm sorry, sir, but I don't think you're feeling quite yourself this evening.'

There was a faint buzz of excitement, of approval.

'Don,' Deepbriar began, but the publican waved him to silence.

'I run a nice friendly pub, and there's some things that are better kept for other places. I'm sure if you want to talk to Mr Deepbriar in the morning, you'll find him in his office.' He turned to the constable, offering him a quick wink. 'Isn't that so, Thorny?'

'Anytime, when I'm on duty, Mr Golding,' Deepbriar said, knowing he was being sensible yet with a faint twinge of regret; it had been alluring, that temptation, just once, to kick over the traces.

Golding gave a quick glance around the bar. George Hopgood and the three men who'd been drinking with him had vanished. The door to the yard was still swinging, suggesting how they'd made their quick exit. Of the remaining customers, none looked particularly friendly, and one or two wore expressions that spoke of their willingness to back their host if necessary.

The huge man gave a shrug. 'Yes, well, maybe Bartle has a point. I'm not in the habit of conducting business in public bars. A man can't rest on his laurels, Constable Deepbriar, you'd best remember that. Results — that's what we need.' He turned and lumbered out, a subdued ironic cheer following him.

'Have a drink on me, Don,' Deepbriar said,

as the buzz of conversation started up again.

The other man grinned, taking down a half-pint glass. 'Cheers. What was that about Harwayes? Did he mean that bank robbery? That wasn't anything to do with Falbrough, was it?'

'No, but it doesn't look good, when three armed men can raid a bank in broad daylight.' Deepbriar pulled a face. 'Doesn't do much for the Belston lads' reputation. Three weeks, and they've not made a single arrest.'

'Well, their coppers can't be as good as ours. You can't be everywhere!'

Deepbriar laughed, the last of the tension easing out of him. 'Thanks for the vote of confidence! And for dealing with Golding.'

'Can't have you getting chucked out of the force, Thorny,' Bartle said, 'not when our Harry's joining the ranks. He'll need a helping hand now and then, till he learns the ropes. As a matter of fact I'd rather have given Golding a proper piece of my mind, but I've my own livelihood to think of. So, will you be going out to see him first thing in the morning?'

'Not unless Ferdy Quinn's prize porkers take to the skies overnight,' Deepbriar replied, setting down his empty glass.

* * *

Mary was already in bed when he got home, although it wasn't full dark. Deepbriar crept around in stockinged feet, trying not to disturb her. He'd been a little surprised when she'd refused to go to the meeting with him. She'd been a bit low the last few days, and he thought she was looking pale. When he asked, she insisted she was feeling quite well. He had to take her word for it; he'd been out of the house so much he felt he'd hardly seen her since the fête.

Within minutes of slipping stealthily between the sheets Deepbriar was asleep. He woke with a start, only a short time later, staring at the paler square of the windows, wide-eyed. He could have sworn he'd heard somebody crying. Holding his breath he listened, but there was nothing. With a sigh he decided he was dreaming; probably those damned traps again. At least no bloody corpse had been involved this time, which made a change. Turning over he was instantly asleep again. When next he opened his eyes the sun was streaming in and the sounds downstairs told him that his wife was already brewing tea. It was almost 7.30.

Mary greeted him cheerfully. 'How did the meeting go?'

He wasn't going to be sidetracked. 'Did you turn off the alarm?'

'Yes.' She turned to face him, saying nothing more, her expression hovering somewhere between defiance and uncertainty.

Recalling how nearly he'd lost his temper in the Speckled Goose the night before, Deepbriar drew in a long breath. The decent night's sleep had done him a power of good. With luck Billy Tapper was right, the wet weather would have kept their madman indoors. 'Right.' He stepped around the table and gave his wife a quick hug. 'Sorry, love, have I been a bit cranky?'

'That's one word for it. Sit down, your bacon's done.'

They sat companionably over breakfast and he told her exactly what had happened the night before, including how close he'd come to punching Phil Golding on the nose. Yawning widely, Thorny leant back in his chair. 'I don't know if he'll come calling, but I hope not. There's nothing I can do anyway. He's not a popular man; he must have made quite a few enemies over the years. I'm sure it was somebody trying to get their own back.'

'I've never liked him,' Mary confided, nibbling at a bit of toast.

'Have we run out of bacon and eggs?' Deepbriar asked suddenly, realizing that she'd hardly eaten anything.

'No, I just didn't fancy them this morning. I'll have something for elevenses.'

The morning was fresh and damp after the rain. For the first time in days Deepbriar made no attempt to patrol any of the footpaths and back lanes, but contented himself with walking his official beat. The subject of Mrs Twyford's will was on everyone's lips, and he was stopped half-a-dozen times by villagers wanting to chat.

'It's such a lot of money, and what a strange thing, leaving it all to the village.' Young Mrs Watts spoke so rapidly the words nearly fell over each other. 'I mean, everybody is so excited, and there are so many different things that the council could do. Mrs Tapper said she thought we could have our own cinema, imagine that! And Miss Cannon was telling me the church tower used to be higher. Maybe they'll build it up again!'

Deepbriar extricated himself with what grace he could, reflecting again on how different Sylvia Watts was from her taciturn husband. Quite the gossip. Could she be the originator of the letters? Somehow he didn't think so. She liked to talk, but he'd seen no sign of any malice in her. And he wasn't sure she would know some of the words the writer had used, as she seemed neither very worldly, nor particularly bright.

He bumped into Miss Cannon by the church. Having glanced around to check that nobody could overhear, the woman confessed that she had no news to offer, though she'd been trying to find out who might have known that her child was a daughter. 'This sort of thing sounds easy when you read about it in books,' she said, with a rueful smile, 'but I don't believe I'm cut out to be a detective.'

Deepbriar smiled. 'Miss Cannon, don't tell me you're a fan of whodunits.'

'Now and then,' she replied. 'Agatha Christie is rather clever, don't you think?'

'Too clever for me,' Deepbriar said. 'We're hoping to get a lead from your letter. Evidently the envelope is rather unusual, not commonly available like the paper. The writing was no help though: our expert said it was probably disguised, although that's a difficult thing to do. Our villain isn't giving us much to work on.'

'I suppose it must be a woman?' Miss Cannon asked. 'I don't know why, but there was something about the language that made me feel it could be a man.' She gave him a piercing look. 'You'll doubtless tell me to rely on facts.'

'That's the official line, but I confess I'm a great believer in hunches. Trouble is, I can't see a man getting to know so much of the local gossip, can you?'

A sudden scream severed their conversation, sharp as a knife and almost as painful to the ears. It echoed across the valley. A woman? A child? The constable froze for the length of a heartbeat; there were two voices he realized, blended in fear or pain or desperation. Even before he reached this conclusion, Deepbriar was on the move.

The sounds were coming from beyond the village, up on the hill. Almost submerged beneath the dreadful appeal, he could hear the frenzied yelps of a dog. The woman was crying hysterically for help, begging that somebody, anybody, should come, while the child's voice wailed its own awful summons.

He ran flat out, horror nipping at his heels as he recognized the voice of Mrs Rose. That meant the child must be Oliver.

Dear God, he'd told them the boy would be safe. And this morning he'd slept late instead of patrolling the footpaths. Maybe Billy Tapper had done the same, convinced that nobody would be out laying traps in a thunderstorm.

The quickest way lay across the fields, and Deepbriar took the shortest route he could, leaping over a garden gate to run through Susan Hopgood's vegetable patch, half seeing her out of the corner of his eye, where she stood open-mouthed at her back door. Then he was jumping over the church brook and hurling himself across the meadow towards the house on the hill.

His heart pounding, his feet feeling as if each weighed a ton, the constable drove himself up the hill, wishing he was ten years younger. As if invoked by the thought, a slight figure came alongside him, arms and legs pumping. Deepbriar had no breath to spare, or he might have called out in surprise. Fred Tapper hadn't been seen in a week, and yet here he was, racing up the steep slope as if it was level ground, or as if a dozen gamekeepers were on his heels. He went by in silence, barely even sparing Deepbriar a glance, his expression intent, as he kept up a pace worthy of an Olympic sprinter.

A hedge loomed ahead, barring the way. The poacher slowed just a little before he launched himself into the air. It was an ungainly leap, all arms and legs, yet somehow his feet no more than skimmed the topmost leaves, and he vanished out of sight.

Knowing his limitations, Deepbriar slowed, his lungs heaving painfully, and detoured to the gate, grabbing the top rail and vaulting over it. He staggered a little as one foot hit a rut, then came upright and began to run again.

They were on the footpath now, and there was Mrs Rose, at the very end, where the path turned at a right angle to follow the hedge down the slope and across towards Will Minter's farm. The woman was on her knees, her arms around something, somebody, that half sat, half lay, upon the ground. Deepbriar felt as if his heart would burst. Not Oliver. Let it not be Oliver with his leg in a trap.

Mrs Rose was clinging to her son, shouting and sobbing by turns. The boy was struggling in her arms, screaming, lashing out, his hands beating at her.

Fred Tapper reached them. Deepbriar stared in total bafflement as the young poacher went straight past the two figures on the path. He appeared to run headlong into the hedge, but had actually thrust his way through a narrow gap without pausing, vanishing again from Deepbriar's view. Seeing that help had arrived Mrs Rose stopped shouting. From the other side of the bushes came the pitiful cries of an animal in pain.

The dog! It was the dog that was hurt, not the child. Deepbriar hadn't the strength left to laugh or cry, and wouldn't have known which to do even if he had. 'Keep him there,' he gasped, diving after Fred and hearing his shirt rip as it caught on a branch.

Barney was yelping, trying frantically to pull loose from the trap that had firm hold of his leg, tearing the flesh with every heave. 'Jesus!' Fred Tapper had been circling, trying to catch hold of the frantic mongrel. Now he flung himself on top of it, pinning it to the ground. The dog responded by grabbing hold of the poacher's arm and biting down hard.

'Get it out of the trap,' Fred ordered through gritted teeth, and Deepbriar hurried to obey. It was difficult enough releasing a dead animal from a gin trap, and it seemed to take forever to free Barney, who continued to struggle despite all Tapper's attempts to keep him still. Blood from the dog's mangled leg sprayed them both, along with droplets from the deepening wound on Fred Tapper's arm.

At last it was done. Deepbriar ripped off his shirt and tied it tight round the dog's head, to act as a muzzle. Fred removed his jacket and wrapped it around the mongrel's body. Captured, tied up tight, Barney was finally silenced.

Blood flowed freely down over Tapper's hand from his injured arm. He grimaced at it briefly, then turning to Deepbriar he lifted Barney in his arms. 'Get 'er to phone the vet,' he said, with a jerk of his head towards the hedge. 'I'll take the dog down to my gran, see if there's anythin' she can do until Mr Foster gets 'ere.'

He was gone, running as if he hadn't already had a gruelling 400-yard dash up a steep hill, not to mention a wrestling match with a dog that had left him with a nasty open wound. Deepbriar watched him disappear from sight, then did his best to clean himself up with his handkerchief before he squeezed back through the hedge.

* * *

'Where's that grandson of yours got to this time?' Deepbriar had stopped Ada Tapper on the street, giving her his most intimidating look, but the old woman merely scowled and shuffled a couple of steps as if inclined to push past him.

'Our Fred comes and goes as he pleases,' she said, when Deepbriar refused to give ground. 'Ain't beholden to nobody, don't owe you no account of where 'e goes, nor why.'

'Ada, he was hurt. It's been two days. Dr Smythe told me he wouldn't wait to get his arm stitched once the dog was taken care of.'

'And since when did you care? It ain't no business of yourn. Done nothin' wrong, 'as 'e?' Ada was defiant, but he could see the worry in her eyes.

'I'm not saying he's done anything wrong. I just want to talk to him,' Deepbriar said. 'I seem to remember you telling me you'd worked in a hospital back in the First War, Ada, so you know neglecting an open wound is a bad idea. A bite from a dog can be downright dangerous; his arm could get infected.' He sighed. 'As far as I'm concerned, Fred's a flaming hero, there's no need for him to hide from me. But if he's got himself in trouble then maybe I can help. Do you think it's anything to do with the traps?'

'It's not the traps,' Ada said firmly. 'Fred may 'ave got up to a bit of mischief in 'is time, but 'e wouldn't set no gin traps. I don't 'ave a clue where 'e's been this last few days, nor yet where 'e's gone now. Billy might know,' she added grudgingly. She glanced down the street and dropped her foghorn voice to a harsh whisper. 'I could tell 'e was scared, before 'e took off, but 'e wouldn't tell me nothin'. Come to the 'ouse early this mornin' an' grabbed a mouthful to eat, then 'e was gone. That dog all right, is it? Fred was proper upset.'

'It'll have to learn to run on three legs, but it won't be the first to do that,' Deepbriar replied. 'Bob Foster would have put it down, if it had belonged to anybody but young Oliver. The boy's had a bad time, Dr Smythe said losing the dog could set him back years.'

'Poor little lad.' Something approaching softness crept over the fleshy features, making Ada look suddenly old. 'If our Fred comes back I'll tell 'im what you said, Thorny. Can't do no more.'

Deepbriar returned to the police house via the back lanes, telling himself it was to check for traps, although in truth he wanted to avoid meeting anyone. He felt horribly guilty about Barney. True, the dog hadn't been on the public path; Mr Rose had checked the route that morning before his son was out of his bed and declared it safe, but he still felt responsible.

Once the boy had completed his walk to the end of the footpath he had turned his dog loose as usual for the return journey. A rabbit had run across in front of them and Barney had chased it through the hedge. If Mrs Rose hadn't stopped him, Oliver would have followed, before the little animal began to yelp in distress. Deepbriar shuddered. It could so easily have been the boy's leg that had been beyond saving and requiring amputation.

Reporting the incident by telephone, Deepbriar had asked Sergeant Hubbard to relay his concerns to Inspector Martindale, but he knew it was a waste of breath. No matter how near they had come to disaster, no matter that a child already crippled by disease might have been seriously injured, the fact remained that the only casualty had been a mongrel dog. That wasn't enough to change Martindale's mind about interrogating the suspects on Deepbriar's list.

Letting himself in through the back door, Deepbriar was surprised to hear sounds from upstairs. Mary had been invited to Bella Emerson's house, for a buffet luncheon, whatever that might be. He could smell the rich aroma of beef stew coming from the kitchen; she'd kept her promise to leave him something in the oven.

He put a foot on the bottom step, which creaked loudly. Deepbriar paused for a second then ran up to the top. He had never been a violent man, but his temper was on a short fuse, and he found himself almost wishing for an intruder to tackle, though it was hard to imagine what sort of fool would risk breaking into a police house.

'That you, Thorny?' Mary called from the bathroom.

'Why aren't you at Mrs Emerson's party?' he demanded bluntly.

She appeared, looking very attractive, he noticed. She had finished the new dress she'd been making, and the pale blue set off her English rose complexion.

'She called it off.' Mary went into the bedroom and began to change her clothes. 'It was all a bit odd. Several of us arrived at the door at the same time. Somebody knocked but there was no answer. We were getting a bit worried, but then Bella opened an upstairs window and said she was sorry but the luncheon was cancelled.'

Deepbriar grinned. 'What had she done, tipped the boiled ham down the sink by mistake?'

Mary shook her head. 'I don't think it was anything like that. I know you get impatient with Bella's histrionics, but I think she was genuinely upset. I'm sure she'd been crying.'

'Hasn't been seeing too much of that Italian, has she? Maybe he's upset her. Slippery sort of chaps, these southern European types.'

'I doubt it. He'd be at work today, wouldn't he? And she was fine yesterday. I did wonder,' Mary mused, pulling her plain dress over her head, 'if it was that husband of hers. I mean, she does enjoy playing the role of the grieving widow, and not everybody knows that Mr Emerson is alive and well and living in Broadstairs with his pet dog. Suppose he came calling?'

'That would do it,' Deepbriar conceded, hiding a grin.

'I thought I'd have a quick bite to eat then pop round. I can understand why she wouldn't want to face a great crowd of us, but she may need to see a friend.'

Deepbriar leant down to kiss the top of her head in a rare gesture of affection. 'You're too good to be true, you are,' he said. 'Bella Emerson's a fraud and a fibber, and you know it.'

'Well, we all have our faults,' Mary laughed. 'Have you been to see Phil Golding yet? He telephoned this morning, asking if you'd go up there again. He wasn't exactly rude to me, but I could tell it was a bit of an effort.'

'I saw him. That's three times in as many days. He raved on about the cost of repairing his damaged greenhouses, and how it's time I caught the chap who did it, but I've no evidence to go on, and no witnesses.'

'Did you tell him your theory about it being somebody with a grudge?'

'Yes. Fat lot of good that did. The only name I've got is Fred Tapper, and that came from George. When I mentioned it to Golding he nearly bit my head off, claimed that he and Fred were on the best of terms. I tried asking him about the shoot as well, and he said he couldn't remember talking to Charles about poachers and mantraps.'

Deepbriar frowned. 'I'm sure he was lying, but I don't see why. It's not as if he could be the one setting traps, he can hardly walk ten yards without stopping, it would kill him walking up to the Roses' place.'

'Maybe he has a guilty conscience about something else,' Mary suggested.

'Hmm. I can't see him writing poison-pen letters, can you? No, I think he's just an all round nasty piece of work. If I hadn't assured him that I'd been questioning all the other guns he'd probably be on the phone to the chief constable right now.'

14

'Morning, Thorny.' Jakes's voice, crackling down the telephone wires, sounded unnaturally cheerful. 'Got something for you. Your poison-pen letter. The envelope was produced by a small company in Devon.'

'Devon?'

'That's right. Newton Abbot. How it turned up so far from home is a mystery. This particular envelope was part of a gift set; you know the kind of thing, twenty sheets of fancy thick paper with envelopes to match, all done up in a leather case. They were only sold in a few shops, and none of them more than twenty miles from where they were made.'

Deepbriar was all attention. 'This could be the lead we've been hoping for. Thank you Sergeant. All I have to do is find someone in Minecliff who has a connection with Devon. Women send that sort of thing to their relatives, don't they? An ideal present for a maiden aunt.' He pulled a sheet of paper towards him.

'Which points at some sour old maid as our poison pen,' Jakes agreed.

'Can I have the address of this firm?'

Jakes read it out. 'I've already spoken to them, and there's no chance of finding the names of individual buyers; the gift sets were made as soon as decent materials were available after the war. Evidently people always use up the sheets of paper first. Those envelopes could have been in the back of somebody's drawer for years. And there's a chance they were bought by somebody who was only in Devon for a holiday.'

'Never mind, it's something to work on.' Deepbriar leant back in his chair. 'While you're on the line, can I ask if you worked on the Harwayes robbery?'

'No, that was nothing to do with Falbrough.' Jakes laughed. 'Lucky for us. Three masked men, two of them armed, and our poor benighted colleagues in Belston never turned up one decent suspect. Why do you ask?'

'Somebody was insulting me, and threw in the rest of the force for good measure. Seems that particular failure has become a byword for police incompetence.'

Jakes huffed a little. 'The gang were pretty clever. They'd hidden a getaway car somewhere, but nobody saw it.'

'Perhaps the vehicle they used was well known. The sort of thing people don't notice.'

'It's a thought. This person who was

insulting you, it wouldn't be a chap called Golding, would it? Owns the nursery out your way?'

'How did you guess?' Deepbriar was genuinely puzzled. Jakes wasn't a local man.

'I was covering a night shift in Belston last week, and since it was a quiet night I read the file on the Harwayes job.' He gave a brief snort of laughter. 'I was kidding myself I'd come up with some clue they'd missed. Fat chance. I could see why they didn't get far. Anyway, Golding was a witness. He gave a fair description of the three men, height and weight, even what they were wearing, not bad considering he couldn't see their faces. Not that it led anywhere. As for guessing it was him who gave you a dressing down, the bloke who interviewed him had left this pencilled note in the file. He didn't seem to like Golding much; evidently he was pretty scathing about the way the police handled things.'

'The man's been pestering me ever since somebody threw bricks at his greenhouses. I just hope our poison pen doesn't target his wife.'

Jakes laughed. 'With a husband like that I shouldn't think she'd risk getting up to any mischief. I'd better go, the inspector's looking for me. Let me know how you get on with tracking down that envelope.'

'I shall, thanks.' Thorny put down the receiver and sat looking at the name and address of the firm in Devon. The trouble was, although he knew nearly everyone in Minecliff by name, this sort of detail wasn't so easy to track down. Village life was changing, new people were coming into the area. Sons and daughters moved away to look for work. Men married sweethearts they'd met during the war and brought them back home; he could think of a dozen women whose origins he couldn't guess. Still, Jakes's information gave him something to work on. He must see Miss Cannon again, and see if she had any ideas.

* * *

'Do you want a biscuit with that?' Mary asked.

'Mmm?' Deepbriar suspected his wife had spoken to him, but his thoughts had been miles away, and it hadn't really registered.

'A biscuit. With your cup of tea.' She stood in the office doorway, holding out the tin. He helped himself to a rich tea.

'Thanks, love.' He looked up and saw that she was wearing her coat. 'Are you going shopping?'

‘No, I’m popping over to Bella’s.’

‘What, again? I thought you did that yesterday afternoon.’

Mary Deepbriar sighed. ‘I told you, she won’t answer the door, though I’m sure she’s at home. Several other people have called too, but nobody’s seen her. I knew you weren’t listening, I don’t think you heard a single word I said at breakfast.’

‘Sorry, love, I’ve been thinking about Phil Golding. His name keeps coming up. And there was something I heard the other day that didn’t sound right. I woke up this morning with this itch inside my head, and I can’t work out why.’

‘You told me you thought he was lying about the traps,’ Mary prompted.

‘Mmm. It’s not that though. Dogs. It’s something to do with dogs.’ He kneaded his forehead with his hand, then suddenly beamed. ‘Got it! Golding’s started using poison to get rid of rats, and that’s supposed to be why he warned Fred not to go to the nursery any more.’

‘What’s that got to do with dogs?’

‘Golding doesn’t give a damn about animals; he wouldn’t care if Fred’s terriers got poisoned. So, that was just an excuse. Then there’s the way Fred’s been acting. He’s been busting a gut to make sure nobody gets hurt by those traps, almost as if he felt responsible for them. I'm sure he's not the one setting them, but I reckon he knows more than he's telling. He's the man I need to talk to.' Deepbriar sighed, his expression sliding swiftly from elation to the habitual slight frown. 'Trouble is, I have to find him first. Apart from turning up to help when Oliver's dog got caught, he's not been seen for days.'

'Poor you.' Mary gave him a fleeting kiss. 'I don't suppose I'll be long.'

Deepbriar didn't see her leave or hear the door close behind her. He had just had a wild idea. The thought of Phil Golding skulking around Minecliff at dead of night setting traps was so ludicrous that he'd never seriously considered the nurseryman as a suspect. But Golding was a very wealthy man. When he wanted something done he could afford to pay somebody else to do it. Golding didn't like people walking on his land, even when they had a right to be there, and he hated animals. Was it such a huge jump to imagine him arranging to have mantraps scattered around the district? Perhaps the whole thing was aimed at keeping people off his land. It was crazy, but more feasible than any of the other explanations that Deepbriar had come up with so far.

Sitting staring into space with the cup

halfway to his mouth, Deepbriar didn't notice the minutes ticking past. The tea grew cold. If Golding was the culprit then he had to be stopped. But how?

The answer lay with Fred Tapper. Deepbriar felt as if another piece of the jigsaw had fallen neatly into place. If Fred knew what was going on but was too scared to talk, that could account for his determination to make himself scarce.

A knock on the door roused Deepbriar from his abstraction, the lukewarm tea slopping over his hand as he jumped.

'Constable Deepbriar.' A strait-laced figure in tweeds stood on the doorstep.

Deepbriar had been so involved with thoughts of mantraps that he was rather bemused at the sight of the elderly woman. 'Um . . . Miss Cannon. Is there something I can do for you?'

'No, there's something I can do for you,' she replied triumphantly. 'I have discovered that another poison-pen letter was sent to somebody in Minecliff, about a week before Mrs Twyford's death.'

'You'd better come in. You're sure this letter came from the same source?' Deepbriar asked, as he led her into the office and offered her a chair.

'Positive. But there is a difference. The

scandal it threatened to reveal was untrue. It never happened.' Miss Cannon sat down, leaning forward eagerly. She seemed to have shed the extra years that had been etched on her face for the last week. 'You remember the stories that were spread about Greta Hutton during the last days of the war, when she first came to Minecliff and set herself up as a hairdresser?'

'I do indeed.' Deepbriar stared at the elderly woman opposite him. 'Are you telling me she got a letter accusing her of being a spy?'

'She did!' Miss Cannon slapped her hands down on her tweed-covered knees. 'And from the way she described the envelope and the writing I'm sure it was sent by the same person. Unfortunately Mrs Hutton tore the thing up and threw it in the dustbin. She's such a good-natured woman, she decided it was some sort of joke. Bless her, she still doesn't understand the English sense of humour.'

'But the rumours about her were scotched within days, everybody knows that.' Deepbriar stood up and went to the filing cabinet. 'I've still got the file here. She'd shown me her marriage certificate and the posthumous commendation awarded to her husband. When that didn't silence the gossips I wrote to the parson who officiated at her wedding, and to Lieutenant Hutton's commanding officer.'

'I seem to recall you gave Miss Jane and her cronies a severe talking to,' Miss Cannon said. 'Some of us were surprised Mrs Hutton stayed on in the village, all things considered. Poor girl. She'd only been married a year when her husband died, then she comes to open her business in a quiet little village and gets treated like an undesirable alien. I still don't see how anyone could mistake a Dutch accent for a German one.'

'People aren't terribly rational at times.' Deepbriar fetched out the folder. He hadn't pursued the matter, since Mrs Hutton had refused to take action against the people who had slandered her, but the evidence was still here. 'February 1945. And the letters are dated early March. So, how did somebody get hold of this story, and not know it was a pack of lies? It has to be a person who wasn't in the village at the time.' He sat down opposite Miss Cannon again. 'Any ideas?'

She hesitated. 'I don't want to make any accusations. This does seem to eliminate a lot of possible suspects.'

'Leaving us with what?' Deepbriar prompted, seeing that she had something on her mind.

'Well, I happen to know that Mrs Emerson

was told about those old rumours. It's possible she didn't hear the whole story.' Miss Cannon looked uncomfortable. 'That doesn't necessarily make her the writer; it seems totally out of character. She is rather an indiscreet woman, though. She might have shared this little titbit. Again, it would need to be someone who didn't know the truth, someone who had moved to Minecliff since the war.'

'I agree, she doesn't seem the type to be sending the letters, but I think you're right, she'd be a good source of unreliable gossip.' Deepbriar hesitated before going on, as if aware he might be treading on dangerous ground. 'Do you know if she has any knowledge of your — '

'My dubious past?' Miss Cannon finished for him. 'It's probable. There are factions within the Women's Institute, Constable, as in any organization. I can't pretend to be popular with everybody.'

'Rather like Mrs Emerson herself,' Deepbriar commented. 'Thank you, Miss Cannon, you've been very helpful. Oh, there was something else I wanted to ask you. Do you know of anybody in the village who has a connection with Devon? A family member living down there perhaps, or a friend?'

'I can't think of anyone. Would it help if I

asked at the WI?' She looked thoughtful. 'It's never easy to find new subjects for our weekly talks, perhaps I might suggest a series by people with relatives in other parts of England, and see if anything turns up.'

Deepbriar couldn't suppress a grin. 'A plan worthy of the illustrious Miss Marple herself,' he said. 'I shall look forward to your next report. In the meantime I'll have a chat with Mrs Emerson. Don't worry, I shan't reveal my source.'

* * *

Since Fred Tapper remained elusive, Deepbriar decided to talk to his brother. It was time to cycle round his beat through Possington; he could call at Will Minter's farm on his way back, and probably catch young Billy while he was eating his lunch.

A car was pulling out of the driveway to the Roses' house as Deepbriar cycled by. He braked, waving the driver down. 'Mr Rose. How's Oliver?'

'Not too good.' The man looked tired. 'I'm going to see Mr Foster. If Barney's well enough we want to bring him back here. Oliver's hardly slept since the dog was hurt.'

'I'm sorry.' Deepbriar was abject. 'I let the lad down.'

'I beg your pardon, Constable, but that's nonsense,' Mr Rose said firmly. 'I walked the path that morning. If anyone should have thought of checking the other side of the hedge it was me. What happened is over and done; it's no good crying over spilt milk. We've had Fred Tapper here too, he seems to think he was to blame for what happened. I told him not to be so stupid. If it hadn't been for the pair of you the dog wouldn't have survived.'

'Fred's been here?'

'I saw him the first time early yesterday.' He gave a wan smile. 'It can't have been much after five. We've not been getting much sleep. And he was back about the same time this morning. My wife called him in and gave him a cup of tea and some toast. We were a bit worried about him to be honest, it doesn't look as if that bite on his arm has been properly tended.'

'I'll get him to hospital if I can find him,' Deepbriar promised. 'Give my love to Oliver. Tell him I'll come and see him soon.'

Possington lay still and quiet under the midday sun, and Deepbriar paused only to wave a greeting to Father Michael, who was trimming the hedge around the churchyard, before heading on to Minter's farm.

He found Billy Tapper sitting against the

wheel of a tractor, working his way through a thick wad of sandwiches. 'Would you like one?' Billy asked. He smiled proudly. 'My Bessy's a treasure, but she tends to overdo it a bit, packs enough for two.'

Deepbriar accepted, taking charge of a cheese and pickle doorstep before lowering himself carefully on to a handy tree stump at the edge of the field, where he'd be out of sight from the road. 'Getting on all right with Mr Minter then, Billy?' he asked, sinking his teeth into the sandwich.

'Fine.' The young man gestured at the tractor. 'I like horses, but you should see what this thing can do in a day.'

Deepbriar sniffed, wrinkling his nose at the reek of petrol. 'Doesn't smell so sweet though,' he said. 'I didn't really come for a social visit, Billy. I want to talk to Fred.'

'You're not the only one.'

'Why, what do you mean?'

Billy hesitated for the smallest fraction of a second before he replied. 'Our gran's going frantic. She reckons Fred's arm will turn black and drop off.'

'She could have a point. Your gran must have seen a few cases of gangrene in her day.' Deepbriar let the subject hang in the air for a moment, noting the small worry lines that had appeared between Billy's eyebrows.

‘I swore I wouldn’t tell,’ Billy said suddenly. ‘He’s in some sort of trouble, Mr Deepbriar, and he’s too scared to talk about it, even to me.’

‘But you know where he is.’ Deepbriar looked at the young man shrewdly.

‘Not for certain. I’ve got a pretty good idea though.’

‘Well then,’ Deepbriar said, getting up and brushing away crumbs, ‘the answer’s obvious. I’ve racked my brains and I can’t see any way to track him down, so it’s up to you. Persuade him to get that arm of his treated. And while you’re about it, tell him I have to talk to him. I can’t make promises, but I’ll do my best to see he doesn’t suffer for it.’

As Deepbriar pedalled away he wondered if it would be worth trying to keep watch on young Billy, and see if he led the way to his brother, but that idea was a non-starter; the Tapper boys were both as slippery as eels. On the other hand, maybe Fred would visit Oliver again tomorrow morning.

It was in a considerably better mood that the constable wheeled his bicycle round the back of the police house. There could be a breakthrough coming in both his outstanding cases; maybe he’d soon be able to spend eight hours in his bed each night.

A sound that was vaguely familiar was

spilling out of the open door. Deepbriar barged into the kitchen. 'Mary!' She wasn't the crying sort. The last time he'd seen her shedding tears had been as he lay in a hospital bed suffering from concussion. But he had the uncomfortable feeling that this was the noise that had woken him in the night, when he'd mistaken it for a dream. 'Whatever's the matter, love?'

'I'm just being silly,' she sniffed, hastily wiping her eyes. 'I don't know what's wrong with me, crying over nothing.'

'I'm sure it's not nothing,' Deepbriar said, taking her rather awkwardly in his arms. 'Come on, tell old Thorny your troubles. If someone's upset you I'll put them under arrest and lock 'em up.'

That brought a watery smile. 'Idiot,' she said. 'I'm perfectly all right, honestly. It's just Bella. I went to her house and got no reply again. Then a few minutes later she cut me dead in the street. She looked right through me as if I was invisible. At first I imagined she hadn't seen me, but she stopped to say hello to Cyril Bostock, and I know she can't stand the man! Then she went and stood at the bus stop, and when I came out of the shop she was chattering away to everybody in the queue, even Ada Tapper, but as I walked by she turned her back on me!'

'The old cow.' Thorny picked up the kettle. 'You're right, it was nothing, because she's not worth crying over. Let's have a cup of tea and — ' He broke off and stood stock still, the kettle poised in mid-air. 'I bet she's had a letter!'

Mary stared at him uncomprehendingly.

'A letter?'

'Yes, like Mrs Twyford and Miss Cannon. And we can guess what juicy little secret our nasty minded scribbler has come up with, can't we?'

'Her husband!' Enlightenment dawned on his wife's face. 'As far as she knows, we're the only people who know she isn't a widow! So she thinks . . . '

' . . . that you are an evil-minded scandalmonger, just like her,' Thorny put in, pouring boiling water on to tea-leaves and putting the lid on the teapot so hard that Mary winced, imagining he'd broken it.

'Well, I wouldn't quite — ' She was silenced as he took her in his arms again.

'No, I know you wouldn't. As I've said many times before, you're too good for this world. As soon as we've had this cup of tea we'll go round and put her straight.'

'We can't. She caught the bus to Falbrough.' Mary sat down suddenly, a rueful smile on her face. 'We'll have to leave it till tomorrow. At least now I know why she was so rude. Poor Bella.'

'Poor Bella my foot! You never did tell me how you knew Mr Emerson was still alive. I think you'd better own up. It could be important.'

* * *

A light mist hung over the village as Deepbriar strode up the lane, keeping to the grass verge so his footsteps were silent. He crept silently past the Roses' house and settled himself between the fence and their garden shed, finding a comfortable position to wait out the next hour; from here he was sure he would see if Fred Tapper came visiting. Down in the valley the clock in the church tower struck four, only the very top of the steeple visible above the swirling vapour.

Above and around him the birds were carolling their song to the dawn. Despite the short amount of sleep he'd had Deepbriar was happy; there was something joyous about being out alone so early on a summer's day and he was sure he was coming to the end of his early morning patrols. He felt no impatience as he heard the clock chime out the quarter and the half hour.

A robin came to take a look at him and

offered a few tuneful notes of greeting. Deepbriar pursed his lips, almost launching into a reply, before he realized that wasn't a good idea; the sound would carry miles in the early morning hush.

The sun was burning off the mist as the three-quarters rang out over the valley. Deepbriar drew further back into his hiding place. There was movement on the other side of the hedge along the footpath, where the trap had been. Somebody was coming.

The poacher ducked through the gap in the bushes and crept stealthily down towards the house. His chin bore several days' stubble, and the clothes he wore were grubby and rumpled. He had his arms folded across his chest; either he was cold or his injured arm was troubling him.

Deepbriar waited until the man was inside the garden, and approaching the back porch, then he moved to block his way out. 'Hello, Fred,' he said quietly.

15

Fred Tapper leapt as if he'd been shot, spinning round to face Deepbriar, his face white. When he saw who it was he let out a groan of relief. 'Mr Deepbriar.'

'Don't you think it's a bit early to come calling, Fred?' Deepbriar tipped his head towards the summer house at the end of the garden. 'We need to have a little chat. Let's go where we won't disturb anyone.'

Leaning back in a wicker chair, the young poacher looked positively ill; his eyes had sunk into his skull and his skin had an unhealthy yellow tinge.

'You haven't had that arm seen to,' Deepbriar said conversationally. 'Your gran's worried about you.'

'I'm all right. I got some stuff to put on it.' Fred touched the filthy rag that was wrapped around his forearm. 'Have you heard 'ow the dog's gettin' on?'

'Vet seems to think he'll do. They'll be bringing him back home tomorrow. I'd say he's probably doing better than you are.'

'Don't reckon you come up 'ere at this time o' day just to ask about me health,' Fred said, his voice suddenly harsh. 'What d'you want?'

'Fair enough, let's talk plain. I want to know how you're involved with Phil Golding, Tapper. I'm sick of being left in the dark. I'm sick of worrying where the next trap's going to turn up. I want some answers, and I want them right now, or so help me, hurt or not, you'll be cooling your heels behind bars.'

Fred's shoulders slumped. 'It took you long enough to get on to 'im,' he said. 'I gave you a pretty good clue. I thought once I'd left that old trap in the greenhouse — ' he broke off. 'I want a deal. If I tell you what I know then you got to let me go. I didn't do much, it was all Golding's idea, an' I never set one of them traps, I told 'im right at the start that I wouldn't.'

'No deals. You tell me about it, then I'll see,' Deepbriar replied implacably. 'Come on, Fred, you can't go on living rough. That bite will be the death of you if you don't get it seen to. Is it Golding you're so desperate to keep away from?'

'Partly.' Fred's glance wandered around the summer house, as if looking for a way out. 'He's got somethin' on me. When the bastard wanted them traps nicked from the manor I couldn't refuse, could I? We took the lorry, 'e parked it just off the road then sat there nice and safe while I broke into the shed. I borrowed a wheelbarrow to get the traps down the drive, then took it back. Never even woke the dogs up,' he added, with a touch of pride.

'But you refused to set the traps.'

'If I'd known what Golding was up to, I never would 'ave done it.' Fred looked across at the constable, his eyes pleading. 'I swear, Mr Deepbriar, that's why I come out every mornin', lookin' for the damn things. I dunno 'ow anyone could put one up the hill, where that poor little kid might've stepped in it — ' Words failed him.

'So if you refused, who's doing it?' Deepbriar asked.

'I reckon it's one of them Italians. Last couple of nights I've been keepin' watch, tryin' to find out. Golding's got the traps hidden somewhere, otherwise I'd 'ave pinched 'em back. I've had a good look round the nursery, but I can't find 'em.' Fred closed his eyes, his head tipping back to rest on the cobwebby wooden wall.

Deepbriar was silent for a long moment, as he thought about what Fred had told him. He would have no case against Golding unless he had proof, and even if he could persuade Fred to give evidence, nobody would take the word of a convicted poacher over that of a wealthy businessman. He must nab the man who was setting the traps. If he was caught in the act there was a good chance he could be persuaded to confess. In his experience, most Europeans had a healthy respect for the law, and if Golding was paying an Italian to do his dirty work, it shouldn't be too difficult to make the culprit talk. Then again, there was a third way . . .

The first thing he had to do was get young Tapper to the hospital. Whatever he was using to treat that arm didn't seem to be doing much good. 'Fred? I think I heard somebody in the house. Reckon we could both do with a cup of tea.'

Fred gave a pallid grin. 'Spot o' breakfast would go down all right,' he acknowledged. 'Not feelin' that great, to be honest, Mr Deepbriar.'

'I'll go and see if Mr and Mrs Rose are up and about. Stay right there, Fred, I won't be a minute.'

There was definitely somebody in the kitchen, and Deepbriar had just tapped softly on the back door when he caught sight of movement out of the corner of his eye. Fred was running across the lawn like a startled deer. He leapt over the fence and was gone, sprinting away over the open field. Deepbriar made a half-hearted move to follow, but he knew it would be a waste of time; sick as he was, Fred Tapper was still fast on his feet. 'Should be training for the flipping Olympics,' Deepbriar commented sourly, as Mr Rose came and stood beside him, to stare after the fleeing figure.

* * *

'Mrs Emerson!' Constable Deepbriar stood on the front lawn of The Lodge and bellowed, until finally an upstairs window was pushed up and the woman, flushed-faced, stared down at him.

'What . . . ?' she began indignantly.

'Kindly come and open the door, Mrs Emerson,' Deepbriar said. He dropped his voice a little. 'Or perhaps you prefer me to question you about that letter from here.'

'Oh.' She put her hands to her mouth. Then, without another word, she closed the window. Deepbriar waited, hearing her heavy footsteps approaching the front door, and the bolt being drawn back.

'I have nothing to say to you,' the woman said, her attempt at haughty disdain somewhat spoiled by the dishevelled state of her hair; one curl stood upright from the top of her head like a question mark, and Deepbriar had trouble keeping his eyes off it.

'I'm here on official business,' Deepbriar replied. 'If you prefer I can request the presence of a female officer, or a member of the CID. I'm sure your neighbours will be intrigued to see a police car coming to the house.'

Scowling, the woman stood aside to let him walk in. Deepbriar removed his helmet, placing it on the hall table. 'Right. Do you still have the poison-pen letter, Mrs Emerson?'

'How do you know I had a letter?' she demanded shrilly.

'I can add two and two and come up with four. You aren't the first person in the village to get one. And when somebody who is normally in the midst of Minecliff's social life starts ignoring one of her closest friends, I'd be pretty stupid if I couldn't work out why.'

'I don't think I should give it to you,' Mrs Emerson said, backing towards the kitchen door. 'You and your wife were the only people in the village who knew — ' She broke off. 'Even if neither of you wrote that letter, you must have told somebody.'

'Neither of us told anybody,' Deepbriar said calmly, 'though I seem to recall you once admitted that you should come clean. Mary already knew that your husband was alive and living in Broadstairs, before you told me. She even knew that Mr Emerson owns a dog, or at least, that he'd been seen walking a dog along the promenade in a certain seaside town.'

'I don't understand. How can she have known?'

'Miss Strathway saw your husband while she was on holiday. She had, I gather, seen the large photograph you keep on your sideboard. At first she imagined it was just an extraordinary likeness — they say everyone has a double, don't they? — but then she heard a passer-by address the man as Mr Emerson.

'Miss Strathway never divulges anything she learns in the course of her work at the telephone exchange, Mrs Emerson, but you were a stranger who had only been in the village for a few weeks. She felt honour bound to reveal your little deception to one or two members of the Women's Institute, including Mary. Being a kindly soul, Mary begged that the information should go no further, but she was too late to stop the story being spread around most of Minecliff.'

'Oh,' Bella Emerson said again, sitting down rather suddenly on a fragile-looking chair, which trembled a little under her weight. 'You mean people have known all this time.'

'They have indeed. And being for the most part good-hearted, they have allowed you to believe otherwise. They have treated you with the kindness and sympathy suitable to a grieving widow.'

'Oh.' Tears leaked down the plump cheeks. 'My friends. And dear Mary . . . '

Deepbriar resisted the temptation to give the woman a good shake. 'So, Mrs Emerson, back to the purpose of my visit. Do you still have that letter?'

* * *

'The style hasn't changed,' Jakes said, scanning the two pages of neat rounded handwriting. ' '*You put on airs and play at being lady muck, but you're just a common lying bitch. What would your snobby friends say if they knew you weren't really a widow? Maybe they should be told that your husband would rather have a dog for company than a snooty cold-hearted shrew like you*'.' The young detective blew out his cheeks expressively. 'And that's mild compared to the rest.'

'It gets pretty vitriolic,' Deepbriar agreed. 'Mind you, in this case I don't have much sympathy. You'll have met Mrs Emerson when we were working on the Crimmon case.'

'I did,' Jakes nodded. 'And I know what you mean. Still, we can't have this sort of thing being sent through the post, can we? Did you ask her about Devon?'

'Yes, there's no connection, as far as she's aware.'

The door opened, and Inspector Martindale appeared. 'Deepbriar.' He gave Detective Sergeant Jakes a faintly mistrustful look. 'I didn't expect to find you in the CID office. Is this something to do with a case you're dealing with?'

'Yes, sir. Sergeant Hubbard suggested turning it over to the CID, and I've just brought in a new piece of evidence.' He indicated the letter that now lay on the desk. 'A second poison-pen letter has turned up, sent to a different person. And I have a statement from a lady in the village who received one some weeks ago. Unfortunately she destroyed it, but I'm sure it was from the same source.'

Martindale picked up the sheets of paper and scanned them briefly. 'I see. Well, now you've handed that over presumably you're finished here. Come to my office.'

Sitting down behind his desk, the inspector folded his arms and glared at Deepbriar. 'I've had another complaint.'

'Sir?' Deepbriar stood at attention, his gaze

fixed on the wall above Martindale's head.

'Mr Golding. Does the name mean anything to you?'

'Yes, sir, I know Mr Golding,' Deepbriar said woodenly.

'He doesn't think you're doing your job properly, Constable. Do you have any comment to make?'

'I've done my best, sir. Somebody damaged some of Mr Golding's greenhouses. He's not happy because I haven't been able to find out who did it.'

'No, you haven't.' Martindale leaned forwards, placing his hands flat on the desk. 'You are neglecting your duty to the people of Minecliff. You are wasting your time trying to track down a lot of rusty old gin traps. Isn't that so?'

'No, sir.' Deepbriar replied stolidly. 'I am trying to find out who stole the traps, and who has been setting them, but I'm not wasting my time. If you saw the last report — '

'I read it. A dog was hurt. Regrettable, but at present the use of gin traps is not illegal. I don't like getting complaints about my officers, Constable Deepbriar, and I can't remember ever receiving two about the same man in such a short time. I warned you to watch your step after you insulted Sir Arthur Drimsbury. In view of your previous good record I shan't be taking any further action, but I expect to hear that you've made an arrest in the criminal damage case. We can't afford to go upsetting people like Mr Golding. Do I make myself clear?'

'Quite clear, sir, yes.'

Outside the office Deepbriar let out a long breath. Golding! If only there was some way to prove the sort of man he really was and put him in the dock. As for making an arrest, all he had to do was lay his hands on Fred Tapper again, but he didn't want the poacher punished, not while a villain like Golding was walking free.

'Thorny!' A hand landed heavily on Deepbriar's shoulder and he whirled around. Detective Inspector Stubbs beamed at him. 'Come back to the CID office for a minute.'

It was the last thing he wanted to do, but Deepbriar trailed miserably behind the inspector. Jakes had gone and Stubbs waved Deepbriar into the sergeant's chair. 'I've got some good news for you.'

'Have you, sir?' Deepbriar tried to sound interested, but his head was still full of Golding and the impossibility of putting him behind bars.

'Cheer up, man. Listen, I'd bet my pension that you'll be joining my department within the next six months.'

Deepbriar stared at him in surprise, but he felt no great elation. He'd thought he was going to get the longed-for move to CID once before, and it hadn't happened.

'Don't you want to know why I'm so sure?' Stubbs asked, looking a little nettled.

'Yes, sorry, sir, it was just — '

'Martindale.' Stubbs nodded. 'He was the one who blocked you, and now he's been giving you a dressing down because you won't kow-tow to the local gentry. This is where my good news comes in. Martindale's about to be promoted to chief inspector, and he'll be moving to Belston.'

'So . . . ' Thorny allowed himself to climb a small way out of the pit of misery he'd been burrowing into.

'So, I know the chap who'll be taking his place, and he's a good man. I get myself a new DC, and you get out of Hubbard's clutches, not to mention the whole lot of us breathing a sigh of relief when Martindale goes! Now, is that good news, or not?'

* * *

'Will it mean moving out of this house?' Mary asked, her head averted as she busied herself with cooking the tea.

'I expect so. But we talked about this

before and you said you didn't mind. At least we won't have people coming to the door at all hours. I'm sure we'll find somewhere else. One of those places in Meadow Row perhaps.'

'Yes. I suppose so.' There was something wrong with her voice. It was quivering, the words muffled. Deepbriar stared at her in consternation. She was crying again!

'What's up, love?'

'It's just that things might change. I don't know,' she gulped. 'There's something I have to tell you. I've been trying to find a way for days.'

'You've not had one of those letters?' Deepbriar demanded, getting to his feet, caught between shock and rage.

'No, of course not. I would have told you if I had.' His obtuseness seemed to stiffen her resolve. She turned to face him, her face streaked with tears but her voice steady. 'I'm expecting a baby.'

'You — '

He couldn't have been more surprised if she'd announced that she was going to sprout wings. Watching his expression a tiny smile broke through her tears; if she hadn't been so miserable he knew she'd have been openly laughing at him, as he stood open-mouthed in shock.

'But that's wonderful!' Deepbriar said,

once he'd got his breath back. He flung his arms around his wife, hugging her tight, then half releasing her as if she might be fragile. 'I mean, after all this time, I'd stopped even thinking about it.'

'So had I.' She nestled against him. 'That's the trouble.' She looked up at his face. 'I'm not so young any more. Suppose — suppose it turns out to be like little Johnny.' The words were suddenly coming in a rush, pent-up for far too long. 'You know how it was with Cousin Joan. She was so happy when she found out she was finally going to have a family. She was only five years older than I am now, but they never told her things might go wrong. They never said it wasn't a good idea to have children when you get to that age. It wasn't till he was born, till they saw his face. Poor little mite. He'll never have a normal life . . . '

The torrent of words came to an end. Deepbriar said nothing, simply holding her, not knowing what he could say. Johnny was a happy little boy now, four years old. His faintly Mongoloid features were usually creased into a beaming smile. But there was no denying his arrival had given his parents a shock.

'Have you spoken to Dr Smythe?' Thorny asked at last.

She nodded. 'I went to see him last week. He doesn't think I should worry, but I can't help it. I'm nearly forty. Suppose it runs in the family?'

'We'll ask him,' Thorny declared. 'I'm sure you're worrying about nothing. And even if we had a child like Johnny, we'd love him just the same. Joan and Bert manage.' He leant back so he could see her face. 'I'm going to be a dad! Me! Tell you what,' he added, suddenly serious, 'if you'd rather stay in this house, if you don't want me to take the CID job, then I won't.'

Mary laughed then, her tears forgotten. 'Oh Thorny, sometimes you're such an idiot. Of course you must join the CID! Come on, let me go or you'll never get fed.'

* * *

There was a definite spring in Deepbriar's step the next morning. They had waited until morning surgery was over then called on Dr Smythe, who assured them that Mary had a very good chance of producing a normal healthy baby.

'I feel a lot better about it,' Mary admitted, as they walked home. 'Evidently women do react in strange ways sometimes, that's probably why I kept crying.'

'You haven't felt like eating any coal?' Deepbriar asked, pausing on the doorstep as he remembered something else the doctor had said.

'No. But I'd love some strawberries.'

'Then you'll have some. If I can't look after — '

'Thorny!' Major Charles Brightman came running from the Speckled Goose, a piece of paper in his hand. He looked drawn, and his breathing was ragged. 'Thank God . . . I need . . . your help.'

'Charles? What's wrong?'

'Elaine,' Brightman gasped. 'Here.' He thrust the paper into Deepbriar's hand.

Dearest Charles, it began.

'Do you really want me to read this?' Deepbriar asked, trying to give it back.

'Dammit, just read,' the major rasped.

I am so very sorry, I had hoped it would all work out for us, but I see now that the past will always catch up with me. I couldn't bear to bring disgrace to your name, I can't let that happen. Please, please forgive me. I hope you will find happiness. It's over. This is the best way, for both of us. In this life and the next, I will never stop loving you. Elaine.

‘How did you get this?’ Deepbriar asked.

‘She left it with Phyllis Bartle.’ The major shook his arm. ‘She’s been gone two hours! Come on, man, don’t just stand there, we have to find her.’

Deepbriar stared at the words Elaine Barr had written. ‘I can see why you’re concerned, but this may not mean — ’

‘You don’t understand.’ Brightman said, his voice anguished. ‘That’s exactly what it means. Elaine had a breakdown a few years ago. She tried to kill herself.’

16

'I think we have to take the matter seriously, Inspector,' Deepbriar said, holding the telephone receiver between chin and shoulder so he could wave Mary into the room. His other hand held the note he had just read out to his superior officer. 'The major tells me the lady may have attempted suicide before. Sorry? Yes, that's right, Colonel Brightman's son. Miss Barr is his fiancée.' There was a brief pause then he exchanged a significant glance with his wife. 'Yes, I'll do that. Thank you, sir, I'm sure they'll be very grateful.'

He put the phone down. 'There are times when being a local personage helps, especially with Martindale. He's taking charge himself; he'll be here within half an hour, and he'll bring as many men as can be spared. Did you find anybody who saw her leave?'

'Maybe. I asked in the shop and the post office, no luck there, but Mrs Harris sent a message round the school, and one child saw a lady walking along the footpath towards the river. That would have been at about ten minutes to nine.'

'Anything to suggest it was Elaine?'

'The child didn't know her. But the lady was wearing green and brown, and a straw hat.'

'Maybe Phyllis can tell us about her clothes.' Deepbriar ran a hand over his head. 'The river. I did wonder . . . I don't even know if she can swim, I'll have to ask Charles.'

'Is that important?' Mary asked, her face pale. 'If she's determined, you know, to . . . '

'It's not easy to drown yourself if you're a good swimmer,' her husband said. 'You'd need to have something weighing you down. Even then, the river isn't running fast, and there aren't many places where it's deep enough.'

Mary Deepbriar shuddered. 'It's horrible to even think about it. The last time I saw her she was so happy, they both were.'

'I ought to go and speak to Phyllis. Will you hold the fort here? Somebody from Falbrough might ring back, and Charles should be bringing the men from the manor soon.'

At the Speckled Goose Phyllis Bartle let the constable in through the back door. 'I feel so bad about this, Thorny. I thought she'd left that note for the major to change some arrangement they'd made, I never dreamt there was anything wrong.'

'It's not your fault,' Deepbriar told her.

'What was she wearing when she left here?'

'A green skirt, a cotton one with a pale cream pattern on it. And a brown cardigan.'

Deepbriar scowled. That matched with the sighting of the child on her way to school. He ought to call the inspector again; they might have to drag the river. 'Did she take her handbag?'

The woman thought for a moment. 'Yes, she wore a big cream shoulder bag. I noticed because the colour didn't match her shoes, which wasn't like her. She had a little straw hat on.' She shook her head. 'I don't understand. She was so cheerful first thing, she came down to breakfast at half past seven with a lovely smile on her face, chattering away as if she hadn't a care in the world. Major Brightman was taking her to Belston; they've started shopping for some bits and pieces for their rooms at the manor.'

'So what happened in the next hour?' Deepbriar asked. 'Was there anything out of the ordinary? Did she receive anything in the post?'

'She might have done. I heard Clive come. He always leaves the letters on the table in the hall. She would have looked on her way back upstairs.'

Deepbriar felt a chill run through him. Dear God, he prayed silently, not Mrs

Twyford all over again. 'Can I see her room?' he said, already on his way, with the landlady following. The bedroom was tidy. Elaine Barr's clothes still hung in the wardrobe. There was no sign of a letter anywhere, and the wastebin was empty. 'Bathroom?' he barked.

'Across the landing.' She pointed. 'What are you looking for?'

'A letter. An envelope, I don't know.' Deepbriar checked the bin in the bathroom. 'Has this been emptied this morning?'

'No.' Phyllis Bartle shook her head. 'If she had an important letter she would have taken it with her, wouldn't she?'

Deepbriar didn't reply, pushing past her and hurrying downstairs, glancing at his watch. He caught up with the postman as the man set off towards Possington, but he wasn't a great help. There had been at least half-a-dozen items for the Speckled Goose, he said, but he wasn't in the habit of studying handwriting, and he hadn't noticed if any of them was addressed to Miss Barr.

Deepbriar was heading back to the police house when Phyllis Bartle came in search of him. 'Look what I found,' she said, holding out a paper bag. 'These scraps had been tossed into the fireplace in the saloon bar. I picked them all up. Look, I think this could say Miss E . . . '

Elaine Barr had torn both the letter and the envelope into tiny fragments, so small it might be impossible to fit them back together, but there was no mistaking the handwriting. The letters were almost childish, round and neatly formed.

* * *

Charles Brightman paced restlessly across Deepbriar's little office. He looked ten more than his forty years; deep lines furrowed his forehead and drew down from the sides of his mouth. Coming to an abrupt halt in front of the desk he glared at the constable. 'Why the hell aren't we looking for Elaine?'

Deepbriar sighed, looking sympathetically up at his friend. 'There are nearly thirty men out there, Charles, most of them know this village just as well as you and I, and the rest are professionals, doing what they're trained to do. I'm here because we're waiting for reports from the men visiting the bus depot and the station, and you're here to give me any background information that might tell us where else to search.'

Brightman put his hands to his head and rubbed them over his greying temples. 'Ye gods, Thorny, I think this is the worst day of my life.'

'Sit down,' Deepbriar suggested, waiting until the major obeyed before he went on. 'You say Elaine's a very good swimmer.'

'Yes, she lived by the sea when she was a child, and she swims like a fish. Is this relevant?'

'Good swimmers usually don't drown,' Deepbriar said shortly. 'I'm sorry, but I have to ask this. You suggested she might have considered committing suicide in the past.'

'The only way to explain is to tell the whole story. Look, couldn't we go and look for her while I tell you all this? I don't think I can stand being stuck in here any longer.'

'I'm sorry, I've got my orders. Unless — '

The door opened and Martindale walked in. Charles Brightman leapt to his feet. 'Any news?'

'I'm sorry, sir, nothing yet.' The inspector looked across at Deepbriar, standing rigidly to attention behind his desk. 'No calls?'

'Not yet, sir. Inspector, the major would like to be allowed to join the search party. He's filling me in on Miss Barr's background, but he thinks we could continue that outside.' Deepbriar kept his expression neutral, knowing that at any other time the suggestion would have earned him a reprimand; Martindale worked by the book.

'I'd be grateful, Inspector,' Brightman put

in, 'I've never been good at sitting still while other men are in action.'

'Of course. Very well, Deepbriar, see Sergeant Parsons, he'll assign you both to an area, but I expect a written report on this desk within the hour, understood?'

The weather had turned hot and sultry again. Deepbriar led the major down the path towards the Dally Pond, his mind full of the fate of Mrs Twyford. He hadn't told Charles about the scraps of paper found in the pub; they had been sent to Falbrough, where some junior constable would be trying to piece them back together. Since there was hardly a scrap more than half an inch across it would be quite a job.

Halfway there they met Terry Watts with another of the colonel's men, poking about in an area of scrub and brambles. Deepbriar hung back to ask where they had searched; no point wasting their resources. 'Not been near the pond,' Watts said, glancing at the major's retreating back. He dropped his voice. 'Women! Got no bloody sense.'

Deepbriar stared at him, surprised by the venom in his voice. 'If Miss Barr has acted foolishly I think it will have been in desperation rather than stupidity,' he said.

'Christ! If my wife — ' Watts began, then he seemed to collect himself. 'Sorry,' he muttered, 'had a few things to do today, could have done without this.' He gave Deepbriar a nod and turned back to his task.

The major was swishing at the reeds with his stick, the muddy water halfway up to his knees. 'Elaine lost her whole family in the war,' he said. 'Her father was in the merchant navy. He was the first to die, then her older brother a few months later, torpedoed on the Atlantic run. Elaine was in the Wrens by then. She was posted to London, then to Portsmouth. Her mother went to live with friends of the family, somewhere in the depths of Hampshire.' He was getting further out, poking his stick into the mud, evidently oblivious of the fact that he had waded into the pond in ordinary shoes.

'Careful, it gets deep somewhere there,' Deepbriar warned, working his way round to the other side of the water.

'I'm all right. Where was I? Oh yes, it was early in 1945. Elaine had a week's leave and went to stay with her mother. She was doing a pretty important job, and she was a bit strung up, really looking forward to a week's peace and quiet in the country. You know, Thorny, there are times when it's very hard to believe in God. A plane, one of those American Flying Fortresses, crashed on the bloody house. Elaine's mother was killed outright, but Elaine had to be dug out of the ruins. It took them several hours to reach her, though she came out with hardly a scratch. She returned to her unit a day early and went back to work. Her younger brother, having joined the merchant navy like his father, vanished in the North Sea shortly after.'

Deepbriar had written brief notes as the major spoke. Now he looked up and saw that his friend's face was set in hard lines, as if it was the only way to keep himself from weeping. 'Elaine carried on at her post until VE day, then she had a total mental breakdown. That's when she tried to kill herself. She took an overdose of some pills the medics had given her.'

'Hardly surprising,' Deepbriar said.

'No. Of course she was invalided out of the service. If it hadn't been for her commanding officer I suspect she'd still be in the asylum. As it was, the woman visited her regularly and after two years she persuaded the doctors to let Elaine try to start a new life. She helped her find a job and a place to live. By then this CO had left the Wrens, and a couple of years later she was married to a friend of mine. Elaine and I met at the wedding.' The major sighed. 'It took me years to persuade her to marry me, and before she accepted she told me all this. She seemed to think it might make a difference to the way I felt, but of course it didn't.'

'Does she still have pills to help her sleep?'

'I don't think so, but it's possible. Thorny, it's all so crazy. She knew I didn't care a fig about her past. After what she'd been through it was no wonder her mind went off the rails for a while, but why bring it up again now? What made her write a letter like that to me?' He waded out of the pond with muddy water dripping from his trousers. 'She's not here, thank God.'

Deepbriar nodded. He knew he would have to tell Brightman about that other letter, found at the pub. But Elaine Barr didn't fit the pattern of the poison-pen's victims; she'd only been in Minecliff a few weeks. 'Where did you say Elaine grew up?' he asked.

'Near Plymouth. Not far from where she was living when I first met her.'

That was the connection. Elaine Barr was from Devon. She could be cleared of any suspicion of sending the poison-pen letters, since Charles had brought her to Minecliff just before the village fête. Elaine couldn't have known about Mrs Twyford's friendship with Gordon Vennimore, and Mrs Hutton had received her letter before Elaine arrived. Assuming that she wouldn't have told anyone about her illness, the only possible explanation was that the author of the letters had known Elaine Barr when she lived in Devon.

'Thorny? What is it?' Brightman shook his arm and Deepbriar jumped.

'There's something I have to tell you,' the constable said. 'This is strictly in confidence, because I'm not sure the inspector would want you to know. There's a case I've been working on for the last few weeks. It has a bearing on Elaine's disappearance.'

* * *

The search went on throughout the long hours of daylight, but no trace of Elaine Barr was found. Dark clouds rolled in before the sun went down. The atmosphere grew heavier when darkness fell and the fields and woods around Minecliff were hushed under a black sky, as if they were holding their breath, waiting for the storm to wash away the tainted air.

Deepbriar didn't go to bed. He stood in the doorway listening for a while, assuring himself that Mary was asleep. Yesterday she had told him she was expecting a child. He'd barely had time to digest that momentous news, and now it felt wrong to be happy, when his friend was plunged into the deepest despair. Charles Brightman had gone, reluctantly, back to Minecliff Manor, but the constable knew he wouldn't be getting any sleep either.

Without any specific aim in mind, Deepbriar fetched his bicycle and cycled out of the village. He had some vague idea that the air would be fresher once he got out of the valley, and he sweated his way up the Falbrough road, stopping to dismount at the top of the hill. Turning off his lamp he pushed his bike on to its stand and leant against the trunk of an oak tree. It was past midnight and there were no lights to be seen in Minecliff. He had no need to see the view, he knew it by heart, every hedge, every field, every tree. One day, he thought, with a sudden guilty surge of joy, he would bring his son here, or his daughter.

The air grew ever hotter, and Deepbriar came out of his abstraction to wipe sweat from his eyes. A tiny light showed somewhere in the valley, then vanished. No, it was still there, the merest glimmer, moving slowly, disappearing when the person carrying the torch passed behind the trees. Deepbriar knew exactly where the man was. He had come along Violet Lane and was heading into open country, using the grass track that had once been a Roman road. The constable fetched his bike and raced back down the hill through the oppressive darkness, eyes straining to see the way, once coming dangerously close to disaster as he misjudged a bend.

Five minutes later Deepbriar breathed a sigh of relief. The light was still there. He was on foot, leaving behind the last dimly seen shapes of houses. He hadn't turned on his torch. It was risky; if the man ahead of him had set a trap in his path, Deepbriar wouldn't know until the jaws ripped into his leg.

Lightning flashed across the distant sky; the storm had broken. Soon it would come this way, following the river. Deepbriar crouched, and moved on slowly, bent almost double, fearing that he might be seen, as thunder rolled ominously around the valley and again lightning wrote jagged threats across the clouds. Any minute now the rain would start.

He was close. Deepbriar held his breath as he listened to the faint sounds of hammering. The figure, half seen by the dim light of the lamp he'd set on the ground at his feet, was anchoring the trap to the ground. A rasp of metal on metal signalled the moment when the contraption was set, its jaws ready and waiting for their victim. The next flash of lightning, much closer, showed Deepbriar a stocky figure just coming upright.

The beam from Deepbriar's torch caught the man full in the eyes. 'Stay right there!' the constable bellowed. 'Police! You're under arrest.'

There was a glimpse of a startled face, a

mouth dropping open in shock, then it was gone, the man turning to run, the lamp going out as it fell to the ground. Swearing, Deepbriar moved to follow, running a few strides. But the trap lay somewhere in his path, and although he shone his torch before him he could see no sign of it. Furious with himself for delaying until the trap had been set, Deepbriar inched forward warily. He focused the torch on the man's back, trying to make out something that would help him recognize the fleeing figure.

He gasped as a dark shape appeared on the path beyond the running man, outlined against the sky for a split second by the storm. The image of some weird creature leaping into the air was etched on to his retinas. Even Deepbriar, most pragmatic of souls, imagined for the length of a long breath that it was some nameless demon conjured by the storm, before he recognized it as a man with arms outstretched and a tattered coat flying wildly in the wind.

A second flash of lightning blazed, right overhead this time, brighter than any daylight, and thunder bludgeoned the men on the ancient track. The heavens opened and rain fell, huge heavy drops coming down like solid bolts upon Deepbriar's head. Deafened and half blinded he peered through the sheeting water, the dim light from his torch seeking out the man he had stalked. The fugitive was running towards him now, mouth open, eyes wide in terror, and behind him came his nemesis, capering down the lane, half staggering, half leaping, arms flailing like a drunken Morris dancer.

As the two drew closer Deepbriar could see that the man who had set the trap was Antonio Bonelli. Now he knew why there had been nobody to hear when Golding's glasshouses were attacked. The man was calling out to him. Deepbriar had no knowledge of Italian, but he guessed Bonelli was begging for help, for the wild scarecrow figure was gaining at every stride, screaming out threats that were drowned by the roar of thunder and the sound of thrashing branches as the wind rose to a gale.

The curtain of rain blew aside for a fraction of a second, revealing that the avenging angel was Fred Tapper, tripping over clumps of grass in his haste. With his hair matted and stubbly beard dripping rain, he charged after the fleeing Italian, his blotched face contorted with fury. Bonelli glanced repeatedly over his shoulder, looking terrified.

'It's all right. I've got him,' Deepbriar called. 'Come on, it's all right.' Bonelli gave a sob of relief, slowing a little.

Lightning slashed down at the village again, hitting a tree in the meadow not far from the strange tableau on the old Roman road. In its brief illumination Deepbriar finally spotted the trap, only a yard from the Italian's stumbling feet. His warning shout was lost as the tree splintered, crashing down and shaking the ground beneath his feet.

Thunder echoed around the valley and rolled away. A split second later Bonelli's scream rent the air, ascending in an unbearable crescendo.

17

'Fred! We have to get him out of there. Help me.' Deepbriar slipped and slithered across to the injured man; the grass track was awash, and still the rain fell as if the sky intended to empty an entire ocean upon their heads. Bonelli had collapsed, and lay in the mire with his hands clutching at his leg.

Deepbriar's foot kicked against the lantern Bonelli had used, but there was no hope of rekindling it. The light from his torch barely penetrated the solid wall of rain beating down upon them.

'Fred!' Deepbriar shouted again, chewing on his lip when a bolt of lightning showed him the bloody jaws of the trap, sunk deep into the Italian's ankle, bare-fleshed above a worn boot. The injured man was weeping loudly, keeping up a shrill lament that made it hard to think straight.

'Why should I help him?' Fred Tapper's voice came out of the darkness, hard and bitter. 'Let the bastard spend the night there, give him somethin' to think about next time he sets a trap.' Deepbriar lifted his torch so its feeble beam picked out the poacher, standing a few yards away. Tapper looked like a wild man, unshaven, filthy, and with the drumming rain plastering his tattered clothes to his skin. His cheeks were flushed and blotchy, as if he had a fever.

'Come on, Fred,' Deepbriar said. 'I can't do it without you. Please. Show him you're a better man than he'll ever be.'

The young poacher grunted something inaudible under the noise of the storm, then he leant down to the trap. 'Give us a light, then,' he demanded.

Once they'd released him from the trap he'd set, Bonelli couldn't walk. The rain had turned the path to a slippery stream. Deepbriar attempted to carry the Italian in a fireman's lift, but his feet slid from beneath him and they both crashed to the ground.

'Here, make a chair,' Fred yelled, holding out his hands to the constable. His arm was massively swollen and he gritted his teeth as Deepbriar took hold, but somehow they got Bonelli seated on their linked arms. It took them an age to reach the outskirts of the village, fighting to keep their footing and leaning into the torrential rain. At last, sodden and exhausted, they arrived at the police house.

Dumping Bonelli unceremoniously in the tiny porch, Deepbriar made Tapper accompany him to his office. 'Sit there,' he ordered, picking up the telephone.

'I'm soakin' wet an' filthy dirty,' Fred protested.

'Sit down before you fall down,' Deepbriar said. 'I'm not letting you out of my sight until you've seen a doctor. The back door's locked by the way.' He spoke to the night duty sergeant at Falbrough, who agreed to send a car and an ambulance, then with a sigh Deepbriar half fell into his own chair, reaching for notepad and pencil.

'What on earth — ' Mary came down stairs in her dressing-gown. 'I was sound asleep,' she said grumpily. 'Thorny, why is the door open? And what's that in the porch?'

'That is an Italian tenor by the name of Antonio Bonelli. But it also happens to be the villain who's been setting mantraps around Minecliff.' He grinned wearily at her. 'Any chance of a cup of tea?'

She stared at him for a moment, evidently torn between concern, anger and curiosity, then she gave a brief nod and vanished into the kitchen.

Deepbriar rose to his feet. With a warning glance at Tapper he went out to Bonelli. The injured man hadn't moved, but sat propped against the door jamb, moaning softly to himself.

The constable cautioned him, saying the

words slowly and clearly. At the meeting of the operatic society the Italian had seemed quite capable of holding a conversation in English, but now that ability had evidently deserted him. 'Come on, Bonelli, did you understand what I just said?' Deepbriar persisted, holding the notepad at arm's length; so much water was dripping off his hair and clothes that it was hard to stop it getting wet. 'Anything you say, I write down, and that information may be used in evidence.'

'*Dottore*,' Bonelli said feebly. 'I need doctor.'

'I know. There's an ambulance on the way which will take you to hospital. While we're waiting you can answer a few questions. Who told you where to set those traps?'

A few minutes later Deepbriar returned to find Fred had fallen asleep, but the poacher woke up when Mary put a tray bearing three mugs of tea down on the desk. 'I don't suppose there's any chance of you telling me what's going on?' she asked, once she'd been out to the porch to give Bonelli some tea. 'Is there a good reason why you didn't bring him inside as well?'

'Several.' Deepbriar replied cheerfully. 'I didn't think you'd appreciate him bleeding all over the floor. Though it's not exactly the right attitude for an officer of the law I also happen to dislike him. He's a nasty piece of work. Plus,' he went on, giving her a pointed look, 'I need to talk to Fred, on his own.'

Mary Deepbriar immediately returned to the kitchen, though she shut the door behind her with far more force than was necessary. Deepbriar grinned at Tapper. 'Well?' he prompted, 'you're going to have to answer some questions under caution eventually, but if there's anything you want to get off your chest, between you, me and these four walls, there's a chance I can smooth some of this over. The criminal damage at the nursery for example. If we can tell the magistrate you only did it to try and stop Golding having any more of those traps set — '

'They'll know I was the one what stole 'em,' Fred objected.

'We might be able to skirt round that, with a bit of help from the colonel, but never mind the traps for the moment. What got you so scared that you wouldn't go home, or call in at the hospital and have your arm fixed up? That wasn't anything to do with Golding, was it?'

'He's part of it. I'll tell you the honest truth, Mr Deepbriar, 'ere and now, off the record like you said, but I'm not puttin' my 'and up for it in court. My life won't be worth a bent farthin' if I do.'

Deepbriar said nothing, waiting for the man to go on.

'It's to do with the Harwayes job.' Tapper said.

'You're not trying to tell me Golding had something to do with that!'

'He was a witness. It was 'im that saw the getaway vehicle.'

Deepbriar stared at him. 'He can't have done. It was never identified; they didn't even know if it was a car or a lorry.'

'Wasn't neither. It was a bloody grocer's van,' Fred Tapper said morosely. 'I was drivin' it. Golding saw me.'

Deepbriar's jaw had dropped open and he closed it with a painful snap. 'He saw you? But why didn't he tell the police that when they questioned him?'

'Give 'im a lever, didn' it? Nasty piece of work, Golding is, for all his money an' posh friends.'

'So that's how he made you steal the traps. Hang on, wasn't Billy driving for a grocer before he took to farm work?'

'If it 'adn't been for that I'd 'ave scarpered, but I couldn't leave our Billy takin' the rap, could I? I borrowed the bloody van while 'e was takin' a break. He never knew.' Tapper sighed. 'Golding tried to force me to set the traps. I told 'im I wouldn't. Said 'e'd find one under his own bloody feet if 'e tried to make me.'

'I suppose it's no good me asking who the rest of the gang were? Look, Fred, if you turn Queen's evidence there's a good chance you'd get off light. You were only the driver; you weren't one of the men with the guns.'

'No chance. If I squeal I'm a dead man, Mr Deepbriar. All I'll say is, they wasn't no pals of mine. An' don't go askin' how I got into a stupid mess like that, 'cos I ain't tellin'.' Tapper sat slumped in his seat, a picture of misery. 'One thing I do know,' he added. 'The blokes took their masks off as they come round the corner to get in the van and Golding got a good look at 'em.'

'Are you sure? I heard he gave a description to the police, but that he never saw the men without their masks.'

Tapper shook his head vehemently. 'He knows enough to put all three of 'em behind bars, I swear it.'

* * *

Deepbriar was finding it hard to stay awake. Daylight streamed into the hospital window. Fred Tapper sat dozing beside him, his arm now enclosed in a clean white bandage, which looked very much out of place, since the rest of him was still filthy. Tapper had refused the offer of a bath and a bed, insisting that he wanted to go back to his grandmother's house, unless he was due to spend what remained of the night in the police cells.

The constable still hadn't taken the poacher's statement, an oversight he knew might get him into trouble with his superiors; his tired brain was chasing round trying to decide how to deal with the information Tapper had given him.

Constable Giddens came into the waiting-room. 'I've left Constable Jones with Bonelli,' he said, 'they want to keep him in for a few hours. Jonesy will fetch him back to the station once the doctor's seen him in the morning.' He tossed some keys in his hand. 'The inspector says I'm to drive you home, if you're ready.' The young constable nodded at Fred Tapper, now snoring slightly as he slid lower in his chair. 'What about him?'

'Reckon we'd best take him back to Minecliff too,' Deepbriar replied. 'There's a chance I'll be charging him with petty larceny, but there's no rush.'

'You'd better have a good story ready for Sergeant Parsons,' Giddens cautioned. 'He'll want to know why you didn't lock him up as soon as his arm was seen to.'

Deepbriar frowned. He was already unpopular with Inspector Martindale and Sergeant Hubbard; adding Parsons to the list didn't seem to matter. All he wanted was to get home, have a bath, and maybe snatch an hour's sleep before he had to be back on duty. 'I'll tell him there wasn't time. Half the Falbrough morning shift will be out looking for Elaine Barr again by the time we get back to the village. I'll be wanted there.'

'Busy couple o' days, eh, Mr Deepbriar?' Fred Tapper had woken up and was grinning at him sheepishly. 'Who did you say they was lookin' for? I saw all them bobbies turn up, an' I thought maybe they was after me. Reckoned I'd got it wrong though, once they started draggin' the river.'

'A woman who was staying at the Speckled Goose has gone missing,' Deepbriar replied. 'I doubt if you know her, she's not local. Her name's Elaine Barr.'

'The major's lady?' Fred sat suddenly upright in his chair. 'Blimey. You ain't gonna find 'er in the river, that's for sure.'

'What do you mean? How do you know she's not in the river?'

''Cos I followed 'er to Derling, that's how.'

'You followed her?' Deepbriar said weakly.

'Yeah. See, she looked proper upset, an' it didn' seem right, her wanderin' off to God knew where. I could see she wasn't out takin' a nature walk. I ain't got much time for the gentry, but the major's a good bloke. I kept an eye on 'is lady for him, made sure she was safe like. It was a real 'ot day for trampin' about.' He shrugged. 'Once I saw she was all right I decided to try an' get a word with me gran, so I come back to the village, but the place was swarmin' with coppers. Legged it, I did. Hid out until it was time to get back to Golding's. I bin keepin' an eye on Bonelli every night and I knew I'd get 'im in the end.'

'Do you know where Miss Barr went once she reached Derling?' Deepbriar asked, suspecting he already knew the answer.

'The station. Looked like her feet were painin' 'er. She was sat in the refreshment room last I saw, nursin' a cup o' tea.'

'It must be nearly twenty miles from Minecliff to Derling,' Giddens said wonderingly.

'Only about thirteen across the fields,' Deepbriar amended, 'but she must have been pretty desperate not to be seen, going all that way to catch a train instead of taking the bus to Falbrough or Belston.'

'Hadn't you better get on the phone and call off the search?' Giddens suggested.

'Might be a bit premature.' Deepbriar consulted his watch. 'We'd best make sure young Fred here hasn't made any mistake. If I have a quick word with the duty sergeant maybe we can take a trip over to Derling for a chat with the station staff, the day shift should be up and about by the time we get there.'

* * *

'The hero of the hour again, Thorny.' Detective Sergeant Jakes clapped Deepbriar on the back. 'You must've been born under a lucky star.'

'Something like that,' Deepbriar agreed, trying to hide a yawn. 'Did I hear the major leaving?'

'Yes, he's taking the eleven o'clock train. He'll be in Edinburgh by three, and he can get a connection on from there. He seems to think he knows exactly where the lady's gone.'

Deepbriar nodded. It hadn't been hard to trace Elaine's progress, once they knew she'd caught the train from Derling the previous afternoon, and the description given to them by the porter had been conclusive. He'd chatted to her as she waited for the train. '*Seemed a bit sad and distracted like*,' he'd said, when Deepbriar pressed him, '*nice lady though, give me thruppence just for openin' the door for her*.'

'She has an elderly great-aunt in Scotland,' Deepbriar said. 'About her only living relative. They were going to invite her to the wedding, so there was a note of her address at the manor.' It was a relief to know that Elaine Barr was probably still alive, he thought, but the affair could still end badly; she might refuse to return to Minecliff. Charles had been eager to take over the estate from his father, but he'd confided in his old friend before he left, insisting he'd rather leave his old family home than give up on his plans of marriage.

It would surely help if they could put an end to the poison-pen letters, but they seemed no closer to catching the evil-minded shrew who had written them than they'd been at the start. Deepbriar made up his mind to call on Miss Cannon; maybe she'd turned up something among the members of the Women's Institute. He was sure that Devon held the key. Pushing wearily to his feet, he turned to Jakes. 'Are you here to see me, or were you just passing through?'

'Inspector Stubbs wants this poison-pen thing sorted out,' Jakes replied. 'And since Minecliff is where it's all been going on, here I am.' He placed a folder on the desk and took out what looked at first sight like a very crumpled piece of paper which somebody had attempted, without success, to flatten out again. Looking closer, Deepbriar could see that it consisted of dozens of tiny scraps, pasted on to a larger sheet. The largish letters in the familiar round hand were legible in places, though there were plenty of gaps.

'This was the best they could do with the bits picked up from the pub,' Jakes said. 'It's the same sort of stuff as before.' He handed it to Deepbriar.

I don't know how you . . . show your face i . . . cent company . . . go back to the loony bin where you belong . . . insane . . . .
After that there was a long gap, then, *psycho . . . good man wh . . . cunning bitc . . . deserve t . . . hell fire . . . tell everybo . . . you've done . . . .*

'My sainted aunt,' Deepbriar breathed, 'it's no wonder the poor woman took off. You'd better know the background.' He gave Jakes a condensed version of the story he'd heard from the major.

'This person is demented, not Miss Barr,' Jakes said, taking back the letter with an expression of distaste. 'Imagine being dug out of the ruins like that.' He shuddered. 'Gives me the willies thinking about it. You'd have to feel sorry for her.'

'The thing is, how did our letter writer know about Miss Barr's past?' Deepbriar extracted a sheet of paper from the pile on his desk. 'This is what I've got on the others. As far as we know, the very first letter went to Mrs Hutton. Our village gossips accused her of being a spy during the war, but everybody knew that was a load of nonsense and the story only lasted a few days. Then there was Mrs Twyford . . . ' He broke off, realizing that he hadn't shared his suspicions about the cause of the widow's suicide with any of his superiors.

'Go on,' Jakes said, 'I haven't heard this.'

Deepbriar shook his head. 'I didn't report it. There's no proof.' He showed the sergeant the tiny scraps he'd rescued from the grate and explained about the words he thought he'd seen on the charred paper before it disintegrated. 'Mrs Twyford did nothing wrong, but unlike Mrs Hutton she wasn't able to laugh off the threat that her friends and neighbours would be told a load of lies. Their good opinion was very important to her. Also, she hated the idea of her fiancé's name being dragged through the mud.'

'Lots of people must have known that she was going out with Vennimore, though,' Jakes said. 'Anybody who spent time in Belston could have seen them together.'

'Yes, from what I've heard, it was an open secret. Leaving that aside for a moment, next we have Miss Cannon, whose past was pretty much common knowledge. I suspect that little bit of tittle-tattle was wheedled out of one of the elderly village gossips, the same as the old invention about Mrs Hutton's wartime activities. Finally, there's Bella Emerson. Half the women in Minecliff knew her husband was still alive, though she herself didn't know that they knew.'

Deepbriar looked at Jakes. 'You see what I'm getting at? Elaine Barr doesn't fit with the rest. How did the person who wrote this stuff know about her being treated in a mental hospital?'

'Isn't there some chance she confided in somebody?'

'According to Major Brightman, he was the only person she ever told.' Deepbriar brooded for a while. 'It all happened a long time ago. We have the connection with Devon, that's where she was in hospital.'

'You think the person who wrote the letters knew her?' Jakes asked. 'But if she saw somebody in Minecliff she recognized, somebody from her past, it's likely she'd have told the major. Writing the letter was quite a risk.'

'Maybe they didn't move in the same

circles. This woman could have been a nurse at the hospital, or even a cleaner. Miss Barr may not remember much about her illness, anyway.'

'True. You say 'woman'. You're still assuming the person who wrote the letters is female, Thorny, but at Inspector Stubbs's suggestion I showed the letters to another one of his useful contacts. This one's an English teacher. He found the style of writing quite interesting, and he said there are signs that suggest our letter writer could be a man. I read him this one over the telephone before I came here this morning, and he didn't change his mind.'

'Miss Cannon had the same idea,' Deepbriar said, thoughtfully. 'And she's a pretty clever woman. But how the heck did a man get hold of all these rumours?'

'Stubbs's expert had some ideas about that, too,' Jakes replied. 'He reckons we're almost certainly looking for a married man, with a very talkative wife. She picks up all this information from her friends and neighbours then passes it on over the tea-table. It's very unlikely she knows about the way he's using it.'

'Only a man who really hated women could write this sort of stuff,' Deepbriar mused.

'Presumably that includes his wife. You

know the locals better than I do, Thorny. Any likely candidates?'

'I was finding it hard enough when I was looking for a scandal-mongering female,' Deepbriar replied. 'Now we're after an unhappy couple. I could name you quite a few, but we're looking for somebody who hasn't been in Minecliff long. I'd say the description fits Terry and Sylvia Watts, but I'm sure it's not her. As for him . . . ' He stared into space, thinking back. Man and wife were rarely seen together. There had been that scene in the gunroom at the manor, but as every married couple had an occasional disagreement, it might have been nothing. Deepbriar sighed. He kept coming up against the same old problem: where was the motive? Why would any man write poison-pen letters to women he hardly knew?

The faintest shiver ran through him as he realized there was a possible answer. In one of Dick Bland's cases a man who wanted to kill his wife had invented a great web of lies, a tissue of falsehood that had convinced all his neighbours that his wife was suicidal. All he then had to do was make it look as if his wife killed herself, and act the part of a grieving husband.

Deepbriar ran a hand over his aching eyes. He'd been through all this when Mrs Twyford died; a detective was supposed to rely on facts, not twist things around until they fitted his pet theories. The handwriting was all wrong. Terry Watts had shown him the names of the beaters he'd listed for the colonel; his letters sloped so far backwards they looked as if they were falling over. Deepbriar had a vague idea that was common among people who were left-handed.

'Well?' Jakes prompted.

'I don't know. Trouble is, I'm so tired if I tried to add two and two I'd probably come up with three.' He shook his head, looking down at his notes again. 'I think I'll have to sleep on it.'

'All right' Jakes put the reconstructed letter away. 'There's one more thing that might help though. Before he left, I asked Major Brightman for the name of the hospital where Miss Barr was treated. I thought I'd try getting in touch. You never know, it's possible the person we're after was another patient.'

18

Deepbriar woke to sunshine and birdsong. His sleep had brought him no insight into the source of the poison-pen letters, but stumbling to the bathroom he realized his subconscious had been at work. He knew how he was going to deal with Phil Golding.

As he brushed shaving soap on to his chin and stropped his razor, Deepbriar hummed softly. The solution he'd come up with would get him kicked out of the force if it was ever made public, but, like the trap which had caught Bonelli, there was a pleasing element of poetic justice about it. Although the Italian's confession had pinned the blame for the illegal mantraps on his boss, there was still a good chance Golding would get off scot free. At the most he'd probably pay a fine, and it wouldn't even put a dent in his spending money. Thanks to Golding's position, the case would be brushed under the carpet or treated as an ill-considered prank.

Deepbriar grinned carefully as he drew the blade across his jaw, pleased with himself for coming up with an alternative. True, it would mean Golding came out of the affair smelling of roses, and it would have been good to see the man's reputation torn apart on the front of the *Falbrough Gazette*, but at least he could make sure Fred Tapper came off lightly.

'You're cheerful this morning,' Mary remarked.

'Bit of sleep does a man a power of good,' Deepbriar replied blandly. What he was about to do wasn't to be shared with anyone, even his wife. 'How about you, are you feeling better, love? Do you want me to cook breakfast?'

'No, I can manage, I'm not feeling sick today, maybe it's getting better.'

Deepbriar nodded, pleased to see that she was cooking something for herself; life, he decided, was good. He put an arm round his wife and gave her a kiss. 'You look better. In fact, you're positively blooming.'

'Get on with you,' Mary replied, though she leant into his embrace for a second before she pushed him away. 'Move over or the bacon will burn. Wasn't it kind of Charles to phone last night? He must have been so relieved to find Elaine. Did he say when they were coming home?'

'Yes, they're staying put to give Elaine a bit of a rest, then catching an early train on Saturday morning. Charles has come up with a story to cover Elaine's disappearance. He'll tell everyone it was a lovers' tiff, and that he overreacted when he found she'd run off. He's happy to take the blame for calling in the police.'

Deepbriar sat down to eat, but although he enjoyed his meal, the bacon being cooked to perfection as usual, he found his high spirits dropping by a couple of degrees. The affair could have been Mrs Twyford all over again, and there was nothing to say the poison-pen wouldn't strike again.

He sat back, watching as his wife finished her poached egg on toast with evident enjoyment and no apparent ill effects. 'If only I could find this wretch who's writing the letters,' he said.

'But if you do, won't the truth about Elaine's disappearance come out in court?' Mary asked.

'No, there are ways to protect victims in those circumstances; she won't have to worry.' Deepbriar shook his head when his wife offered to refill his teacup, and pushed back his chair. 'No, I'll get going, at least I should be able to clear up the business with the mantraps today.'

Apart from the odd puddle, the storm of two nights before might never have happened. The weather was warm and sunny, with light clouds floating slowly on a blue sky.

Deepbriar walked his beat round the village; it was suddenly a pleasure again, with the threat of more mantraps having been removed.

He returned to his office feeling quite cheerful, and telephoned Golding to arrange a meeting.

There were half-a-dozen Italians gathered by the nursery gates when Deepbriar cycled in. They looked at him rather nervously then vanished into the packing shed. He wondered if they suspected the reason for Bonelli's disappearance. The constable strode into the office, smiling benignly at Golding's secretary.

'He wants you to go straight in,' the woman said, rising to her feet. 'I'm off to the village with the post, unless you'd like a cup of tea or coffee before I go?'

'No, thanks,' Deepbriar said, opening the door for her and watching her fetch her bicycle. Then he drew the bolt. Turning he saw that Golding had come out of his office and was standing watching him. Deepbriar offered him a smile which wasn't a bit like the one he'd given the secretary. 'We won't want to be disturbed,' he said. 'Shall we go and sit down, Mr Golding? Might as well be civilized about this.'

'I assume you're here to tell me what's

happened to Bonelli,' Golding said brusquely, easing his great mass into his chair.

'I thought you'd have worked that out for yourself. He's in custody, Mr Golding, since he was caught putting down one of those illegal traps you acquired.'

'Me?' The large fleshy face grew beetroot red. 'Are you accusing me of having something to do with those traps? How dare you!'

'I dare because I have a sworn statement. In fact I have two. You blackmailed Fred Tapper into stealing the traps from the manor, then you paid the Italian the princely sum of a pound for each trap he set. It's a shame he went and put his foot in the last one, otherwise who knows how much longer this business would have gone on. I think it's probably time I read you your rights, don't you, sir?'

Deepbriar had the initiative, and after the rather acrimonious start, the discussion went exactly how the constable planned. Golding saw the advantages of following the course of action Deepbriar suggested, and within a few minutes the nurseryman was making a telephone call to the police station at Belston.

'I have something to tell you about the bank robbery,' Golding said into the receiver, his eyes fixed on Deepbriar. The constable suppressed a grin; if looks could kill he didn't think he'd make it out of the room alive.

'This is information I withheld when I was interviewed. Yes, I realize that. I had a very good reason for keeping quiet, but my conscience has been troubling me.'

This time Deepbriar didn't bother to hide his disbelieving smile, which left Golding grinding his teeth, as he made an appointment to see Chief Inspector Nidthwaite, who was in charge of the Harwayes case.

Once it was done Golding slammed down the telephone and scowled at Deepbriar. 'Was there anything else? I have work to do.'

'You might like to call Falbrough Police Station as well,' Deepbriar said, still smiling, 'and tell them that damage to your greenhouses was a personal affair, the result of a misunderstanding, and that you should never have reported it as criminal damage. With luck you won't be charged with wasting police time. Oh, and see if you can arrange bail for your night watchman, you'll need to find some way to make him change his story. We can't have people thinking you were responsible for those mantraps, can we?'

Deepbriar was halfway to the door when he turned, the anger he'd been keeping under check suddenly coming to the surface. 'Why?' he demanded abruptly. 'We both know you'll never be held to account, not once you've become a hero over this Harwayes business, so you might as well come clean, I'll have no hope of taking it any further. What was the point of those dead animals, and poor little Oliver Rose's dog?'

'My land.' Golding said bluntly, an unpleasant glint in his eyes. 'I work hard for what I've got, and it's mine, not a public park for people to go strolling about in as if they own it. I put up a fence and it didn't keep them out. The law tells me that there's footpaths, and bridleways, that I'm not allowed to stop them. It's nonsense. Give them a scare, that's what I thought, teach them to keep off. I reckon if the other landowners knew what I'd done they'd be pleased.'

'Pleased?' Deepbriar felt ready to explode, recalling Nev Butcher, who had found a trap down the lane where his children rode their ponies every day.

'Yes. You can't tell me I'm the only one. I have to put up with kids pushing through hedges, stealing fruit, causing damage just for the hell of it. Then there's picnickers leaving all their rubbish behind and forgetting to shut the gates. They walk past my garden, with nothing to stop them staring in, gawping as if they're at the zoo. They've got no right.' His voice rose almost to a shout. 'No right!'

'The remaining traps are to be delivered back to the manor so they can be destroyed. And if anything like this happens again, Mr Golding,' Deepbriar said quietly, 'then I'll see you get what's coming to you. That's not a threat, it's a promise.' He wrenched open the door and left, taking a good long breath of fresh air once his feet were safely off Phil Golding's property.

* * *

Elaine Barr looked tired and subdued as she came into the drawing-room at the manor on Saturday morning, but she met Deepbriar's eyes without flinching as he offered her his hand.

'I'm sorry to have to bother you, Elaine,' he said, 'but I do need to ask you a few questions.'

'Of course. I'm afraid I put you to a lot of trouble.'

Deepbriar raised his eyebrows and glanced at Charles Brightman, who had remained, hovering near the door. 'Not at all. Everybody agrees the whole thing was a mistake, this nonsense about you going missing; Charles overreacted. That sort of misunderstanding happens all the time.' He grinned. 'I've had my share of lovers' tiffs, believe me.'

'It's very kind of you, and of Charles,' she added, exchanging a look with her fiancé. 'We've agreed that if there's anything at all I can do to help you, then I shall, Thorny, even if it means people find out about — ' She faltered, then went on more firmly, 'About my unsavoury past.'

Deepbriar smiled, heartened to hear her use his nickname. 'People would have to be very unfeeling to call it that, but I don't think you should worry. I just need to know if there is any way, any way at all, that you might have let some detail slip about what happened to you after the war, particularly the time you spent in hospital.'

She shook her head vehemently. 'No. I never talk about it. And I'm sure the few friends who know the details wouldn't either.'

'Which leaves us to assume that the person who wrote that terrible letter must have known you before you moved here.'

'Yes; Charles and I discussed that on the train.' She drew her brows together. 'I've been racking my brains, but I'm sure I haven't seen any familiar faces in Minecliff. To be honest though, there are parts of those two years that aren't exactly clear in my head. The mind does strange things at times, and it becomes quite difficult to separate dreams from reality.'

Deepbriar nodded sympathetically. 'About the letter you received, you didn't recognize the handwriting?'

'No. I'm sorry.' Again she looked at the major. 'We did have an idea, if it's of any help.'

'I never turn down ideas,' Deepbriar replied. 'It's not as if I have too many of my own, not in this case anyway.'

'I've kept in touch with one of the doctors who helped me,' she said. 'We thought he might be persuaded to supply you with the names of people working at the asylum while I was there. Maybe even the patients, too.'

'You think he would do that?' Deepbriar clutched at the suggestion eagerly. 'Sergeant Jakes has tried telephoning them, but they aren't being very co-operative so far.'

Elaine smiled wanly. 'When you've spent time in a lunatic asylum, you prefer to have it kept quiet. But if I explain, and can reassure him that the details will be kept confidential, I think Dr Whirtle might help.' She gestured towards the phone. 'If you like, I could call him now.'

Deepbriar nodded and stood up.

'Thorny and I will have a cup of tea in my study,' Charles Brightman said. 'Come and join us when you're finished.'

'She's taking it all quite well,' the major

said in a low voice, leading Deepbriar into the hall, 'but I'll feel a lot better once this character is safely locked up. She's putting on a brave face, but if the rumours started I'm not sure she could cope.'

'Despite the threats, no rumours were spread about any of the other women who received poison-pen letters,' Deepbriar said. He rubbed his knuckles across his eyebrows. 'I can't help thinking I'm being slow. There's something not right about the whole business, but I can't figure out what it is.'

* * *

Tuesday morning found Deepbriar at Falbrough Police Station. He'd handed in his incident reports, and was on his way to the canteen when Inspector Martindale stopped him.

'Constable, come in here a moment.' Inspector Martindale sounded positively jovial as he beckoned Deepbriar into his office.

'Morning, sir,' Deepbriar said. 'May I congratulate you on your promotion?' The news had just been made public, which was presumably what had put his superior in such a good mood.

Martindale waved this aside. 'Yes, well, I

shall be sorry to leave Falbrough, of course. But it's you I wanted to talk about. I've reconsidered this matter of your move to CID, and persuaded Sergeant Hubbard that he can manage without you.'

'Thank you, sir.' Deepbriar was shocked; he hadn't really believed Stubbs when he'd told him this would happen.

'The least we can do,' Martindale replied. 'I've had Major Brightman on the telephone twice, singing your praises. And Chief Inspector Nidthwaite tells me you were in some small way instrumental in solving the Harwayes case.'

Deepbriar was surprised; he hadn't expected Golding to mention his name. 'Hardly that, sir. I just discovered that one of the witnesses was withholding evidence, and persuaded him to come clean.'

'Yes, that's what I heard.' Martindale looked puzzled. 'How did you know this chap Golding had seen the gang's faces?'

'It was something he let slip when we were talking about quite a different matter, sir,' Deepbriar lied cheerfully. 'I'm sure Mr Golding feels much better now he's got it all off his chest. Oh, you may have heard he's not pursuing that criminal damage case, it seems he's discovered it was a private matter, something he wants to deal with himself.'

'Really? Seems a bit of a strange chap.' Martindale shrugged. 'Of course, he may have been right to be wary of giving evidence about the Harwayes raid. We've had some nasty cases of intimidation in the past.'

It was a point that had been causing Deepbriar occasional twinges of conscience. 'We wouldn't want his family getting hurt, sir.'

'Don't worry, we'll be keeping an eye on him, give him protection until the case comes to court. As a matter of fact he might be thinking of moving, which might be best in the long run. I gather he's looking into a business opportunity in Essex.' Martindale began shuffling papers on his desk, a signal that the interview was over.

'Keep up the good work, Deepbriar. You'll get notice of your new appointment within the next couple of weeks. Oh, by the way,' he added, as the constable opened the door, 'I'm told a friend of yours is joining the force here in Falbrough, straight out of college. Young chap by the name of Bartle. He'll be coming over from Belston later today to start his probationary period.'

'Really?' Deepbriar beamed. He hadn't thought Harry would be posted to the local station. 'He's a good lad, Inspector, very keen. I'm sure he'll do well.'

Sergeant Jakes was waiting for him in the CID office. 'Morning, Thorny. I'm glad you're here, the list from that asylum in Devon just arrived. It's a long shot, but maybe there'll be a name you recognize.' He handed over two sheets of paper. 'If not, then we've hit a dead end.'

Deepbriar sat down and studied the long list of names. Among the staff who had worked at the asylum during the relevant time, apart from one woman named Smythe, he could see no surname that matched anyone in Minecliff. The list of patients was short. A hand-written note at the bottom explained that these were people who were no longer living. Dr Whirtle had evidently had second thoughts about revealing any more.

'You saw this?' Deepbriar asked, tapping the note. 'We . . . ' The word trailed into silence. A name had leapt off the paper at him. Watts. Male. Age 53. A patient by the name of Bertram Watts had died a month after Elaine Barr left the asylum.

* * *

'We've got him!' Jakes slammed down the telephone receiver and beamed triumphantly at Deepbriar. 'They've confirmed it. Next of kin was his son, Terence.'

'But he's a gamekeeper, a tough outdoor type. If a man like that hates his wife he usually takes a strap to her. He doesn't write nasty letters to her friends. Anyway, the handwriting's all wrong,' Deepbriar demurred. 'Watts was responsible for writing down the names of beaters at the shoot, and he showed me a whole page he'd written. His writing is nothing like the letters.'

'He disguised it,' Jakes said. 'Unless we're barking up the wrong tree and it's his wife.'

'Even less likely, her handwriting looks like a spider's been crawling in the ink. And she's always struck me as a bit too stupid to be our poison pen.'

'This can't be a coincidence.' Jakes tapped the list of names.

'But there's no motive. No demands for money, and — ' Deepbriar broke off, his mouth dropping open. 'That's it! Dear heaven, it's all about money.'

'Blackmail?' Jakes hazarded.

'No. It's been staring me in the face. Sylvia Watts has had a legacy. Suppose it's a large sum of money? She's running into town spending money on hats and dresses every couple of days. Her husband's not going to be impressed at seeing a small fortune squandered, so he decides to put her out of the way.'

'But what's that got to do with the poison-pen letters?'

'That's what's so clever. With several other women having received these letters, suppose his wife is next? And suppose she is then found dead, apparently at her own hand? Everyone would assume that she'd been driven to suicide, just like poor Mrs Twyford.'

'It's a heck of an idea, Thorny,' Jakes said, getting to his feet. 'We have to follow this up. I'll go and have a word with the boss, I think we could get a search warrant.'

While he was gone Deepbriar sat lost in thought. If he was right there was still a piece of the puzzle missing; how had Watts disguised his handwriting?

Jakes came hurrying back. 'It'll take about an hour,' he said.

Deepbriar nodded. 'If it's all right with you, I think I'll get back to Minecliff. I'd like a word with Sylvia Watts first, before we question her husband.' He looked at the clock. 'The WI are meeting this morning, she'll be in the village hall. I'd like to check that I'm right about that legacy being a serious amount. If it is then I'll feel more confident that we're not barking up the wrong tree.'

'Not a bad idea,' Jakes conceded, 'We don't want any mistakes. Where shall I meet you?'

* * *

The sound of many voices greeted Deepbriar as he pushed open the door of the village hall. About thirty pairs of eyes turned his way as he stepped inside, taking off his helmet, and the talking gradually stopped. 'Sorry to interrupt,' he said. The ladies were busy sorting jumble. He couldn't see Sylvia Watts, so he went instead to his wife, working at a long table with Miss Cannon and Miss Jane. 'Ladies,' he nodded. 'I was hoping to have a word with Mrs Watts,' he added, lowering his voice.

'She didn't turn up today,' Mary said. 'I wondered if she'd gone to The Lodge. Mrs Emerson doesn't come to our working sessions.'

'Hmm, there's a surprise,' Deepbriar muttered, unable to resist the opportunity to snipe at his enemy.

'I don't think she has,' Miss Jane put in. 'I met Bella Emerson on my way here; she was catching the bus to Falbrough, and she didn't say anything about Sylvia joining her.'

'It doesn't matter,' he said. 'I'll just borrow my wife for a moment instead, if you don't mind.'

'Is something wrong?' Mary asked, following him outside.

'You know I wouldn't usually ask you to pass on the local gossip,' Deepbriar said, 'but have you heard about Sylvia Watts inheriting some money?'

'Yes, she told me herself.' Mary smiled. 'I think her husband wanted to keep it quiet, but she's such a chatterbox.'

'She didn't tell you how much it was?'

'Not in so many words. But she did say, sort of jokingly, that she was worth more than poor Gladys Twyford.'

Deepbriar let out a long low whistle. 'So that's it. I think I'd better go and call on Mrs Watts.'

He had almost reached the manor before it occurred to him that Sylvia Watts's absence from the WI meeting might have a sinister significance. Suppose her husband had chosen this very day to do the deed?

Deepbriar raced through the gates of the manor, turning off the drive to take the track that led to the cottage where Terry and Sylvia Watts lived. He braked, skidding on the gravel, and pushed his bike out of sight before the cottage came into view. Then he ran, keeping to the grass verge so he wouldn't be heard. The place looked empty, with all the windows shut and the downstairs curtains drawn.

The constable went to the front door and

raised his hand to knock, freezing as he heard a slight sound from inside, as if something heavy was being dragged across the stone flags. Then there was a long silence. Very gently he pushed open the letterbox and peered through; a piece of heavy brown material blocked his view, presumably hung there to keep out the draught. He could hear nothing from inside but the deep slow ticking of a clock.

Deepbriar found he was holding his breath. The hairs on the back of his neck lifted. The cottage wasn't empty, he was sure of it; the stillness spoke of a tension in the air, a presence, watching and waiting. Perhaps he was already too late. He dithered on the step, unable to decide what to do. Until Jakes arrived with the search warrant he had no right to enter the house, and yet his every instinct told him that something was seriously wrong.

Letting the letter box flap close quietly, Deepbriar straightened, staring around him. How had Watts planned to kill his wife? It was a long way to the river, and the cottage wasn't connected to the gas. A knife perhaps, slashed wrists while she lay in the bath? Dear God, what should he do?

Gingerly, he set a hand to the door handle and turned it. Locked. He was moving away, intent on trying at the back, when a faint cry reached him. The sound was cut off abruptly, leaving a ringing silence behind; it might have originated anywhere, but some gut instinct told him it had come from inside the cottage.

Hurrying back to the front door, Deepbriar heard that same rasping noise as if something was dragging on the floor. There was a gasp, followed by a terrible sound he couldn't begin to identify and a crash. Running footsteps echoed in the hall, then came the slam of a door from the back of the house.

Deepbriar didn't wait to go around, he picked up the boot scraper and smashed it into the glass panel in the top half of the door, his other hand reaching inside for the lock before the last shards tinkled to the ground. He burst into the hall, then came to a dead halt as movement halfway up the stairs caught his eye.

19

Mrs Watts was hanging over the stairwell. By the neck. Her body swung as she struggled, choking gasps issuing from her throat, while her hands clawed frantically at the rope digging ever tighter into her flesh. There was no time to make use of the fallen stepladder which lay blocking his path. Deepbriar leapt over it and hurtled up the first three stairs; the woman's face was swelling, turning purple.

It might already be too late. He threw his arms around Sylvia Watts's thighs and lifted her, taking her weight. His face was buried in the folds of the long dressing-gown she wore; he was blind and half-suffocated. After a moment he heard, felt, that she was still alive, for she was moving, air was somehow still passing in and out of her straining lungs.

'Mrs Watts? Can you get your hands up to the rope above your head, try to hold some of your weight? If you can, maybe I can help you down.' The answer was a choking sob, but the burden became no less, and Deepbriar could do nothing but remain where he was. Long minutes passed. The discomfort in his muscles and tendons was almost unbearable.

Deepbriar bit down on his lip. He could hear the woman's harsh arduous breaths and feared that with any more pressure from the rope they would stop. It would have taken him just a few seconds to reach the ladder but he hadn't dared risk the attempt. To distract himself from the pain in his straining muscles, Deepbriar began to count, slowly. He determined that he would reach 100; Jakes was on his way, surely he would come soon.

When he reached 100, with his shoulders on fire and his chest feeling as if a hot band of metal was gradually being tightened around it, Deepbriar went on counting.

His own breathing now almost as ragged as that of the half-hanged woman he was supporting, Deepbriar counted to 100 yet again. And still Mrs Watts drew in rasping slivers of air; through the dressing-gown he could feel shudders as she moved a little in his grasp. Another 100. And another. Deepbriar had lost all sense of time, and he'd forgotten about Jakes, forgotten about the man who had run from the back of the house as he stormed in at the front. His existence was focused on enduring the agony that racked him, and the absolute necessity that he should endure. He would have given anything to be able to move, even to release the grip of one hand, to drop one shoulder the merest fraction of an inch. There was a taste of salt water on his tongue; involuntary tears of pain were soaking the cloth that smothered his face.

Deepbriar heard the approaching car though he was no longer able to think what it might mean. He was barely aware of Sergeant Jakes's horrified curse as footsteps dashed past him. 'Dear Lord! Grab the ladder, get it up to that rope.'

The weight lessened as Jakes came to his side. There was the familiar sound of wood scraping on the tiled floor as the ladder was lifted into place, and then at last Deepbriar was free, his burden lifted from him.

'Mr Deepbriar?' He hadn't realized that he'd screwed his eyes tight shut, but now they flew open, and focused in bewilderment on the man before him, his appearance at once familiar and yet strange. Harry Bartle's face looked incredibly young under the police helmet. 'Are you all right?'

'I'll live.' The spasms in his tormented muscles and sinews took a while to subside, and Deepbriar gritted his teeth as he finally lowered his arms. Sergeant Jakes was kneeling by Mrs Watts, who lay on the tiles at Deepbriar's feet. 'How is she?'

'Alive, thanks to you,' Jakes said, struggling to remove the rope from her neck. 'Bartle, get up to the big house, telephone for an ambulance.'

As Harry ran out of the front, Deepbriar went upstairs, fetching a blanket to put over Sylvia Watts where she lay in the hall. That done, he bent to pick up a sheet of paper that was lying on the floor.

''*Your neighbours will soon know the truth*',' he read. ''*They will find out that you are a wicked wanton whore . . .* '' There was a whole page of it, in the familiar childishly neat handwriting. Deepbriar passed the letter to Jakes. 'Can't say it's much comfort to find I'm right,' he said. 'Mrs Watts was the next target for our poison pen, and probably the last. I'm willing to bet we'll find the envelope too, posted in Belston, just like the others. I still don't understand how he managed to disguise his handwriting so well, but I think we know who wrote this. Watts can't have gone far, I heard him run out at the back of the house as I broke in at the front.'

'So he'll know we're looking for him,' Jakes said flatly.

'I imagine he must have heard me,' Deepbriar confirmed. He glanced out through the open front door. 'If he thinks he's killed her and we're right on his heels he could do something stupid.'

'Let's hope not. Before we start looking for Watts we'd better get her away from here,'

Jakes said. 'We'll take a quick look round while we wait for the ambulance. The search warrant's in my pocket.'

They found what they were looking for in the bottom drawer of a desk in the parlour. Deepbriar prised open the lock with his penknife and lifted out a leather-bound case. It held a pad of writing paper, the sort that could be bought at any number of shops in Falbrough or Belston. It also held two very distinctive envelopes.

Jakes meanwhile was scowling over a diary that lay on top of the desk. There wasn't much in it, only an appointment to see the dentist, and a record of the bag at the last two shoots of the season, but it was enough. 'Look at the writing,' he said. 'Like you said, there's no similarity at all. Is there anything here that was written by his wife?'

By way of answer Deepbriar handed him a half completed letter in a spidery hand. '*Dear Josephine, thank you very much for the bath salts. It was very kind of you to think of me. We are settling down well in the village. The people are so nice. I do lots of things with the Women's Institute . . .* '

'You only have to look at the style,' Deepbriar said. 'She couldn't have written that other stuff.'

'No. Make sure she's all right, will you,

Thorny? I'll have a quick look upstairs, see if there's anything else of interest.'

Deepbriar went to crouch at the woman's side and she stared up at him, her mouth working. 'Best if you don't talk,' he said, 'the ambulance will be here soon.'

'I heard what you said. That letter,' she whispered painfully. 'It came in the post this morning, but he took it before I could open it.'

'We think your husband sent it to you.'

She nodded. 'Terry wrote it.'

'But it isn't his handwriting,' Deepbriar said. 'Look, we can do this later, when you're feeling better.'

'I'm all right. They made him use his right hand at school, Constable, but he found it hard because he was left-handed. He can write with them both, but the writing's different.' Tears squeezed from the corners of her eyes and dripped off her face.

Deepbriar laid a hand on her arm. 'That's enough for now; don't upset yourself. We'll take care of things,' he soothed.

Jakes came back empty handed and beckoned Deepbriar to the front door. 'Where would Watts go?' He stared outside; the manor house was out of sight behind a bank of trees and shrubs, but no more than 200 yards away.

'He's a loner. Might have run to the woods.

Right now I'm more worried about Harry. It's time he was back; it shouldn't have taken him more than a minute to get to the manor house. It's possible Watts went there first. And he's got the key to the colonel's gun cupboard.'

'You don't think Bartle met up with him?' Jakes looked alarmed. 'It's the first day of his six-month probation, we can't have him tangling with an armed lunatic!'

'Do you want — ?' Deepbriar broke off as a figure appeared through the trees, glancing nervously back in the direction of the manor house. It wasn't Harry Bartle.

'Mrs Brant.' Deepbriar went to meet her, with Sergeant Jakes on his heels. 'Is something wrong?'

'I'm not sure. Young Harry Bartle turned up. I started telling him how smart I thought he looked in his new uniform, but he said he was in a hurry and that he had to use the telephone. I'd have taken him to the colonel, but he's away to Belston today, and of course Major Brightman's gone riding with Miss Barr, so, since there wasn't anybody home, I took Harry into the hall, and he called for an ambulance, then we were just going back to the kitchen when we heard noises from the gun-room. I told him there shouldn't be anyone in there. Do you think it's burglars?' Mrs Brant asked, pausing for breath. 'And who's been hurt? Is it Sylvia? Has there been an accident?'

'Where did Harry go?' Deepbriar demanded, cutting across the flow.

'I don't know where he went. He told me to go out of the front door and come down here. He said run, but I'm not built for running. I did hurry though, I thought — '

It was Jakes who interrupted her this time. 'Come in here. You can keep an eye on Mrs Watts for us. The ambulance shouldn't be long now.' He jammed the stepladder across the front door on the inside. 'Once we've gone you're to bolt the back door behind us. Don't open it to anyone, except Constable Deepbriar and me, or the ambulance men.'

Deepbriar looked dubiously at the sergeant. 'What if . . . ?' he began.

'It's up to us to make sure he doesn't come back,' Jakes said tersely. 'You understand, Mrs Brant? Just stay in here and keep Mrs Watts company.'

The two policemen ran through the belt of trees, towards the manor house.

'The front door?' Jakes queried.

'I'd suggest the back,' Deepbriar replied, breathing hard. 'If he's been in the gun-room we need to find out exactly what we're dealing with.'

'All right, but let's take it slow and easy, he

could still be in there.'

The door to the service area of the house stood wide open. They stood listening for a while, hearing nothing. 'About five yards straight along the passage, then left,' Deepbriar said in a low voice. 'Gun-room's the first door on the right.'

Jakes nodded. 'Come a few paces behind me,' he ordered, 'no point giving him more than one target.'

Reluctantly Deepbriar hung back until he saw Jakes ease himself round the corner, then he followed. When he reached the gun-room the sergeant was in the entrance, looking for him. 'Been and gone,' Jakes said, gesturing at the open door of the gun cupboard. 'Any idea what he's taken?'

'Shotgun,' Deepbriar said, looking at the empty space in the rack. 'Twelve bore.' The drawer underneath was open too, several cartridges spilling out of a box inside.

'Then it looks like we're in trouble.' Jakes said. 'Where the heck is young Bartle?'

'The house is like a rabbit warren; we'll never find Watts if he's gone to ground inside,' Deepbriar said. 'Somehow I don't think that's likely; it's not his home territory.'

'That's no comfort, Constable,' Jakes observed, leading the way back along the corridor, 'if he's taken to the woods we're even worse off. I don't fancy trying to track a gamekeeper on his own ground. We'll — '

He was interrupted by the sound of a shot, echoing as if the gun had been fired within a narrow space.

'The yard,' Deepbriar said, pushing past his superior officer and running outside, leading the way towards the stables. As they rounded the corner a small figure appeared at the further end of the block. His back turned to them, the man ran as if his life depended on it, heading towards the barn.

'Who was that?' Jakes breathed.

'The colonel's groom, Ernie Pratt,' Deepbriar replied.

'Can you skirt round the outside of the buildings and catch him?' Jakes asked. 'We need to know what's going on in there. If that bastard has shot young Bartle . . . '

Deepbriar didn't wait to hear any more, his heart in his mouth as he ran, his head full of nightmare visions.

'Ernie,' he called breathlessly, seeing the man hesitating, evidently torn between taking refuge in the barn and going on towards Home Farm.

'Thank the Lord you're here,' Ernie said. 'Young Watts has gone mad. Did you hear? Fired both bloody barrels into the floor, he did.'

'Into the floor? You're sure about that?'

The old groom's face was pale under its lined and weathered surface. 'Wasn't more than ten foot away when he did it. He's in one of the open stalls, Gawd knows what he thinks he's doing.'

'You didn't see Harry Bartle?'

'Young Harry? Why the heck would he be here?'

Deepbriar didn't bother to answer, dashing back to Jakes. He found the sergeant chewing worriedly at a fingernail.

'Well?' Jakes demanded.

'Watts didn't shoot anybody. But Pratt didn't see anything of Harry.'

'Right, we'd better get in there. I take it there are stables inside, how are they laid out?'

'Watts is in the old stalls.' Deepbriar bent down and drew in the dust with his finger. 'Look, those three outer doorways all lead into a passage that goes along the front of the building and down this side, with open stalls leading off it, about half a dozen of them. I'm not too sure what's behind the stalls, but the back walls aren't solid like the sides — there's gaps I reckon a man could climb through. That last door leads to the tack-room. You can get into it from inside as well.'

'And you said the house was a maze,' Jakes

grumbled. 'There could be half-a-dozen people hiding in there and you wouldn't know. Is there another entrance at the back?'

'No. Do you want me to get to the other side? We don't want him taking off.'

Before Jakes could reply a shout resonated from the stables. 'I know you're there, copper!' This was followed by another explosion of sound, not a shot this time, but a crash as if something heavy had been overturned.

'Christ,' Jakes swore. 'He's after young Bartle. I'll try talking to him. Nip round to the other side and see if you can get inside while I distract him, Thorny, but for God's sake don't let him see you.' Jakes ran across the yard and flattened himself against the wall, alongside the first of the open doorways.

'Mr Watts! I'm Sergeant Jakes, Falbrough CID. I need to talk to you.'

There was no answer. Not a sound from within.

'Mr Watts? I've just seen your wife. She's not badly hurt. She's gone off to hospital in an ambulance. Do you hear me? She's going to be all right.'

The silence dragged on. Deepbriar sprinted right round the outside of the building, to the opposite end of the block from the place where Jakes stood spread-eagled against the sun-warmed bricks. Signalling to Deepbriar to stay where he was, Jakes launched himself across the yawning darkness of the doorway, aiming to take refuge behind the next solid length of wall. The blast from the shotgun sounded horribly loud as it echoed within the enclosed space, a scatter of shot peppering the solid door frame while most of the charge thudded into the wall of the feed store on the other side of the yard. The sergeant yelped as he measured his length on the ground.

Deepbriar stared at Jakes, and let out a long relieved breath when the sergeant pulled himself up to stand against the stable wall. He didn't seem to be hurt. 'Watts,' Jakes called, 'you're doing yourself no favours. Come on, be sensible.'

There was still no reply. After a moment's reflection Deepbriar ducked through the door of the tack-room. Luck took him past the opening and into the shadows. Jakes was pinned down, helpless, since Watts could cover both openings from inside the stalls. The constable refused to think what might happen if Watts simply decided to step outside and let fly.

His eyes adjusting to the dim light, Deepbriar crouched low and peeped into the passageway. It was empty; Ernie had got it right, Watts was in one of the stalls. The gamekeeper had the advantage of knowing the building better than Deepbriar. As children, he and Charles had only played together in the stables once; the game, which involved climbing around among the roof beams, had ended with his friend breaking his collar bone, followed by the threat of a hiding from the colonel if they tried it again.

Deepbriar looked up, but instantly dismissed the idea of repeating his childhood stunt; he couldn't hope to take Watts from above. Clambering around in the roof was all very well for a small boy, but there were signs of rot in the ancient timbers and they wouldn't support fourteen stone.

The wall of the tack-room was made of rubble and sandstone, while the partitions between the stalls were timber boards, over an inch thick, strong enough to withstand the kick of workhorses weighing nearly a ton. Deepbriar crept into the passageway, his ears stretched, hearing for the moment only the pounding of his own heart.

'Watts, you're not a murderer. Why don't you put the gun down and talk to — ' Jakes's words were cut off by another blast from the shotgun, so loud that Deepbriar ducked, clapping his hands over his ringing ears.

'Shut up, copper. No more of your lies or I'll come out and give you both barrels, right in your ear. Reckon that'll be plain talking enough for you?' Watts's voice was high with strain.

Steadying himself, Deepbriar let out the breath he didn't know he'd been holding, and drew in another. Looking out of the stall where he'd taken refuge, he stared at the gouge in the floor made by the shot. At least now he knew exactly where Watts was. He moved back into the passage and stepped cautiously past two empty stalls, then ducked into the next. Now only the thickness of a wooden wall separated him from the armed man.

Deepbriar swallowed hard. 'Terry?' he ventured. The gun stayed silent and he went on. 'This is Thorny Deepbriar, Terry, you remember me? I've been wanting to thank you for the way you helped me. I caught that bastard who was setting mantraps, did you hear about that?'

There was what seemed like an endless pause, and Deepbriar tried hard not to think about the effects a shotgun could achieve, when fired at close range into a human body.

'I heard,' Watts said at last.

'Then you know I owe you a favour. I can't blame you for not trusting Sergeant Jakes, the man's a townie, born and bred, but you and me, we're country folk. You've got my word,

Terry, I swear, your wife is going to be fine. Be sensible and we can get you out of this mess. All you have to do is put down the gun.'

'And if you're telling the truth, then what?' Watts demanded roughly. 'I can't face being locked up, I need air, room to breathe, and not too many damn people. I don't reckon I'd last long in prison.'

'A few years in prison is better than the alternative,' Deepbriar said. 'Shoot a copper and there's nowhere to run. You can't hope to escape, half the county constabulary's on the way. It'll go easier with you if you give yourself up nice and peaceable, before they get here.'

'There's another way,' Watts said. His voice was pitched low now, as if he was talking more to himself than to Deepbriar. He gave a strange little laugh. 'What I had planned for Sylvie, the silly bitch. You don't find out what a woman's like, not until you've lived with her a year or two. And by then it's too late, you're trapped. You know about the money, don't you, Constable? That was the last straw. A bloody rich uncle, leaving her a fortune. Well, maybe this is the best way out, after all. Nice and neat and tidy.'

'Now then, Terry, you don't mean that,' Deepbriar said, eyeing the partition between the two stalls, knowing he couldn't hope to clamber over it quickly enough to do any good. 'Put the gun down, there's a good lad. You won't be facing a charge of murder, and I'll do my best for you when it comes to court. I'm sure — '

'Stop lying to me!' Watts's voice rose to a scream.

Something caught Deepbriar's eye. Up in the shadows above his head, a shape was moving slowly across the roof beams. He caught his breath as a little cloud of dust drifted down, but Watts hadn't noticed.

'Bloody coppers! Just like bloody women, always telling you what to do!' Watts was moving. Deepbriar heard the scrape of his boots on the cobbled floor. 'I've heard enough of your bloody lies. My wife's dead, so what difference does it make if I shut your mouth too!'

'Terry, for God's sake! She's alive. She told me about the writing, how they made you use your right hand at school. How would I know that if she hadn't told me?' Deepbriar felt sweat prickling down his back. He was running out of time, running out of words.

Up above, Harry Bartle had come upright. He was poised directly over the stall where Watts was hidden, shifting his feet very slightly, finding his balance.

'Give yourself a chance,' Deepbriar began

again, raising his voice to cover any sounds Watts might hear from above his head. 'There's no need — ' He broke off as Harry Bartle was launched into the air, but not in the smooth leap he'd doubtless planned. The beam he stood on gave way and he plummeted headlong, crashing down among the rending of splintering wood and a cloud of dust. Deepbriar had no time to jump out of the way. He flung his arms above his head as half the stable roof came down and buried all three of them.

* * *

'He's not happy with you,' Sergeant Jakes said, absent-mindedly helping himself to a grape from the bowl beside Deepbriar's bed. 'Reckons he'd rather be dead than facing a long spell behind bars for attempted murder.'

'Tough luck,' Deepbriar replied, more than half his mind occupied with the terrible itch underneath the plaster encasing his leg from ankle to hip.

Jakes shrugged. 'Can't say I've got any sympathy for him. They say he's sane, despite what happened to his father. Cunning though; what sort of brute thinks up a scheme like that? Mind you, I understand how that wife of his got him down. I took her statement a couple of days ago. Being rich hasn't made her any less silly.' The sergeant ate another grape with evident relish. 'She plans to leave Minecliff, she fancies living down on the South Coast. Says she'll spend her legacy on a nice little bed and breakfast establishment.'

'I hope she'll let us know where,' Deepbriar said gloomily. 'So we can give the place a wide berth.'

Jakes chuckled. 'Constable Bartle sends his regards, says he'll call in tomorrow. Funny the way he got off scot-free. And even Watts only got a knock on the head.'

Deepbriar sighed. He had thought the same thing a dozen times, coming to the conclusion that he was just born unlucky; he would be spending six weeks in plaster, then several more getting fit enough to return to duty. 'Every time it looks as if I might finally join the CID something goes wrong. At this rate I'll never get transferred to plain clothes,' he complained.

'Oh, I nearly forgot.' Jakes reached into his pocket and pulled out a brown envelope. 'I knew I'd come to see you for a reason. Last thing Martindale did before he left for Belston. Welcome to Falbrough CID, Detective Constable Deepbriar.'

Other titles published by
The House of Ulverscroft:

MURDER SOLSTICE

Keith Moray

Museum curator Finlay MacNeil had spent years trying to decipher the markings on the Hoolish Stones, the stone circle which for millennia had stood on the West Uist. He was suspicious of the cult-like group at Dunshiffin Castle, which was preparing to celebrate the summer solstice. It seemed that his fatal mistake was to challenge their beliefs on Scottish TV. Yet Inspector Torquil McKinnon had many other things on his mind. So when attractive Sergeant Lorna Golspie arrived on the island to investigate the way he ran his station, was it enough to distract him from the forthcoming Murder Solstice?

DOWN A NARROW PATH

Faith Martin

A sniper is at large, killing police officers all over the UK. The atmosphere at Thames Valley Police HQ is tense and DI Hillary Greene is feeling the strain. But it's business as usual when a wealthy woman is found murdered in her home in the village of Bletchington. The victim was unpopular and suspects are thick on the ground. Things don't improve as Hillary faces the secretive DC Keith Barrington and her underhand sergeant, Gemma Fordham. But even as Hillary searches for a cold-blooded killer, a tragic event will rock her world. Will this be the end for her?

AN EVIL REFLECTION

John Paxton Sheriff

A tragic road accident on a bleak moorland road lures PI Jack Scott to the Isle of Mull, and into a web of intrigue stretching back thirty years. On the island he's soon convinced that the crash that killed Bridie Button was no accident. He and his colleagues investigate possible connections with crimes in Mull, Oban and Liverpool as the death toll mounts. Then in another road accident that almost mirrors Bridie Button's tragic end, Scott's close friend Sian Laidlaw is injured. The violence is too close for comfort. A solution must be found . . . a murderer is on the loose.